A Wedding
in the Keys

≈ A COCONUT KEY NOVEL ≈
BOOK SIX

HOPE
HOLLOWAY

INTRODUCTION TO COCONUT KEY

If you're longing for an escape to paradise, step on to the gorgeous, sun-kissed sands of Coconut Key. With a cast of unforgettable characters and stories that touch every woman's heart, these delightful novels will make you laugh out loud, fall in love, and stand up and cheer...and then you'll want the next one *right this minute*.

A Secret in the Keys – Book 1
A Reunion in the Keys – Book 2
A Season in the Keys – Book 3
A Haven in the Keys – Book 4
A Return to the Keys –Book 5
A Wedding in the Keys – Book 6
A Promise in the Keys - Book 7

For release dates, excerpts, news, and more, sign up to receive Hope Holloway's newsletter! Or visit www.hopeholloway.com and follow Hope on Facebook and BookBub!

CHAPTER ONE

"*H*ere we go, Lovely Ames." Beck Foster backed away from the overflowing buffet table, looking over the exquisite setting to meet her mother's gaze. "We are ready to open the doors of Coquina House Bed and Breakfast—at least for our first real event."

"And then for the soft opening you're so determined we have in this not-quite-ready-for-prime-time B&B?" Lovely's green eyes widened. "You know I'm not a fan of that idea."

"What are you afraid of?"

"Failure," Lovely admitted. "Aren't you?"

"I'm not afraid of anything," Beck proclaimed. "And I've done a ton of research and talked to other inn and B&B owners. A soft opening will help us work out the kinks, and determine how to arrange the breakfast room—"

"That's what we're calling the dining room, right?" Lovely stroked the tiny white terrier in her arms, getting as much comfort from Sugar as the dependent little dog got from her owner. "It's been the dining room my whole life."

"It's a Bed and *Breakfast*, Lovely. Not a Bed and Dinner." Beck stepped closer to gently ease Lovely's long gray braid over her shoulder, wanting to add to that comfort. "Are you worried we can't do this?"

"It's getting real," she said. "Can we do this without a staff of any kind? You're busy, I'm old, and we both agreed we have the budget to hire at least one person."

"When we have paying customers, we will. Until then, I can do it. We always said soft opening in March, and start taking reservations to open in April."

"Um, Beckie? It's February fourteenth."

Beck shrugged. "So, we're pushing it a few weeks. But this wedding is the perfect launch for the B&B, since it's all friends and family. Anyway, as far as a soft opening with 'beta' guests? It might take a few weeks to find the perfect, most understanding—but still incredibly honest —test patrons. We have three rooms completely ready on the second floor."

"Yes, we do. And I adore the carved signs on the doors, each with the name of a palm. I just love that we picked the Queen, the Royal, and the Canary, with Coconut and Foxtail on the third floor. They came out perfectly."

"And so did your paintings of each of those palms. It's that personal touch that is making our dreams come true," Beck assured her.

"Mine came true when you walked through my door, sweet girl," Lovely said on a sigh. "This is just icing on the cake of my life."

"Aww." Beck tilted her head, thinking. "Can you believe I walked through that door a year ago this month?"

"Best year of my life," Lovely cooed.

"True that, Aunt Lovey." Beck added a hug with the childhood nickname.

In the year since newly separated and freshly heartbroken Rebecca Foster and her daughter, Peyton, had impulsively come to Coconut Key to visit Lovely Ames, so much had changed.

Not long after she'd arrived and fallen in love with the dreamy tropical island in the lower Keys, Beck had learned that Lovely wasn't her estranged and distant aunt, but her biological mother. As a teenager, Lovely had given her baby to her sister to raise, and Olivia Mitchell had taken Beck away from Coconut Key when the resemblance between real mother and daughter became too noticeable. Lovely had kept the secret for fifty-five years.

But after a near-death experience, Lovely finally told Beck the truth, and they'd grown incredibly close—close enough to embark on the adventure of transforming the Ames family home that Lovely still owned into a beachfront B&B.

Their enthusiasm and energy for that project hadn't waned a bit, but a hurricane had slowed things down. The remodel had been time-consuming and expensive, and Beck had discovered that Lovely wasn't quite the risk-taker she seemed to be at first.

Beck had also discovered that she, herself, was downright fearless, a fact that had put a smile on her face no matter what happened around them. And she was more than ready to get this new phase of their lives underway.

"Come on, let's finish helping Peyton in the kitchen so we can have plenty of time to set up your cottage as the bride's dressing room." Beck guided Lovely back to the kitchen, giving her arm a pat. "Trust me, we'll find the right guest or two, but not today. Today, we get Jessie married again."

Lovely sighed. "I still think we should wait until we're one hundred percent ready before we start taking guests."

Beck's oldest daughter, Peyton, was at the counter skewering some shrimp hors d'oeuvres that would be served to the guests during the post-ceremony cocktail hour.

"Lovely!" Peyton exclaimed, brushing back some long hair that seemed to have gotten a little lighter after a year in the sunwashed Florida Keys. "Do I get my 'I'll wait for the right time' gene from you? If I can beat it, so can you."

Lovely laughed. "You haven't waited for anything since you got here."

Peyton rolled her eyes, because they all knew she'd waited for some*one*...but Valentino Sanchez had returned to Miami to deal with personal and family issues many months ago, and he still hadn't come back.

"Well, I haven't waited *professionally*," Peyton mused. "Now that I'm the assistant manager at the Coquina Café and signed up to start night classes in the Key West Culinary School, I feel like Mom. Now I zoom along and don't wait for anything."

Beck walked up behind Peyton and gave her a hug. "You know, I was just thinking of all I've accomplished this year, but you're the one who's really changed her life."

"I'm working on it, Mom." Peyton gave a warm smile. "No more desperation for marriage and kids. I have plenty in my life with work, this family, and now I'm Aunt Peyton to Dylan, Ava, and Beau. They're taking care of my maternal needs."

"That makes a mother happy."

"You have a lot to be happy about, Mom. New business, new family, new friends...new man." She dragged out the last one, eyeing Beck for a response.

"Josh isn't new," she said. "I've known him since I was a little kid and he was trying to impress me on his skateboard right out there on Coquina Court. Also, we've been seeing each other for a year now. Nothing new."

Beck let a sigh slip that she probably shouldn't have, because Peyton abandoned the shrimp, and gave a curious look.

Peyton leaned a centimeter closer. "Or maybe I got my *waiting* gene from my very own mother?"

"Maybe," Beck conceded. "I sure am...waiting."

And again, last night, she'd sent Josh home with a warm and caring goodnight kiss, unable to miss the disappointment in his eyes when she didn't invite him to stay with her in the owner's suite on Coquina House's first floor.

"And what *are* you waiting for, Mom?"

A few feet away, Lovely steeped her tea, listening but not opining, like Beck frequently did with her own daughters.

"If I knew," Beck finally said to them, "I'd tell you. I love being with Josh, but..." She shook her head. "Some mornings I wake up remembering those empty, aching, dark days after Dan announced he was leaving me, and I'm just terrified to take a chance again."

"There's no timeline for love, Mom."

"And no pressure," Lovely added. "You just let your relationship grow at a pace that feels right. But who knows? Maybe today's wedding will make you feel differently."

"How?" Beck asked.

Lovely shrugged. "Maybe you'll see yourself walking down that aisle again at your own wedding."

Beck just stared at her, trying to imagine feeling that way...and failing.

But Peyton picked up a skewer and pointed it at Lovely. "You guys have to stop calling it a wedding. Today's ceremony is a *vow renewal*, not a wedding."

"Today's ceremony is a miracle, whatever you call it," Lovely said, settling onto a counter stool. "And if we're comparing who's had the most change in her life in the past year? Jessie Donovan might win that one."

"No joke," Peyton said, returning to the icing. "When I met Mom's childhood best friend, she was a widow with a struggling high-end restaurant."

"Not a widow anymore." Beck chuckled softly, thinking of how Chuck had returned to "life" after four years—a single father living in St. Bart's, suffering from amnesia, and a completely changed man. He'd been back in Coconut Key, with his three-year-old son Beau, for four months, and he'd so easily fit into their world that it was hard to think of life without him.

And that made today's vow renewal ceremony, held on Valentine's Day just like the first time they got married more than thirty years ago, all the sweeter.

"I think Jessie's true joy will be when Beau finally calls her Mom," Lovely said, a slow smile pulling. "It's quite a milestone in a woman's life."

"You want me to call you Mom?" Beck asked, half joking.

"I don't care what you call me, darling girl. As long as you're here, I'm a happy woman." Lovely lifted her teacup in a mock toast. "But I wouldn't hate it at all."

"Okay, *Mom*." Beck came around the counter and gave her a kiss. "But don't you need to get home and start getting ready? Peyton and I will be over as soon as we're dressed to set up pre-wedding mimosas for the unofficial bridal party."

"Not a wedding, a vow renewal," Lovely reminded her.

Beck made a face. "That's too hard to say. It's a wedding, and a joyous one. Hang on. I have a call." She reached into her pocket and glanced at the phone, smiling at the name. "Oh, speak of the devil."

"Jessie's freaking out?" Peyton guessed. "Heather got in last night and is supposed to be keeping her calm and happy this morning."

"No, it's Josh," she said. "Jessie called a few minutes ago and her sweet sister must be doing her job, because that woman is beyond calm and content. 'Scuze me."

She tapped the phone, walking to the French doors that led to the large veranda, already set up with tables and chairs and flower arrangements for the guests who'd gather there after the ceremony.

"Good morning," she said brightly, slipping onto a chaise and looking out over the azure water of the Atlantic Ocean. Her gaze was focused on the dance floor and additional tables set between the house and the beach. Coquina House really made for a spectacular small reception venue, so she hoped they'd book more of these events.

"How's the brother of the bride?" she asked. "Ready to walk our girl down the aisle?"

"Completely," he said. "I've got on a replica of what I wore thirty-two years ago the first time my sister married Chuck Donovan—only no mullet and my Hawaiian shirt is a little less *Magnum P.I.* than back in the day."

"Wait. You had a mullet?" She gave a throaty laugh. "I'd kill to see that."

"Pretty sure there are going to be pictures on display on the beach today. Anyway, Toni just arrived and isn't quite ready, so we might be a few minutes late for that little pre-party you're having at Lovely's cottage."

"Toni's running late?" she asked with dry laugh, not the least bit surprised that Josh's thirty-year-old daughter would push her entrance for her aunt's ceremony to the very last minute. She'd only met Toni Cross once, when she'd blown into town for a few days during the holidays. It was long enough to learn that the aspiring actress ran on her own clock, set an hour later than everyone else's.

"She just told me she's thinking about staying in Coconut Key," he added.

"For the weekend?"

"For...a while. She's not committing."

Beck sank back on the chaise, processing this news. "I thought she said she was headed to Hollywood to give it a go as an actress."

"Turns out she needs money to do that, and the bank of her mother has truly dried up. She wants to look for seasonal work in Coconut Key. Maybe Jessie's café, if she's hiring."

Seriously? "Somehow I'm having trouble imagining Toni Cross slinging crab cakes benedict and refilling coffee." The stunningly attractive model/actress who'd supported herself with a series of wealthy boyfriends didn't seem like she was cut out for food service.

"She said every aspiring actress waits tables."

Sure they did. In L.A.

Beck tamped down the comment. Toni was his daughter, and if Josh was going to be in Beck's life, then she needed to treat his daughter with the same love and respect he treated all of hers.

He was quiet for a moment, then said, "She won't be here long. Coconut Key isn't exciting enough for her. I think she's hoping Nick might give her some advice before she heads to L.A. Maybe he can introduce her to some people, since he's our local celebrity."

But Nick Frye was so much more than a famous guy who lived in Coconut Key. He was happily living with Beck's middle daughter, Savannah, and raising their five-month-old son. Was it right for Toni to exploit his fame and connections?

Again, she swallowed the comment. "It's fine," she said instead. "You can get to the pre-party anytime. The service can't start until you have Jessie on your arm."

"All right. Save me a few dances, Rebecca Foster."

And somehow, like always, he made her smile, the way a good friend did. It would have been nice if that comment gave her butterflies, too, but...it didn't. Maybe Lovely was right. Maybe after she saw her best friend "remarry" the love of her life, she'd look at Josh differently. As more than a friend.

"More than a few," she promised.

But the truth was, she had no idea what the day held, but with the strong and supportive group of friends and family, she wasn't worried in the least. Beck Foster was fearless.

Well, mostly.

"*W*ho's got a poo-poo? Dylan's got a poo-poo. Who's gonna change him? Daddy's gonna change him!"

"*Staaaahp.*" Savannah pulled her pillow over her head, but that didn't completely block out the light or the view of Nick Frye standing over a changing table, removing a diaper with the skill of a trained nurse. And it certainly didn't block out his singing...if you could call it that.

Whatever it was, Nick's ridiculous serenade put a big smile on the face of the giggly, kicking, gurgling bundle of perfection who they both adored.

"And Mommy is starting today in a bad mood." Nick flashed his million-dollar Hollywood smile, angling just enough so the light spilled over his bare chest and abs.

Talk about things she *adored*.

"I'm in a great mood, but you're waxing poetic about his poop." She shoved the pillow away and blinked. "I didn't even hear him cry."

"He didn't cry." He leaned over to get right in the

baby's face. "Did you, big man? Not my wittle bitty Dyl."
Baby talk. Now he was killing her with baby talk. "He just
turned over in his crib and said, 'Yo, Daddy, my pants are
full.'"

She snorted and fell back, never quite used to the
bliss that had filled her heart every morning since Nick
had left his old life and announced he wanted this one. A
life with Dylan, the child they'd conceived as strangers on
a one-night stand. A life with her, the woman who never
stayed still long enough to figure out where she belonged.

Apparently, she belonged here, in a luxurious Gulf of
Mexico beach house—*mansion* would be more accurate
for The Haven, a five-bedroom estate with a guest house
—in the Keys. With Nick, former celebrity actor and
heartthrob. Well, he was still a heartthrob. She had the
pulse rate to prove it every time she looked at him.

This. This was Savannah Foster's life. How had she
gotten so lucky? And how long could it possibly last?

She didn't know, so she was just going to live in this
moment and enjoy the hell out of it.

"Let me run to the bathroom," she said, sliding the
covers back. "Then he can have breakfast."

With one hand on the baby, Nick watched her get up,
his gaze sliding over her T-shirt and sleep shorts like *he*
was the one who wanted breakfast...in bed. He lingered
on her bare legs for just a fraction of a second too long,
then looked up at her with a now-familiar heat in his
blue eyes that made those legs nearly buckle. And
usually got them wrapped around him in a hurry.

But only when Dylan was sound asleep, which he
most certainly wasn't right now.

With a playful wink, she headed into the bathroom

and closed the door with a sigh, still warmed by the appreciative gaze from her...

What the heck was he, anyway? Other than baby daddy, lover, best friend, co-parent, source of endless amusement, make-out buddy, bed cuddler, confidante, and midnight snack sharer...

Yep, Nick had become a lot of things to Savannah during this blissful interlude. But she couldn't seem to put a label like "boyfriend" on their strange and unique relationship.

That kind of permanence would jinx this wonderful thing they had, and she *so* didn't want anything to burst her bubble.

As she brushed her teeth, she thought about the last few months, truly the halcyon days that poets write about.

In mid-November, after taking off to L.A. to make major career and life decisions, Nick had returned to Coconut Key in true Hollywood style. He'd arrived in a helicopter that landed on the beach, bearing gifts and the news that he had refused to sign a contract to continue his hit TV show. He wanted to retire from acting to live here and raise Dylan with her.

And since that moment, Savannah had fallen into his arms and given herself mind, body, and soul.

With the exception of the occasional weirdo paparazzi type who managed to find him and try to get pictures, life with a former household name was pretty darn normal. He'd made a clean break with everything in his old life, avoided calls from his manager long enough that they'd stopped, and put his laser focus on being a father and Savannah's...

What *should* she call him today when she introduced him to all those people?

The question teased her enough that when she stepped back into the oversize main bedroom, she was ready to just ask. Jinxing be damned.

"Nick," she said, coming over to the rocker where he sat cooing—yes, *cooing*—to a baby who cooed right back. "I have a question for you."

"Then I have an answer." He got up and handed her the baby, all of thirteen pounds now since he'd been born slightly premature, and nothing short of glorious.

"Hello, sweet little French Frye." She kissed his downy head. "Did you let your mama sleep in today? What a good baby angel you are."

Yeah, she was as bad as Daddy.

As she settled into the rocker in the sitting area, Savannah felt her heart fill with a love that was indescribably perfect and real. She never failed to get a little breathless every time she saw, touched, smelled, heard, or kissed this tiny creature who had Nick's eyes and her mouth and, well, some bald guy's head.

"And the diner is officially open for business." Sliding Dylan into nursing position, she lifted her top to take him to her breast, sighing as he latched.

Nick, of course, watched with his goofy grin—not that anything on that handsome face could truly be considered "goofy."

"So, what's your question?" he asked.

She searched his face, taking her time to enjoy that journey and consider his response.

He lifted his brows. "Something wrong, babe?"

"No, I'm just wondering how you'll answer."

"Um, honestly?"

"Yes, but..." She stroked Dylan's head lightly, but looked at his father. "I still don't know you completely," she admitted. "Somehow you constantly manage to surprise me. But I like that. I love anything unpredictable."

"So, ask me and I'll surprise and delight you."

"Okay, so today, when we meet lots of people—"

He looked skyward. "I hope they're normal and not picture-takers."

"Same. But when we do, and I intro—"

"Hang on." He held up a hand to stop her, fishing for his phone from his sleep pants pocket. "Let me just send this to voice mail, so..." His voice trailed off as he stared at the screen. "Huh. What do you know?"

"Who is it?"

He let out a slow, steadying breath. "It's Diana Frye, mommy dearest."

"Oh?" She sat up straight, eyes wide. "Really?"

She saw him swallow and recognized the discomfort —some might call it pain—in his expression. "Let me take this outside, Sav. I won't be long."

She lifted a brow, knowing he very well could be. His mother had barely talked to him for the past three months, openly furious that he'd given up the career that she had worked so hard to help him build from childhood.

"Take your time." Savannah gestured toward the large, covered patio that overlooked the water. "My question can wait."

He nodded, tapping the phone screen on the way out.

"Well, hey, stranger," he said as bright and charming as possible.

Her heart folded a little as she resituated Dylan against her breast, stroking his feathery three wisps of hair.

"I will never be that mother," she whispered to him. "I'll never push you to some dumb career just because you're jaw-droppingly good-looking and can deliver a line. I'll never withdraw my affection when you do things I don't like. And I will never, ever, ever give you the silent treatment. You have my word, dear sweet son. No manipulating you to get what I want, I promise."

He whimpered as if her word mattered, but it was the juice making him respond, and she knew it. But someday, some distant day, he'd be a grown man and she wanted to still be close to this boy, to never judge him, and always love him.

She wanted to be just like her own mother.

Her heart swelled at the thought of how Rebecca Foster had managed to be such a great mother, so on her game. All Savannah wanted was to be exactly like her.

Did Mom pass judgment on Savannah when she showed up in Coconut Key almost a year ago, literally jobless and pregnant by a stranger? No, nor did she even demand to know who the father was.

"Remind me to give that dear sweet grandmother of yours an extra kiss or six today," Savannah said, easing the baby away when she sensed this plate was empty and it was time for a mid-way burp.

As she lifted Dylan to rub his back, she stole a glance out to the patio, where Nick paced with the phone to his ear. She could hear the tenor of his voice but couldn't make out the words. He didn't sound angry or frustrated, just that he was trying to make a point.

It sounded like he wasn't succeeding.

The little she knew about Diana was not great. An aspiring actress whose fledgling career had been derailed by an unexpected pregnancy that left her a single mom who'd used her wits and resources to survive. And her best resource was a kid the camera loved who became a child actor who could deliver a line and steal a scene.

If Nick Frye had been born to be a star, then Diana Frye was Central Casting's Ultimate Stage Mom. His father remained out of the picture, although he apparently tried to cash in on the family fame and fortune when Nick was still a teenager and had been on a hit TV show. Nick said he'd really wanted to meet the man, and hoped they could have a relationship.

So Diana had taken him to meet Oliver Jones, Nick's father. The meeting, he'd told Savannah, had not gone well, and that was that. But having an absentee father was, according to Nick, what drove him to turn his life upside down so he could be the most present father possible for Dylan.

But while that decision thrilled Savannah, it had infuriated his mother. And, as punishment, Savannah presumed, Diana refused to come to Coconut Key to meet her grandchild, and rarely even called.

Who did that to a son?

"Not me," she swore to the baby. "I'll never hurt you like that."

Yes, Nick was a grown thirty-three-year-old man, who didn't need his mother's approval or advice. But, he was a human—and one who'd been raised with no father—and he *did* want Diana's love. To cut him off was purely heart-less, Savannah decided, and made her intensely dislike the woman. No matter how many stories Nick told her that he thought painted his mother in a positive light, she always sounded like a conniving, controlling witch to Savannah.

So why was she calling on Valentine's Day, moments before the "what are we, really?" conversation?

"Maybe I jinxed it after all," she said to Dylan, who looked up at her with adoration in his blue eyes, ready for round two. "Let's hope not."

She watched as Nick finished the call, holding the phone as he walked to the railing and looked out over the Gulf. His broad shoulders rose and fell with a sigh she couldn't hear, but definitely felt.

That was not a happy man.

After a moment, he turned and came back in. He didn't fake a smile, which she appreciated so much. That proved, as he so often did, that he was not the "man who was paid to lie" as she used to think of him because he was an actor.

"So...how'd it go?" she asked when he silently returned to the chair across from her.

"She's on her way here."

"*What*?" Savannah sat up, making Dylan jerk a little and flatten his sweet baby hand against her as if trying to keep her from moving.

"This afternoon," he added.

This time, her "What?" was just mouthed, silent with shock.

"Yup." He dropped his head back as if the news physically hurt him. "And she won't be alone. Max Meadows is in the car with her."

His mother *and* his manager? "Where are they?"

"Driving down from Orlando, where they flew in from L.A."

"Why Orlando?"

"They thought it was close to the Keys." He straightened his head and looked at her. "Or she's lying about that."

"Why would she lie?"

He just closed his eyes. "Nothing my mother does is without an agenda. Nothing. She manipulates like other people...breathe."

"So what is she coming to manipulate you into doing?"

He shot her a "get real" look from under thick lashes. "She said something about Max having a new project up his sleeve. God knows he's desperate."

Savannah frowned, thinking of everything she knew about his manager. Honestly? Very little. Nick loathed his acting career so much, he preferred to talk about anything else. He did share some stories about Eliza Whitney, his agent. But that was a wholly different job from what Max did, as she understood it.

"Why is he desperate?" she asked.

"Because I was his number one client and he gets a percentage of everything I make. And he's got a sixteen-thousand square foot house in Beverly Hills, four cars, a lawyer on retainer, and alimony payments that would curl your hair."

"So they are coming here to do a full-court press to

get you to go back," she said, not bothering to make it a question.

"That would appear to be the agenda du jour."

"Did they say that?"

"Oh, no. Not my mother. She claims she can't go another day without meeting Dylan."

Seriously? "Well, I guess it's about time."

"I can't let you be that naïve with her, Savannah. I'm certain she has a scheme up her sleeve, and we'll figure it out soon enough. But just to make things more awkward, they're going to arrive smack dab in the middle of the reception."

"Of course they are."

"I told them we would be at a wedding at Coquina House, so she's going to text me when they get to Coconut Key. I'm sorry I'll have to leave early and come back to meet them here."

"It's fine. I'm sure Dylan will have had enough by then, and I'll come back with you. No reason to greet them alone."

He angled his head and looked at her. "Why are you the greatest thing that ever happened to me?"

She laughed softly, letting the thrill he always gave her dance over her every nerve ending. "Is that what I am? I was just wondering."

"Oh, what was that question you wanted to ask me?"

She stared at him for a long time. *The greatest thing that ever happened to me.* How could she want to be anything else? Labels, like permanence, had never mattered to Savannah Foster. Why would they now?

"Nah, not important. I need to get this baby fed and

changed and put on my fancy dress with the breast-accessible easy-open access."

He grinned and got right in front of her, dropping his hands on the rocker armrests to roll her closer as he bent over. "That is my very favorite kind of dress." Then he leaned in and kissed her. "On my very favorite woman."

Was she his favorite? Guess she was about to find out.

She kissed him again, hoping like hell she hadn't jinxed this by even *thinking* about what they should call their relationship.

Because she was crazy about Nick Frye and had never been happier. Was his mother about to do everything in her considerable power to put an end to that?

CHAPTER THREE

KENNY

Be cool. Be chill. Be unfazed when you see her.

Right. Like that was possible when Kenny Gallagher was just moments away from seeing Heather Monroe at her sister's vow renewal ceremony. Like he could be chill when he was about to see the woman he'd thought about every day and night since she left Coconut Key on January first, six weeks ago.

Oh, Heather. "Why are you so under my skin?"

"Did you say something, Dad?"

Swallowing a curse at his stupidity, Kenny turned from the entryway mirror to watch his daughter, Ava, as she came down the hall, a dress the color of sunshine clinging to a body that shouldn't be quite that, uh, grown-up at sixteen. The flirty little skirt skimmed thighs that looked like they belonged on a supermodel, and how the hell could she even walk in heels that high?

"I said you're showing a little skin, A."

She straightened a shoulder strap that revealed a tan

she'd worked long and hard to get. "Grandma Beck helped me pick this dress."

He always smiled when she called Beck by that name. Yes, Beck was his biological mother, so it was accurate. But before they'd come to Coconut Key, her most beloved grandmother was Grandma Janet, his mother. What foresight Janet Gallagher must have had when she wrote a letter to his birth mother and asked Ava to deliver it in person. She had to have known it would change both their lives. Well, no, she hadn't. But she trusted God, and He knew.

"And Savannah said I could totally carry off yellow," Ava continued, stepping next to him to glance in the mirror.

"You carry it off, all right. And I'll be carrying off every guy who gawks at you."

She rolled her eyes. "Relax, Daddy. Maddie will be there and if anyone is getting gawked at, it's her."

"Maddie..." *Heather's daughter.*

"Maddie Monroe? Sister of Marc? Daughter of Heather? Don't tell me you've forgotten these people who lived here for, like, four months."

If only he could. "Of course not. I'm really looking forward to seeing Jessie's sister and her kids." There, that was cool and chill.

"I just wish Maddie could stay longer than the weekend, like her mom is."

"Her mom is staying?" He didn't know that. "How long?"

"A couple of weeks, until Maddie and Marc's spring break. Then they're flying down all by themselves and spending spring break here. Maddie and I are thinking of going to Key West alone. You'd let me do that, right?"

"She's staying in Coconut Key until March?" Oh, *man*.

"Right? It doesn't seem fair that Maddie can't stay, but she has school, so she and Marc will live with Shelley, that lady who works for Heather in Charleston. But we can go to Key West in March, right?"

"Yeah." That could be three weeks of...Heather.

"Really?" She gave him a hug. "I knew you'd be cool with it."

"Wait, what am I cool with?"

She gave him her best "are you serious" look and God knows she had a lot of them. "Are you okay, Dad?"

"Of course, yeah, why?"

"You look...weird."

"It's the tie." He straightened it. "Can't remember the last time I wore one of these things. And what did I just agree to?"

She laughed and jabbed his arm playfully. "Maddie and me going to Key West."

"Alone?"

"Look, if it's a huge deal you and Heather can drive us down but, yes, please leave us alone for the day. We won't do anything bad."

But would he? He just stared at her, head buzzing at that thought.

"You two can walk around or, like, go to church. That seems to be what you and Mrs. Monroe like to do."

Mrs. Monroe. That cleared up his thoughts in a hurry. "We'll see, A. That's three weeks from now." Three *long* weeks.

Whoa, he needed to do a better job of hiding his feelings. The beautiful woman who'd invaded his every thought while she stayed here last fall and through the holidays was still a darn near fresh widow, in mourning after losing a husband about six months ago. For that reason, she remained off limits, no matter that they'd become good friends and "church buddies."

In the time she'd been gone, he'd thrown himself into his job as a general contractor, pushing his crew to finish the B&B for Beck and Lovely. He'd been at the site ten, twelve, sometimes fifteen hours a day, twisting arms and prodding trades and forcing himself to think about only that house. He'd even met with the local fire chief and discussed getting on the roster as an EMT, like he had been in Atlanta.

And, he was still a single dad. Sure, he had plenty of back-up from Beck, Savannah, Peyton, and Jessie, but Ava was ultimately his responsibility and spending time with her was still one of his favorite things to do. Even more so now that she'd mellowed so much.

But at night, alone in his bed, his brain went back to sweet blue eyes and soft blond hair and those precious questions Heather would ask about the Bible as she fell in love with Jesus...and he fell in love with...

No. *No.*

"So can we leave early?" Ava asked, checking her phone before dropping it into a little straw bag. "Maddie said they're already there down at the beach in front of Lovely's cottage, where the wedding is. I want to hang with her. I've missed her so much."

"Sure." He didn't hate the idea of arriving early, maybe getting that first sight of Heather over with to see just how chill he really could be.

He did want to tell her he'd continued going to Our Redeemer Church even after she left. Maybe he was dipping his toes back into his faith, or maybe he was just there because it reminded him of her. Either way, he was in "their" pew every week, and he'd missed hearing her sing, or talking about the sermon over coffee afterwards. He'd even gotten Ava to go a few times, but church still reminded her too much of her mom, and he noticed she'd be blue on Sunday afternoons. So, he stopped asking, and she didn't push it.

"We can leave any time," he said.

Ava took a few steps closer, standing right next to him so they could see themselves in the mirror. "Look at how cute we are, Dad."

He gave a dry laugh, but the smile he flashed in the mirror was genuine. "You're cute. I'm a forty-year-old in a sports jacket I haven't pulled out since I got roped into that Bachelor Auction last summer."

"Nope. You're cute." She dropped her head on his shoulder, her blond hair tumbling, the last vestiges of the hideous pink and purple coloring gone.

Her nose diamond was gone, too, he realized as he looked down at her. Along with her hatred of hugging and fears that had sent her spiraling into anxiety attacks after her mother and brother were lost in a house fire six years ago.

Coconut Key, and the family they'd become part of, had been so good for his little girl.

"You'll look really nice when you dance with Heather, Dad."

"What?" He croaked the word.

"Well, who else are you going to dance with?"

"There's dancing?" He blinked at her.

"It's a wedding...ish thing. Isn't there always dancing?"

"It's not technically a wedding, and the reception is at Coquina House." He scowled. "If anyone dances on that hardwood floor I killed myself to get refinished, they will personally answer to the General Contractor on that renovation." He tapped his chest. "And he will not be forgiving."

"They're putting a dance floor outside on the sand," she said. "No one's going to dance on your hardwood floor. Come on, Dad. You need to chill."

"Trust me," he mumbled in agreement as they headed out the door. "I'm trying."

CHAPTER FOUR

*W*ait for it now. Here it comes. Any second... the thud of sadness and disappointment.

But nothing happened.

Peyton gripped the patio railing a little tighter, bracing for the sensation when her heart dropped into her stomach, the feeling she had every single time she attended a wedding. The pang of envy, of longing, of wanting it to be her turn.

But none came today. Maybe because that sweet wedding venue that Jessie and Chuck had created—technically re-created—on the beach wasn't really for a *wedding*, per se. Although no one walking by would know that.

The sands of Coconut Key had been scraped and cleared of the seaweed, leaving the wide beach white and inviting from up here at Lovely's cottage all the way to the edge of the Atlantic Ocean. There, forty white chairs wrapped in bright pink ties were lined up and separated to create a tulle-trimmed aisle. Jessie would walk down the sandy aisle barefoot, like she and Chuck had all those years ago when they did this the first time.

They'd meet under the arch of a trellis bursting with baby's breath and roses, where they would say an updated version of the vows they'd taken a lifetime ago. A lifetime and one death...that never happened.

Chuck's return to Coconut Key after Jessie and everyone else believed him dead at sea for four years had the true feeling of a miracle. And this "wedding that isn't a wedding" was a culmination of that.

So maybe that was why Peyton didn't have her usual bout of jealousy. Or was it something else? Had she truly changed in this past year in Coconut Key, like she swore she had to her mother and Lovely?

Did saying she was a new woman really make her one? Had she found herself, and stopped waiting for the perfect man and fantasy life? Had Peyton Foster finally come to terms with the fact that she might not ever be the bride or wife or mother she always thought she'd be? Maybe. And that was okay. Better than okay, actually. It was—

"If I take one sip..." Savannah surprised her by sidling up to the railing, reaching for Peyton's barely touched mimosa. "Would you tell anyone?"

"You've got five bottles of breast milk pumped out and in the fridge at Coquina House, and Nick is ready to do every feeding." Peyton offered the orange juice and bubbly to her sister. "Drink up, buttercup. It's a vow renewal."

Savannah took the glass and sniffed it. "I don't want to turn Dylan into a mad mimosa drinker like Mom."

Laughing, the two of them turned to see their mother

gathering up flowers to take inside, chattering away with Lovely and Heather, Jessie's half-sister. The three of them were all flitting around in their roles as "co-attendants," so named because Jessie couldn't decide who should be her woman-of-honor.

"Oh, Mom," Savannah sighed on a whisper. "She's so cute, isn't she?"

"She's blossoming before our very eyes," Peyton said, turning back to the beach to study that pink trellis and wait for...nope, nothing.

"She's changed so much since those dark days when Dad ditched her," Savannah mused. "So happy, with friends, and a new business, and new...Josh."

"Who she says is not 'new' because she knew him when she lived here as a kid."

"You know what else he isn't?" Savannah muttered. "Mom's lover."

"Savannah! Not our business," Peyton said. "She's not ready."

"After a year with the guy?" Savannah shrugged and eyed Peyton. "And speaking of people who've changed, so have you, you know."

"We were just talking about that," Peyton said. "I think I'm finally free of my burning need to validate myself by getting married and raising kids." She added a laugh and leaned into her sister. "Just in time to watch you do both."

"How's that for irony?" Savannah mused. "Remember when we used to play bride when we were little?"

"All too well," Peyton admitted, images of the childhood dress-up game crystal clear in her head.

"You would stand at the top of the stairs at the house and use an entire roll of toilet paper as your train."

"And you would always be waiting at the bottom as the groom," Peyton said, no small amount of wonder in her voice. "You never wanted to be the bride."

"As if you'd let me."

"You never asked." She frowned. "Did you want to be the bride, Sav?"

Savannah took a deep breath, then sniffed the mimosa again as she contemplated her answer. She closed her eyes as if tempted, then lowered the glass without drinking.

"No," she said simply. "I didn't want to get married. It felt like prison to me."

"And now?" Peyton asked, fairly certain her smitten sister would sigh and say *yes* the minute her dream man dropped to his knee.

But she just stared out at the water. "Maybe not prison," she said. "But...still very scary."

"Why?"

She cocked a brow. "Two words: *Mom* and *Dad*."

"Nick is not Dad," Peyton said. "And they had a pretty good run of thirty-four years until Dad hit his mid-life crisis."

"Would you settle for a 'pretty good run'?" Savannah challenged.

"No." Peyton didn't even have to think about it.

Savannah handed the flute back. "I'll wait till he's weaned." Then she slid her arm around Peyton and rested her head lightly on her shoulder. "I wish Callie were here today."

"She wanted to be," Peyton said, thinking of her

morning text exchange with their youngest sister. "But she has three mid-terms on Monday."

"So she's gone back to her overachieving ways. At least one of the Foster women hasn't changed."

"Deep down, we're all the same, only better."

Savannah eyed her. "So, no wedding blues today, Peypey?"

Peyton smiled. "No, actually, none at all. I guess that part of my brain has died. Or my heart. Whatever controls...desperation."

"The part that's figured out that there's more to life than having a man and a baby."

"Says the woman who has both."

"Yeah, yeah." Savannah gripped the railing and leaned back, staring out at the water. "I also have a lot of stress about the mother and manager who are on their way."

"Hey, you two." Mom stepped out on the patio, her jade green eyes dancing with excitement. "Here comes the bride! Ta-da!"

She made a sweeping gesture and Jessie walked out to the patio, flanked by Lovely and Heather, making Peyton totally forget about everything but how completely beautiful the woman who'd become her friend, mentor, and boss looked right then.

"Jessie!" she exclaimed, walking over with her arms outstretched. "You are radiant!"

She threw her head back and laughed, her brown curls threaded with flowers bouncing over her shoulders. She'd chosen a pale pink dress with accents the same fuchsia as the ribbon and tulle on the beach. The silk fell gracefully, almost to the ground, with a handkerchief hemline that added to the nostalgic, vintage vibe she was going for.

She extended one pink-tipped bare foot, jangling a sea-shell anklet. "I wore this the first time," she said on a playful laugh.

"I'm so happy for you, Jessie." Peyton hugged her, careful not to mess with the perfection that was her hair and makeup. "I love you so much."

"You love me?" Jessie whispered. "Really?"

Peyton drew back slowly, not even sure she'd heard that right. "With all my heart, why?"

Jessie winced. "I, um, have some news."

"What?"

"Val's coming today."

Peyton stared at her. "Val...he is?" Damn it, her voice cracked.

"I guess he didn't tell you."

Peyton could feel the blood drain from her face, leaving her a little lightheaded, but that was probably because the women she loved and trusted most in the whole world were staring at her with...pity.

"Of course not," she said lightly. "I haven't heard a word from him in weeks." But that was typical of Val Sanchez. And when he did text, he was...friendly but distant.

After they'd dated for a few months, Peyton had made the huge mistake of telling him she was in it for the long haul. After years with a commitment-phobe boyfriend in New York who ultimately betrayed her in the worst way, she wasn't interested in casual dating.

That was when Val confessed that a few years ago, he'd lost his fiancée and lifelong girlfriend to leukemia.

Not only was he not ready to commit again, the deep conversation had made him realize that he had a lot of unfinished family business in Miami. So, he decided to leave his life as a fisherman in Coconut Key and go back to address the loss he'd tried to ignore, and the two deeply intertwined Cuban-American families—his and his fiancée's—he'd tried to forget.

In the eight months since he'd been gone, he'd texted sporadically and called...rarely.

"I hardly even think about him," she added when they all still stared. "You guys, I'm fine."

"I sent him an invitation but never dreamed he'd come," Jessie said. "It was just out of our old friendship from when he supplied fish to the restaurant. Then this morning, he texted and said he was sorry he never replied, but he'd be here. I wasn't sure if I should tell you or just let you be surprised."

"I convinced her to tell you," her mother said. "Was that the right thing to do?"

"Of course, Mom. I don't want to stand there and sputter and drool all over him."

"And if that boy is anything," Savannah added, "it's drool-worthy."

Yep. Val was one fish pun-making gorgeous hunk who Peyton had fallen for way, way too hard.

"Enough about Val," she said self-consciously, waving off the conversation. "Let's get some pictures. Look at you, Jessie."

"Look at this!" Heather held up a wedding picture where a much younger Jessie glowed next to a big, burly young man. "Her hair's almost the same, only a little more contemporary."

"It is!" Peyton exclaimed, but her gaze was on Chuck, who looked like a different person. She could see his eyes and smile, but "new Chuck"—who'd arrived with the name Rafe Mercier, but decided to drop that—was the only one Peyton ever knew. And he was a truly wonderful man, a doting father, and would be an adoring husband. And who didn't want one of those?

Like always, she waited for the thud, but...nothing.

Thank *God*.

Using her professional Nikon, Savannah started taking pictures, taking advantage of the beautiful beach as a backdrop, catching some candids before she took some more formal shots.

Another round of mimosas was poured, dozens of hugs were exchanged, and Peyton laughed and wiped enough tears to have to touch up her makeup just as the seats on the beach begin to fill with guests.

When she came out of the bathroom, Jessie's brother, Josh, arrived, his warm smile mixed with his own moist eyes when he looked at his sister.

"Jessie," he said on a raspy, emotional voice, reaching out to her. "Look at you, turning back the hands of time."

She grinned up at him. "Last time you weren't in the wedding, this time you're giving me away."

He looked around at the group and, as always, his gaze fell on Peyton's mother, who was sitting on the sofa holding one of Lovely's little pups.

"And speaking of beautiful," he said on a sigh of pure admiration. Then, as if he realized they were all looking at him, he glanced around. "This room is overflowing with it."

"Where's Toni?" Mom asked. "She's welcome to join this little pre-party."

"She saw someone she knew in the crowd, so she's already in her seat," he said, holding out his hand to draw Mom off the sofa. "Dang, Rebecca Foster."

She gave a self-conscious laugh, and Savannah slid a secret look at Peyton, her expression echoing their conversation. What *was* holding Mom back from going all in with this awesome man?

The question faded while they made a few more quick toasts, took more pictures, then headed down to the beach, all barefoot like the bride. They were all sitting together in the front row, escorted down the sandy aisle by Marc, Jessie's nephew, and Linc, her line cook and one of the Coquina Café's best employees.

Waiting for their turn, Peyton scanned the back of the guests' heads, recognizing some friends, neighbors, and customers, but not...Val.

"I don't see him either," Savannah whispered as they stood and waited for Marc to come back and take each of them on one arm.

"Who?" Peyton asked, getting a dry snort from her sister. "But there's Nick and the boy wonder." She cocked her head toward the handsome movie star swaying slightly with the infant in his arms as he looked across the sand at Savannah with nothing but anticipation and...love.

Oh, boy. Here it comes. Envy. Longing. Desire. Resentment.

But, no. She just watched Savannah give him a little wave and joke around with Marc as the three of them walked down the aisle. Peyton didn't want to make her search obvious, so she kept her gaze on the trellis and the water behind it, resisting the urge to stop, drop, and search for the man who'd stolen her heart so completely.

Instead, she simply reveled in the feeling that she could enjoy a wedding and not get attacked by the case of "when will it be my turn" blues. This was a massive victory, and cause for celebration.

That heartfelt joy continued when Chuck came out, holding Beau's hand, the toddler uncharacteristically quiet at the sight of so many people and the chorus of "awws" that accompanied the sight of him in a little white suit.

Then the music changed, the small jazz quartet sliding into an updated version of "The Wind Beneath My Wings," since it was the song that played the last time Jessie walked down the aisle. Cheesy as all get out, but there wasn't a dry eye in the place as everyone turned to watch Jessie.

Wiping a tear, it wasn't difficult for Peyton to keep her gaze locked on the "bride."

As Jessie reached Chuck under the archway, the whole group of guests let out a collective sigh.

Many of them had been in a local church for a memorial service four years ago, weeping for a man lost at sea. But today, the tears were for nothing but joy and gratitude.

Jessie greeted Chuck with a smile, then reached down and hugged Beau, who'd already become the son she never had. She whispered something in his ear and he nodded, then stepped back and did his signature fist in the air move.

"Ava!" he called just as Peyton's niece popped up and

snagged his hand, as they'd rehearsed. She managed to corral him to the seat saved next to her, somehow working her magic to keep the exuberant child quiet.

A former mayor of Coconut Key officiated, as he had all those years ago. Now, he was a weathered old Conch classic who looked like he'd spent forty years on a fishing boat. But his voice was booming and warm as he welcomed them and began the ceremony.

Every single muscle in Peyton's body wanted to turn and search the small crowd behind her. Val was here. Somewhere in one of these rows, on one of these seats, Valentino Sanchez was sitting. If she could just glance over her shoulders and see him...but she resisted, listening to the vows instead.

"As everyone gathered here knows, I don't remember the first time we did this, Jessie." Chuck's voice, which seemed louder than usual, completely hushed the mesmerized crowd. As he spoke words of affirmation and love, the only sounds were the soft splash of the waves behind him, the squawk of a distant gull, and the burning whisper in Peyton's head that she should turn and *look*.

Gritting her teeth, Peyton forced her gaze on Jessie's glowing face during Chuck's heartfelt speech.

"For me, this *is* the first time." Chuck leaned in as he concluded. "And I can honestly say, to the world and our friends, that I love you, Jessica Cross Donovan, and I am thrilled to make nothing but memories with you until death parts us. For real, next time."

A soft laughter rolled through the small crowd at that, and it would have been a perfect time for Peyton to peek over her shoulder and find him.

But she fought the temptation, giving herself a mental

high five for the self-discipline. Instead, she actively listened to every word Jessie said as she told Chuck how he'd changed her life twice.

"As strange as this sounds," Jessie said, looking up at Chuck, "I'm kind of grateful for the weird twist of fate that we've endured. Mourning your loss was the darkest time of my life, but falling in love with you for a second time? Pure bliss." She reached for his hand as if she simply couldn't resist the need to touch him.

Everyone "awwed" and still Peyton resisted.

"Charles Donovan, I *do* remember the first time we did this," Jessie continued. "And I can honestly say I love you today as much as I did when we stood here as very young adults, not knowing the ups and downs ahead of us. Maybe more," she added on a whisper that only the people in the front could hear. "And that love is forever."

After a beat, the former mayor started the exchange of more formal vows, and Chuck and Jessie promised to love, honor, cherish, and respect, and gave each other new rings. Then they kissed to a noisy, happy, enthusiastic applause.

As everyone stood, Peyton lost the battle. She turned to her right and scanned the crowd as everyone rose and applauded the couple coming down the aisle.

And there he was, tall, dark, and unspeakably handsome, clapping and smiling at Jessie, not even glancing her way.

Then she noticed the woman next to him. Was that... Toni, Josh's daughter? The statuesque blue-eyed blonde leaned into Val's shoulder and said something that made him laugh. Then she slid a possessive hand around his arm, holding his gaze for one too many heartbeats.

And there it was. The thud of her heart falling into her stomach. The punch of envy, longing, resentment, desire, and the bone-deep ache.

So she hadn't changed all that much after all. But maybe Val had.

CHAPTER FIVE

BECK

*T*he afternoon went by in a whir of guests, greetings, toasts, hugs, happiness, and plenty of kitchen work. Although Peyton had handled the menu and décor, Beck had hired help to serve the food and drinks, and still hadn't stopped or sat down for what felt like hours. That explained why her feet were on fire and her back was aching. Outside, the music started, the beach dance floor filled, and the last of the dessert trays were readied on the kitchen counter.

"You need a break." Josh came up next to her and put one hand on her lower back, knowing exactly where it ached.

"And a hot bath." Beck sighed. "I'm feeling every one of my fifty-six years today."

She leaned against the counter, eyeing the gorgeous dessert charcuterie boards, all Valentine's Day themed. "Gosh, when did Peyton manage to make these?"

Each white wood tray included slices of the red velvet wedding cake, kabobs of pineapple, coconut, and berries, decadent cream puffs and petite fours, bowls of chocolate for dipping, and a smattering of pink candied hearts the same two colors as Jessie's dress.

"She hasn't left the kitchen all day," Josh said. "Every time I'm in here, so is she."

"I think she might be avoiding Val," she said.

"Not that she could get close to him." He looked skyward. "Toni was pretty darn happy to see him."

And hadn't left his side to the point where it looked like they'd come as a couple. "How do they know each other?" Beck asked.

"Toni worked as a temp in his accounting firm a few years back," he said. "To hear her, they're long-lost friends."

"Did you tell her he and Peyton used to go out?" she asked.

He shook his head. "Didn't have a chance, but I will if you'd like me to."

She let out a sigh. "I hate stepping into our kids' lives," she said.

"I know. It feels like elementary school, when the parents had to smooth out their problems. You probably didn't have to do that much with your girls, but Toni? There was no shortage of drama and issues."

"At least she's not breathing down Nick's neck for acting advice," Beck said, looking for the positive.

"True, but...is it my imagination? Savannah seems tense, too. The mother and manager?"

"She's dreading it." Beck pushed off to find her second wind and instruct the wait staff to start serving dessert. "I can no longer lollygag."

He put his arms around her, holding her in place for a

few more seconds. "Didn't we hire help so you could lollygag with me?"

"But it's the first time people have seen Coquina House finished. I want to be the hostess with the mostest."

He tipped her chin so their lips were close. "I wish you'd sit down, have a drink, and rest up for a dance with me."

She smiled up at him. "You had me at sit down."

"Then we'll skip the dance." He pulled her in closer. "But are you too tired for a kiss?"

"I could probably handle that."

"Now we're talkin'." He closed the space between them and gave her a sweet, slow kiss, which was interrupted by a noisy throat clearing.

Surprised, they broke apart to see Savannah with her arms crossed, a look of disbelief on her face that cracked them up.

"What is it with you two and kitchens? Always kissing."

"Not always," Beck said, feeling a slow warmth crawl up her cheeks.

"Well, if you don't mind, my life is about to fall apart in..." Savannah glanced at the big farmhouse clock Beck had brought from her house in Alpharetta, which looked so good over the table. "We're leaving for The Haven in ten minutes."

"Oh, honey, you haven't had cake."

"The least of my problems," she said, eyeing the spread on the island. "On second thought, I should take some with me so I have something to give my guests. Besides, you know, tickets on the red-eye back to L.A."

"How long are they staying?" Josh asked.

"Not a clue, but ugh..." She dropped her head back and looked skyward. "I hate the idea of them invading my peace at The Haven."

"Honey, you haven't even met the woman yet," Beck said. "You might like her. And the manager? Nick said Max Meadows is a good guy."

Savannah's shoulders sank a little. "Can I be honest? And don't take this the wrong way, but you've moved in here. And Lovely's back in her cottage. Peyton's living in The Haven guest house, so we are really kind of digging the alone mommy-and-daddy-and-baby life."

Which they'd never really had, since they'd never even been a real couple, and so richly deserved.

"Then maybe they should stay here," Beck said, the words out before she could take any time to think about it.

"Here?" Savannah blinked.

"Why not? I need beta guests and you need privacy."

"Oh, God, Mom. Could you be any more amazing? I doubt they'll go for it, since The Haven certainly has enough space and she probably wants to breathe down Nick's neck, but...we'll see. I'm going to check on Dylan. He conked in the portacrib half an hour ago, but I didn't bring the monitor. You may resume kissing."

She slipped out and Beck gave Josh an apologetic look. "I need to—"

"You'd do anything for your kids, wouldn't you?" he said, touching her face tenderly.

"Yeah, I guess I would."

"Savannah's right. Could you be any more amazing?"

She rolled her eyes but couldn't resist smiling. "If I

were amazing, I'd have all the tables cleared on the veranda and make sure the breakfast room is ready."

"I'll handle the veranda, you take the breakfast room." But before he stepped away, Josh gave her one more hug. "By the way, you were born for this."

"Seriously?" And just like that, all the stress washed away. "Oh, Josh, I want this B&B to be a success."

"It already is," he assured her. "I'm so proud of what you've done."

"With a lot of help," she added, not willing to take the credit for what was a group effort. Not to mention the tremendous financial assist when her ex-husband's infidelity guilt translated into a big divorce settlement. "I could never have breathed life into Coquina House alone."

"But you're the driving force behind it, and your signature is all over the place." He leaned down for one more light kiss. "It's not only a success, but might be my biggest competition for your time."

Before she could respond, one of the servers came in and the kitchen revved back to life. After Beck instructed them on how to handle the dessert boards, she turned the corner to check the breakfast room. Taking a few steps, she was already envisioning her overnight B&B guests arriving for scones and coffee, raving about the rooms and the service.

Maybe she'd—

She sucked in a breath when she darn near collided with Val Sanchez.

"Oh! Oh, sorry." She inched back and he did the same.

"Hi, Beck. I've been wanting to get a chance to see you."

Maybe you were too busy with Toni. She swallowed the retort and gave a tight smile. "I've been swamped."

"This place looks fantastic," he said, gushing a little too hard. "I mean, wow. Kenny took me all around and showed me the guest rooms and the new third floor. I can't believe what you've done in six months."

"It's been quite a ride." *That you missed.*

"Look, I really want to talk to Peyton. Have you seen her?"

"I think she's talking to people out on the veranda now."

"I was just out there, but she got away." He angled his head, concern etched on his strong cheekbones, darkening his ebony eyes. "Is it my imagination, or is she avoiding me?"

"I don't know. Is it her imagination, or have you had Toni Cross draped all over you since this thing started?"

He made a face. "I know her from a long time ago, but I sure hope Peyton isn't misreading that."

What about the months of silence or the sporadic texts? Had Peyton misread those? Beck swallowed the question, knowing it wasn't her place.

"I don't know," she said instead. "Peyton's swamped with this event. She's made everything, you know."

"That's amazing. I remember when she was learning knife skills."

"She's a natural," Beck told him.

On a sigh, he glanced past her toward the kitchen, where one of the servers was barking orders. "I really want to talk to her, so—"

"¡Ahí esta! Era buscándote." Toni waltzed into the dining room with her laser blue eyes trained on Val. *"Quiero bailar."*

He flashed a dark look at her. "I don't want to dance, Toni. I'm talking to Beck."

Toni looked undaunted by the rejection, taking his hand. "Did Val tell you we go way back together?" she asked Beck.

Beck gave a non-committal smile, digging for the right thing to say. Josh told her Toni and her mother frequently spoke Spanish as a way to block him out of the conversation, and Val had been raised in a fully bilingual Cuban-American home.

"He did," Beck finally said. "What a small world."

Toni pulled Val a little closer and let out a string of Spanish that went right over Beck's head. To his credit, Val shot Beck an apologetic look.

"Thanks for your help," he said. "If you see her, can you tell her I'd love to talk to her?"

She nodded, but turned as Savannah came in from the living room, her eyes wide. "Change in plans. Big."

As if she sensed her opening, Toni wrapped two hands around Val's arm and dragged him away, but Beck had to forget that problem because, by the look on Savannah's face, there was a bigger one.

"What's going on?" she asked.

"They're coming *here*. Diana claims she got completely confused by the two names—because Coquina House and The Haven sound *so* much alike—and the GPS is sending her here. So, good news. Put Coquina House in GPS and it sends you here now. Bad news? T-minus one minute until they get here."

"That's good, Savannah," Beck assured her. "Better that you're surrounded by us. Where's Nick?"

She angled her head toward Beck's first-floor owner's suite. "With the baby, who is asleep but is making threatening wake-up noises."

"Then why don't I go out and greet our guests, and you and Nick can join me with the baby when he wakes up?"

Savannah closed her eyes. "I have a bad feeling about this, Mom."

Beck put her hands on Savannah's shoulders, narrowing her eyes. "Honey, if this pushy, ambitious, judgmental might-someday-be-your-mother-in-law tries to break you two up? She'll have to go through Rebecca Foster first."

Savannah blinked, shocking Beck with some rare tears in her eyes. "All day I've been meaning to tell you how much I love you, but I've been too busy fretting."

"We've got your back, baby."

"And your front, side, top, and bottom," Nick said, cruising around the corner, no baby in sight. "He went back to sleep, and I'm not waking him. No reason everyone's world should be turned upside down by Hurricane Diana."

As he walked to Savannah, Nick's blue eyes were full of concern and caring, as if he, too,

was ready to battle with anyone trying to separate him from Savannah. Another one of the many reasons Beck adored this man.

Watching them hug, Beck said, "You guys are strong. No matter what gets thrown at you, I think you'll survive it."

Nick smiled and added her into a group hug. "Momma Beck," he said, his voice husky with affection, "you are the best. Maybe my mother can take some lessons from you."

"Aww, you're sweet." She inched back. "You know, Sav, you've got a keeper here."

"As if I don't know that."

At the sound of a car door, they separated and looked at each other.

"Game time," Savannah whispered.

BECK LED the way to the front entryway, opening the door to see a gray sedan parked in the shell driveway. Diana Frye was already out and looking toward the beach, where she could no doubt see she was walking into a private wedding party.

As she walked down the steps to do her hostess thing, Beck took a moment to assess Nick's mother. She knew nothing about Diana except she was a powerhouse who never let anything get in her way. But she *had* to have a chink in her armor, right?

That "armor" currently included an outfit of silk pants and a drapey top that even Beck could recognize as Chanel. Shiny auburn hair was styled in a classic bob, angle-cut around an attractive jaw and mouth that had nary a wrinkle, flaw, or minor sign of natural aging. She wore large sunglasses, hiding her eyes, but her body was slender and toned, and she moved with grace and confidence. It was instantly obvious where Nick got his extraordinarily good looks.

"You must be Diana," Beck said, extending both hands as she reached the bottom of the stairs. "Welcome to Coquina House."

The other woman barely managed a tight smile as if Beck were no more than a valet. Then she zoomed by, tearing off her sunglasses to exclaim, "Nicky! Oh my God, it's been so long!"

Nick jogged down the last few steps with a cool smile in place. "Way too long." Points to him for not pointing out that the months of near silence were on her part, not his. Did this woman think they didn't know that?

Diana threw her arms around Nick and squeezed, whispering something in his ear.

"Yep. Glad you finally made it," he said, easing her away. "I want you to meet Savannah."

She was a few steps behind him, but Diana didn't take her eyes off Nick. She pressed both hands on Nick's cheeks and squeezed like he was a seven-year-old.

"You should use sunscreen, Nicky. You don't want to look like Robert Redford by the time you're forty. Old and withered Redford, I mean. Not *The Way We Were* Redford."

He deftly stepped out of her touch, ignored the comment, and backed up one stair. Very deliberately, he reached for Savannah's hand. "This is Savannah Foster, my—"

Diana held up her hand, cutting him off. "Savannah." She held out a hand. "The woman who stole my son. A pleasure."

Beck waited for the usual Savannah quip, nailing the woman with a perfect nickname, or deflecting the passive aggressive insult by making everyone laugh.

But Savannah just took Diana's hand and nodded, murmuring, "It's nice to meet you."

Come on, Sav. Don't let her bulldoze that spunk out of you.

Dropping Savannah's hand, Diana turned to the car. "Max! Get off the phone, please."

The driver's side tinted window lowered, revealing a silver-haired man with a phone to his ear. He held up one finger and mouthed, "Just a second" to Diana, then zipped the window back up again.

"Oh, every other client is so important to him now," Diana said. "Just because you left him in the dust, Nicky."

"And you haven't met Beck," Nick continued, undaunted by her.

Still holding Savannah's hand, Nick brought her down the stairs, past his mother, forcing the woman to face Beck.

"This is Rebecca Foster, Savannah's mother, and the owner of the beautiful B&B. Beck, this is Diana Frye and that will be Max Meadows, who you will soon learn has a phone growing out of his head."

"Hello, Diana," Beck said, not bothering to attempt another handshake. "We're so happy you're here."

She finally looked directly at Beck, her eyes blue like Nick's, and the skin around them as smooth as baby Dylan's backside. She'd had work done, that's for sure.

"Ah, the other grandmother," she said. "What's the kid call you?"

Beck blinked. "He's not talking yet."

"Good, because the first human to call me 'grandma' is going to suffer my wrath." She added a fake laugh and looked at Nick. "So where is he? I didn't fly commercial across the country to stand in this wretched heat. Show me the baby. I have gifts. Max! Get the bags!"

"Dylan's asleep, inside," Nick said. "Why don't we—"

Just then, the car door opened and an older man stepped out, brushing off expensive khaki-colored trousers as he stepped on the broken coquina driveway.

"Sorry about that." Then he beamed at Nick. "There he is! Looking like a million bucks, as always."

He instantly swept Nick into a bear hug, patting his back and looking over his shoulder and winking at Beck. "Or ten million, on a good year." He chuckled and pushed Nick back. "Good to see you, kid. Very good."

"You too, Max. Sav, this is Max Meadows, my former manager."

Max stabbed his chest with a pretend dagger. "Former. Darkest word in the English language." Then he grinned. "Kidding. Kind of. Savannah. You're gorgeous. No surprise. Hello."

He shook her hand with visible force, then turned to Beck as Nick completed the introductions.

"No way you're her mother," he said. "Did you have her at ten? Pleased, Beck. Pleased."

She smiled and shook his hand, amused by his staccato delivery.

Next to him, Diana was fanning herself with her hands. "Please, God, tell me there's air conditioning in this cute little bungalow."

Cute little bungalow? Beck stole a look at Savannah, who secretly rolled her eyes.

"Just inside," Beck said, ushering them all to the steps. "But be warned, we're celebrating a wedding."

"As long as it's not Nick's, I couldn't care less." Diana

marched toward the stairs, leaving the rest of them in the dust.

"A wedding venue, huh?" Max said, lingering and looking around. "How frequently do you have them here?"

"This is our first," Beck said. "We aren't officially opened yet, just launching this spring."

He nodded. "Interesting. How many rooms?"

"Five bedrooms with en suites, gorgeous views, and beach access," she said, using the words from the website they'd been working on.

Max looked impressed. "Nice. That could work. That could work quite nicely."

"For what?"

He gave her a slow smile, pinning her with an intense gaze. "I'm letting Diana handle the timing. You'll find that's very important to her."

"The timing...of what?"

"You'll see."

Confused by the answer, Beck hustled to catch up and jump back into hostess role. Slipping past the others, she managed to get up the stairs first, talking as she walked.

"Today's event isn't technically a wedding," she said, "but a vow renewal. However, there is dancing, champagne, and the cake's been cut. Please join us and get comfortable after your long drive."

Just then, Peyton stepped outside to the covered porch, holding the baby. "Someone's awake," she announced.

That stole everyone's attention, as Savannah leaped toward her sister.

"There's my little man." She practically siphoned the

baby out of Peyton's arms like he was her personal security blanket.

"And not even crying," Beck said with forced happiness. "He's such a good baby."

"He is that." Nick followed Savannah and stood next to her, putting his arm around her and gazing down at Dylan like they were posing for a Christmas card.

"Cute kid," Max announced, climbing a few stairs to get closer. "Looks like a chip off the old Frye block."

They were all at the top of the stairs now, but Diana hadn't moved. She stood at the bottom, looking up at them, an unreadable expression on her face.

"Come on, Mom," Nick said, his voice softer than it had been. "Meet your grandson."

Her eyes glimmered at that, and she finally took a step forward, then started up the stairs, silent and staring.

Savannah swallowed and held the baby a little tighter. "Let's go inside where you can sit with him."

They all headed into the entryway and Savannah walked right to the overstuffed sofa in the living area and angled her head for Diana to sit down.

"If you want to hold him," Savannah said, "you have to sit down."

"I want..." Diana walked through the small group and sat on the sofa, dutifully following orders. Her gaze was still locked on Dylan, who, remarkably, hadn't fussed. It was as if he knew he was about to be judged and had to be on his very best behavior.

"Here you go." Savannah slowly lowered the baby into Diana's arms.

Beck realized she was holding her breath, and maybe so were the others. Nick, Max, Peyton, and, of course,

Savannah, all watched as Diana Frye held her grandson for the first time.

"Oh." Diana let the word out on a sigh as she let the baby settle against her. "Oh, my. He's...he's..."

"Perfect," Savannah supplied.

"I was going to say small." She looked up. "Is he okay? Surely it isn't normal for a child this age to be this small."

Good heavens, Beck thought. If her own grandchild doesn't soften her, what will?

"Well, he was pretty anxious to get out and came a few weeks early," Savannah said, her voice tight with nerves that just broke Beck's heart. Savannah shouldn't have to be scared of this woman.

"He looks just like Nicky," Diana said. "He's a clone, in fact. An absolute clone."

Irritation snaked up Beck's spine. Dylan *was* half Foster.

Suddenly, the baby's little face got red, as if he, too, were protesting the clone remark. Then, with a strangled sound, he turned his head left then right, then squeezed his eyes shut.

Savannah sort of lunged forward, but Dylan opened his mouth and spewed his last meal with some projectile force. It landed right on Diana's silk top, a splotch of milky white vomit against creamy Chanel.

Beck just backed up and bit her lip. Sometimes karma was a bitch. And sometimes, she was just a five-month-old baby who had something to say.

CHAPTER SIX

NICK

*W*hen his mother didn't react at all to a shirt full of Dylan barf, Nick knew something was up. Way up. Like scary up.

Savannah leaped into action and Beck and Peyton gasped. Max barked a laugh, and everyone sort of descended at the same time. But Nick didn't move, carefully scrutinizing the face he knew so well, looking for her tell.

How he longed to trust his mom the way, well, the way Savannah trusted hers. But she'd always been more of a manager than a mother, which was why he'd called her "Diana" instead of "Mom" since he was a child. Back then, she'd insisted on being called by her first name in front of all the "important people" so she had legitimacy and didn't get treated like just another stage mother.

So, she was Diana. And he was still on guard with her. Always, always on guard.

So when Diana *used her fingers* to wipe Dylan's mouth, he really took note.

"Well, you made a mess of me, didn't you?" she whispered.

Nope. Not normal. His mother didn't care one whit for a baby, unless she thought she could get him cast in a diaper commercial, which would happen over Nick's dead body.

"I'm so sorry, Mrs...Diana," Savannah sputtered, reaching to take him from Diana's arms. "He never...well, he does do that, but, oh my gosh, your beautiful top. I'm so sorry."

She gave him up without a fight. "Max, get my suitcase so I can change. Nick, grab me a towel so I can clean up. Is there a room I can have for privacy?"

"Absolutely." Beck came forward with a kitchen towel Peyton had magically produced. "Let's get you upstairs to the Queen Room."

"I'll take him while you go upstairs," Savannah said, rocking him gently, although he was already calm. That always happened after he got rid of whatever was upsetting him.

Diana leveled her gaze at Savannah. "You'll come with us. You'll need to be in on the conversation. Give him to your nanny."

"My..." She glanced at Nick for help.

"No nanny," he said coolly, coming closer as if his very presence could protect his woman and son. "What's the topic of the conversation?"

Diana smiled as she stood. "Your wedding. The one you're having in, what is it, Max?"

"Two weeks, well, three. It takes a little time to sign the contracts."

Nick blinked in shock, then looked at Savannah in

time to see her jaw drop wide open. Behind him, he heard Beck gasp.

"Excuse me?" Savannah managed to ask, which was better than Nick. He was literally speechless.

"Live on national TV." Diana said. "You've heard of *Celebrity Wedding*, the reality show. You're about to star in it, my dear. Oh, there's my suitcase. Beck, is that what people call you? Lead the way to your Queen suite," she said. "I really do like the sound of that."

"It's just the Queen Room," Beck murmured, gesturing for Max to follow her with the bags. "After the palm tree, not the guest."

Savannah still looked like a deer in headlights, but Nick just watched Diana, his brain ticking through what game she was playing, and what strategy was on the table.

Reverse psychology? Bluff calling? A surprise twist? She had all the moves at her fingertips.

"Did...did you know about this?" Savannah whispered when Beck led them out.

"No," he said. "I know what the show is, but..."

"Nick. You're not going to let her talk us into...that, are you?"

Something told him that wasn't what Diana was up to. Talk him out of it, more likely. Yes, that made sense. She'd back him into a corner and expect him to howl and run. Corner-backing was a favorite move of hers.

But she didn't know him at all. And she really didn't know how much he loved Savannah. Married in three weeks on TV? In fact, the truth was...he didn't *hate* the idea at all.

"Would it be the worst thing in the world, Sav?"

Her eyes widened. "Getting married or doing it on live TV?"

"Both."

She searched his face, still in low-grade shock. "Why?"

"Um, because I love you and want you to share my life and last name?"

She stared, silent, shocked, and then her eyes narrowed with suspicion. "You're really good at delivering a line, Nick."

"Especially when it's true." He took her hand. "I know the host of the show," he said. "Sunny Washington is another client of Eliza Whitney, my agent. I'm surprised Eliza didn't call me herself, but her husband's very sick." He gave her fingers a squeeze. "Sav, we've never been conventional. Not from day one. Why would we start now? Let's hear them out."

"You can't be serious."

"If I know my mother—and I do—there's so much more to it than what appears on the surface. Let's find out and drive her crazy by doing the opposite of what she thinks we'll do."

A smile threatened as she looked at him, her beautiful hazel eyes locked on his and hitting the target of his heart.

"Okay, but let me give the baby to Peyton. I don't want to drop him when I hear about this...insanity."

"Insanity." He put his arm around her, already seeing a way to move fast and efficiently to get what he wanted —because what he wanted was the woman who'd been pretty damn hard to pin down. "Savannah. Is marrying me so insane?"

She didn't answer. But there was enough spark in her eyes for him to know he had a chance of convincing her that maybe this wasn't a terrible idea. And he had a feeling that *was* exactly the opposite of what his mother had planned.

DIANA CHANGED in the bathroom while Max Meadows, true to form, was on not one, but two calls simultaneously, out on a small balcony overlooking the mangroves and a warren of canals visible from this level.

Savannah and Nick settled into the two small chairs in the sitting area, sharing a secret smile like a couple of bad kids who'd been called into the principal's office.

"Love that plan! Love it! Call you soon, Jack! Promise!" Max's voice floated through the not-quite-closed French doors, then he signed off and joined them, beaming at Nick. "Kid. You look amazing! This fatherhood thing agrees with you!"

Every sentence, every single one, was an exclamation, making Nick remember how exhausting this man could be. As he spoke, Max perched on the end of the bed, moving one of Diana's Louis Vuitton bags, which were already open and spilling clothes.

"So, *Celebrity Wedding*. Great idea, huh?" Max asked.

"It's interesting, I'll give you that." Nick glanced at Savannah, who just bit her lip. He could read her mind, though. He knew she was wondering how he could get behind a live wedding on television. Wasn't that everything he'd just walked away from?

Not exactly. Reality TV wasn't a role. And this wasn't a game...it was marriage, and exactly what he wanted.

"Sunny Washington's the host," Nick said, "and she's Eliza's client. Funny I haven't heard from Eliza about this, not even a text."

Max shot him an enigmatic look that didn't feel...right.

"Sunny's not hosting?" he asked. "Or she and Eliza parted ways?"

"Eliza is—"

"Wait!" Diana called from behind the bathroom door. "Do not decide a single thing without me."

"Like that's possible," Max mumbled with a sly smile to Nick.

"I heard that, Maximillian!" The door popped open, and Diana appeared in a completely different outfit, this one the color of a ripe peach, a skinny column of a floor-length dress with gold chains draped over her flat chest. She exuded L.A. skinny-chic, with red-framed glasses now and equally bright lips. Was all that make-up necessary? He loved his mother, but, like Max, she exhausted him.

"Is there room service?" she asked, sweeping into the room. "I need some sparkling water. With a lime. And no ice. Not in a stemmed glass, please."

Savannah started to move, but Nick reached out and put his hand on her arm. "Don't leave."

She blinked at him, then fell back in the chair. "I'll text my mom," she said. "I'm sure she can have something brought up."

"This little inn is *cute*," Diana said as she looked

around the shiplapped room with coastal décor. "Farm-house on the sea, I'd call it."

Savannah shifted in her chair, no doubt resenting having to hear her mother's classy and creative design ideas reduced to an HGTV cliché. But she kept her eyes on her phone, thumbing a text to that very mother who would certainly leap to comply with Diana's requests. The good mother. The one Nick loved more each day.

"So, what else can you tell us about this *Celebrity Wedding* idea?" he pressed.

"Ahhh...wedding." Diana let the word out on a sigh, falling onto the bed and dropping back on the mountain of pillows. She shoved one of the bags back at Max with her foot. "Quite the idea, isn't it, Nicky? Married on national television."

Quite. "I gotta admit, Diana. I didn't think you'd embrace something so...tacky," he said, dancing around the obvious question of *Why?*

"Because I've..." She gave a tight smile to Savannah. "I don't want to say *lost*. That's harsh. But if you really aren't coming back to Hollywood, Nicky, then my gut tells me you should go out in style. Tell him about the show, Max."

His manager nodded, always ready to do Diana's bidding.

"Ratings are sky high, Nick," he said. "Sky freaking high. These are like *Bachelor* numbers, and if they get *you*? The money is nutso, buddy. Oh, and they pay for every single detail. All you have to do is agree to have some cameras around for the big stuff, you know? Proposal, dress shopping, rehearsal dinner. They tape that business the first week, edit it all into a package, then air the ceremony live as the last half hour of the show. Wham, bam, done and done. Easy peasy."

"It can't be that easy," Nick said.

"Well, Sunny's gonna sniff out juice," Max replied with a dry laugh.

Savannah leaned forward. "I don't speak Hollywood. What does 'sniff out juice' mean?"

Max shrugged. "You know, the action. The drama. The emotion. She'll look for cracks in the foundation, but if she doesn't find them, you're fine."

Where would his cracks be? "I'm not leaving Coconut Key," Nick said simply. "I'm here. Savannah's here. Dylan's here. And our wedding, on or off screen, will be here."

"Crystal clear and that's easy to negotiate," Max assured him.

But Savannah's frown deepened as she looked from one to the other. "Nick, we're not..."

"Engaged?" Max interjected. "Thank God. You'd just have to re-enact it for the cameras if you were."

"On live TV?" Savannah asked.

"No, that part's taped," Diana said, with a little impatience in her voice. "Weren't you listening?"

"But it's on TV," Savannah clarified. "For the world to watch?"

"Oh, honey." Diana sat up. "You're not part of Nicky's world, so it's understandable you'd be scared to death. But this is what celebrities do. Isn't it, Nicky?"

Okay, now he was beginning to get an idea of what this was about. Diana had long ago turned reverse psychology into an art form. In this case, she fully expected that forcing him to marry Savannah would make him change his mind. And, while she was at it, she'd make Savannah doubt him—and herself. Which wasn't going to happen and, damn it, he'd prove it to her.

"I'm still surprised you're behind this, Diana," he said to his mother.

"As you know, my darling son, my every decision has been for your good." She sat up and her eyes tapered as she sliced him with a signature Diana Frye look. "Your name, and mine, I might add, is mud in Hollywood right now. Lower than mud. Cesspool level. Tell them, Max."

Max nodded. "You took a hit, Nick. Not gonna lie. Netflix is furious to lose *Magic Man,* which was making a freaking fortune, so this could appease them."

"Why didn't Eliza call me?" he asked again as the question tweaked him. His agent might not have brokered the deal, but she would handle certain aspects of it, especially with Sunny Washington's involvement as the show host.

He didn't like the look on Max's face, though. "Eliza Whitney is about to get shown the door at AAR."

Wait, *what?* "Eliza? Fired?" Nick demanded, curling his lip at the thought of the machine that was All Artists Representatives. Eliza hadn't been happy there for years, but stayed for the amazing money and benefits, too wrapped up in her husband's illness to look for another job.

Diana lifted a bony shoulder. "They know she didn't exactly strong-arm you to stay on *Magic Man.*"

"The decision was *mine*," he said. Eliza had just been the only human with a heart in the process of making that decision. She had confided in him that his unexpected family and new life gave her...hope. That was her exact word.

"Someone has to pay for this loss."

"Someone other than me," Diana ground out.

"You?" Nick asked.

"Did you forget that I spent thirty years building your career?" she demanded. "I've attached my reputation, my friendships, and all my heart to your career. And now that your name is garbage, so is mine. I can't walk into a salon, a restaurant, or a fundraiser without knowing what people are saying."

He didn't really care about the gossipmongers at his mother's spa, but Eliza? That bothered him. "Would doing this show really help?" Nick asked Max.

"It can't hurt," Max said. "And it definitely would save Eliza's job."

A tendril of guilt wound through him. Firing Eliza was inexcusable. Especially when her husband was literally on his deathbed. Damn it, he hated them all. "Well, I owe her something, after all she's done for me."

Diana snorted. "Not to mention me."

"I don't have to mention you," Nick said dryly. "You will."

"Okay, then." Max slapped his hands on his thighs. "Let's just nail down a date. They can be here in a week, once we dot *i*'s and cross *t*'s on the paperwork."

"Wait a second." Savannah turned to Nick. "Are you *sure* about this?"

"About marrying you? As sure as I am about taking my next breath."

Diana stifled a moan and shifted on the bed.

But Savannah bit her lip and studied him. "You think we're ready to take that step?"

"I am." Nick leaned over to take her hand, holding her gaze. "Are you?"

So ready. She managed a nod, not trusting her voice.

"And this show?" He squeezed her hand. "It'll be fun and maybe help someone I care about."

For a long moment, they looked into each other's eyes and just as Savannah opened her mouth to respond, Diana shot to her feet.

"There will be a prenup, of course. Detailed and specific. You can get out of this at any time, but—"

"Then what's the point?" Savannah asked.

"Oh." Diana crossed her arms. "You hear the word prenup and have second thoughts?"

Nick turned to her and narrowed her eyes. "You don't know a thing about her, Diana. You think you do, but you don't. She's not in this for money, or fame. She cares about Dylan."

"And you," Savannah whispered, the soft words touching his heart.

He squeezed her hand. "You're a hundred percent sure, babe?"

"Let's talk tonight and make a final decision tomorrow."

"Excuse me?" Beck tapped on the door and came in with a wooden tray holding two cold Pellegrinos and glasses—not stemmed—with limes. She'd also added a mini charcuterie board with fruit and desserts. "Some refreshments for my guests."

"Oh, lovely, Beck. Is that right? Beck?" Diana asked for at least the second time. "It's such an unusual name."

"Short for Rebecca," she said, setting the tray on the

table between Nick and Savannah's seats. "Are you comfortable in here?"

"Define comfortable," Savannah murmured, giving her mother a wry look.

"I love it here," Diana said. "It's darling."

Beck straightened slowly, sliding a secret look to Savannah. "And your bags are already up here. Why don't you stay and be our inaugural guests? At no charge, of course."

"Mom, you don't have to—"

"Lovely and I are looking for beta guests, so all we'd ask for is some positive critique."

"Oh, I can critique," Diana said, making Nick snort. "And I do like the idea of not moving again. What do you think, Max?"

"Is there another room?" he asked. "Diana and I are strictly platonic."

"Of course," Mom said quickly. "The Royal Palm Room has an ocean view. And there's a very small room next to it, the Canary Palm. You can take your pick. I'd love to have you as my first guests."

Now there was a mother, Nick mused, always amazed at Beck Foster's singular and nurturing brand of love. She was protecting her daughter and grandson—and Nick—with one unselfish and brilliant suggestion.

"It really would help me out so much," Beck added.

But convention dictated that Nick put up some kind of fight, even though he personally loved the idea. And the woman who'd suggested it.

"We have a lot of room at The Haven," Nick said.

"But do you have staff?" Diana demanded.

"No staff, but—"

"Turn down service? And food like this?" She lifted a plate of pastries. "We'll stay here, and everyone will be more comfortable." She took a delicate bite of cake. "Delish! We'll have to get this baker for your wedding cake."

Beck's eyes flashed. "You're going to do it?" she asked in a shocked whisper.

"We're going to talk about it," Nick said.

She turned to Savannah. "Are you sure about this, honey?"

"No." She directed the answer to Diana. "And I'm not easily bulldozed."

"Neither am I," Diana said, the faintest challenge in her voice. "Now you two go home and chat. Max will email you the details and contract. We'll reconvene tomorrow. I'm exhausted from that flight and this bed is divine." She literally shooed them out as she fell on the bed with a dramatic sigh. "Leave the cake, though. Goodbye."

And just like that, they were dismissed. Nick was used to it, but he took Savannah's hand, sensing she was left reeling.

As they walked out, Nick leaned close to Beck and whispered, "If I didn't already love you, I would now."

She smiled up at him. "Protect my daughter, or you're dead."

He laughed because he knew she was kidding. Kind of.

CHAPTER SEVEN
PEYTON

"*W*ell, there's a sight for sore eyes."

Peyton looked up from the baby and darn near dropped the bottle she held. And somehow managed not to say, *So are you*.

"Hey, Val. How'd you find me in here?"

He looked from side to side around the large master suite where she'd slipped away to give Dylan a bottle while Savannah dealt with the new arrivals.

"It wasn't easy," he said. "You have been elusive today."

"Just so busy with the event," she replied.

"I know. I tasted everything you made." He took a few steps closer to the sitting area, hesitant as if waiting for her permission. "You always knocked Jessie's crab cakes out of the park."

"Thanks."

"Salmon had to say it," he teased, his dark eyes dancing with the first fish pun they'd shared in a long, long time.

And it was just enough to soften her heart. "Have a seat, Valentino," she said. "I just started and Dylan's a slow eater."

He sighed as he dropped into the chair across from her, studying her intently. "It's a good look for you," he finally said, nodding toward the baby. "I know you..."

Always wanted one, she mentally finished when he didn't.

"He's a great baby," she said, trying to stay non-committal.

He leaned in to really look at him. "He's seriously cute."

She beamed with the pride of an aunt. "He's the king of Coconut Key, that's for sure." After a beat, she added, "Are you having fun at the wedding?"

"No," he said simply. "I came expecting to spend the whole day and evening with you."

And spent it with Toni Cross instead. But she tried not to react. "You should have let me know you were coming."

"I didn't know until the last minute," he said, finally relaxing enough to sit back. "And all the way down here, I still wasn't sure."

"You didn't want to come back to Coconut Key?" she asked, purposely keeping it not-too-personal.

"I was scared," he said softly.

She just looked at him, confused by the answer.

"I was afraid I'd take one whiff of hibiscus or feel the first tropical breeze or catch sight of a big old trawler bouncing on the waves or...see Peyton Foster looking like a dream and *pffft*. I'd be right back where I was eight months ago."

She tried to swallow, but hit a lump in her throat the size of a golf ball. "So, where are you now that you are terrified of memories?"

He studied her face, quiet for a long time. Long enough for her to take in the angles of his cheeks and jaw, the shape of his mouth, the bottomless black eyes trimmed in bottle brush lashes. Time and distance had only made him cuter, sadly.

"I'm where I belong," he said quietly. "In Miami, with a family that needs me, in a job that's making me financially secure, and in a city that has always been home."

Damn it. She hated every word of that answer. "Well, that's good," she answered with impressive cool. "How is your family?"

"Abuelita is not feeling great, and my mother is...overwhelmed."

"Oh, no." He'd told her so much about his grandmother, she felt she knew her. "What's wrong?"

"Many things. She's eighty-two." He just kind of waved his hand, as if he didn't want to get into the details. "And Papi, my grandfather, had to retire, which he hates. They live with my parents, you know."

She nodded, remembering. "And Ramon?" she asked, remembering his brother, who she'd met briefly once.

"Actually, Gabriella is pregnant, so they're good."

But there was another family. Marisa Vega's family. He'd told her that his late fiancée had lived next door to him growing up, that the two families were deeply connected. One of the reasons he'd gone back was for them, because he'd left suddenly after Marisa had passed away.

"Anyone else?" she asked, purposely vague.

He glanced out the window and sighed. "The Vega family hasn't quite recovered from their loss. As a matter of fact, Marisa's parents split up and sold their house. Their other daughter, Natalia, is trying to hold things together..." He shook his head. "It's hard when you lose a child. Even a grown one."

"I can't imagine," she whispered, looking down at the baby. "But you're glad you went back?" She had to know the answer to that. He'd left Coconut Key and their budding romance for all of these people. Was it worth it?

He shrugged. "Like I said, I'm where I belong and where I'm needed, doing the right thing for people I love." He turned his gaze from the window and looked directly at her. "Some of them, anyway."

What exactly was he saying? She waited, the only sound her heartbeat and the soft suckle of Dylan's lips on the bottle she held.

"Those people don't keep me warm at night, Pey," he finally said, his voice thick.

"In Miami?" She dug for a light tone. "Just open the window and you should be warm."

But Val, the king of the joke, wasn't smiling. "You know what I mean. I'm there, but I spend a lot of time remembering...us."

She frowned at him. "I hardly ever hear from you. You barely text, and never call, and..." She shut herself up, sounding like a nag.

"Because it's too hard," he said. "I'm trying to forget, but I can't. When Jessie invited me here, I had to come. I had to try one more time."

"Try...what?"

"For us again."

"Val, there was barely an 'us.'" They'd dated less than three months. Yes, it had been lovely and romantic, but she'd blown it with her ultimatum, telling him she was looking for...the whole package. A few days later, he was packed and saying goodbye. And she couldn't forget how much that hurt.

"Anyway, you just said you're where you belong. How is that CPA firm?"

"Let's just say...the net income beats fishing." He winked. "See what I did there? Net?"

She couldn't help smiling. "So, the money's good."

"It's great," he said, "and that helps my family, which is what really matters."

"And Miami? It's home, you say." If he loved it so much, what was he asking her?

"It is, but...what's the expression. Home is where the heart is?" He inched forward, putting his elbows on his knees. "Peyton, I'm just gonna come right out and put my cards on the table. I miss you."

She didn't respond, but let the words roll over her, wanting to wallow in them for just a moment since she'd dreamed of hearing them for so long.

"I've missed you, too, Val," she finally whispered. "But I had to move on."

His eyes widened and he inched back. "Are you with someone else?"

"Actually, no."

His visible relief touched her.

"But I *am* someone else." She sat a little straighter, shifting Dylan in her arms as she made the proclamation. "I'm working as the assistant manager at Jessie's newly reimagined restaurant, the Coquina Café, and I cook there a lot. I'm about to start a culinary program in Key West, and I have my own dreams of maybe opening a restaurant or writing a cookbook like Jessie did. I'm living in the guest house at The Haven, but only until next month, when my condo will be ready. I got in on a new build near the marina, so I'm a homeowner now."

It was like he actually fell with each word she spoke. His jaw loosened, his eyes softened, and his shoulders seemed to drop with disappointment. "Wow. That's...a lot."

She was also starting to consider having a baby on her own, but wasn't quite ready to share that with anyone yet. It felt like a little bit of an admission that she'd failed, and the idea was too new to share.

After a moment, he huffed out a breath and threaded his fingers through his hair, which was much shorter now than when he'd lived in the Keys, but no less silky looking. "Man, I blew it."

Wow. There should have been so much victory coursing through her when he said those three words, but she didn't feel that way at all. Instead, she tipped her head and gave a sad smile, slowly pulling the empty bottle from a sleeping baby's mouth.

"You made the best decision you could at the time," she said, looking down at Dylan.

"Ouch."

She looked up.

"It hurts when you let me off the hook like that." He winked and stuck his finger in his cheek, pretending to have a fishhook in his mouth.

"I'm not letting you off the hook," she said. "You hurt me and I cried. A lot."

"Pey, I'm so sorry."

She lifted one hand to stave off the apologies. "It was exactly what I needed, Val. I had to stop looking for a husband and start building my own life. I have quietly done that, all while the spotlight was on Savannah and her baby and the aftermath of the hurricane and the B&B and the new restaurant and Chuck. All that time, I have just very carefully created a life for myself. I've watched my mother do the same and now I'm here. Where *I* belong."

He didn't reply for a moment, but she could see the words deeply affected him.

"Well, I guess I wasted this trip, then," he said huskily.

"How so? You didn't want to come to Jessie's vow renewal ceremony?"

"I came to see you, Peyton. We didn't have enough time together. I left before I should have, at least as far as our relationship was concerned. I can't leave Miami—my family needs me and I need this job. But..."

She waited, watching him, not quite sure where he was going—because if it was where she thought it was? She wasn't sure what to say.

"I didn't realize you had so much going on," he said. "Which was damn stupid and selfish of me. But I came to ask you if you'd consider...trying again? With me."

How many times had she dreamed of him saying those words? Too many to count. But...

"You're not moving back here," she said.

"No, and I don't want to do long distance, not if we can avoid it." He leaned forward.

"What are you asking me?"

"Come to Miami, Pey. Let's try this for real. I want to

be that man you asked me to be that night down on the beach." He leaned even closer, as if the force of the words were just too much for him. "We don't know each other well enough to make that commitment yet, but I want to try. At the risk of making a bad fish pun, I really want to test the waters."

"Val," she whispered and leaned closer. "This is my home now. This is my family. This is my life. I'm not going to Miami."

"I didn't imagine you had serious feelings for me when I was here?" he asked. "You told me you did."

She stared at him, a little lost in those eyes. "Of course I did. I...still do."

He let out a little grunt like the admission had shot right through him.

"I just don't know what those feelings are," she finished.

"So there's a chance? Please, Peyton, all I want is a chance."

She just took a slow breath, not answering.

"This is what I want to ask you," he said. "Would you consider just spending a few weeks with me up there? Maybe before you move into the condo? Just see what it's like. Meet my family. Be with me again. Peyton, you can't make a decision for the rest of your life without knowing. You'll always regret it. You'll always wonder."

Was that true?

Would *not* going to Miami with him for a few weeks amount to "waiting" again—waiting for love, waiting for life, waiting for her dreams to come true? Wasn't that the very character trait she'd been determined to change?

"I have to think about it," she whispered. "How long are you here?"

"This weekend. I have to be at work on Monday. Can I see you tomorrow? I think I can snag us a boat for the day."

Very slowly, she nodded, a million questions in her mind. Only one needed to be asked, though.

"But, Val, what if I like it? What if we do belong together? What if this test turns into...everything?"

His lips lifted in a slow smile. "Would that be so bad?"

"But you won't leave, and I want to stay here."

"Let's talk tomorrow."

"Okay."

But what if they *did* belong together? Then getting everything she ever wanted would cost her...everything.

CHAPTER EIGHT

BECK

*B*y the time the sun disappeared and twilight fell over Coconut Key, the party was just about over. Coquina House was immaculate but for a late dessert and coffee bar Peyton had set up in the kitchen. The staff was gone, the music had ended, and the guests had left. All but Beck, Lovely, Josh, and Peyton, who all rested on the veranda.

From her chaise with her aching feet up, Beck sipped some decaf and peered out toward the dark water, spotting her granddaughter, Ava, along with Heather's kids, Maddie and Marc, tossing a football on the sand. Kenny spent more time teaching Marc how to throw a spiral than actually playing, while Heather, Maddie, and Ava chased two of Lovely's terriers. The third, Sugar, was plopped on Lovely's lap, recovering after a busy day.

Upstairs in the Queen Room, Diana apparently slept and Max was...somewhere. Beck had lost track of him after Savannah, Nick, and the baby took off, and Jessie and Chuck left. They'd headed home to get Beau in bed before they took off the next morning for what Savannah had dubbed the "familymoon"—a weeklong trip to Blackbird Beach on the west coast of Florida.

"Where's Toni?" Josh asked, looking around as if he were doing the same family and friend inventory that Beck had been.

"I haven't seen her for ages."

"She better not be with Val," Peyton murmured, speaking up for the first time in a while and adding a pretend frown.

Beck eyed her daughter, trying to decide if her long period of quiet was due to exhaustion—it had been a very busy day—or the fact that her ex-boyfriend had been here.

Toni seemed to finally let go of him later in the day, and Val had made a point of finding Beck to say goodbye before he left alone.

"Did you ever get a chance to talk to him?" Beck asked when Peyton didn't elaborate.

"For a little while," she said, sounding awfully vague.

"And how is he?"

"He's fine." She took a long sip of water, then pushed up. "I'm going to put the desserts away now."

As she walked by, Beck reached out her hand, all of her maternal instincts—and God knows she had those—on high alert. "You okay, Pey?"

"Sure. But I want to be sure everything is ready in there for your first breakfast. You have guests now, Mom."

"I can do that."

"I want to."

Because she did not want to talk about Val, Beck mused. "Peyton."

"Mmm, yeah?"

What had Val said to her? Whatever it was, she wasn't sharing. "You did an amazing job catering today. Somehow you managed to make it look effortless."

"I really enjoyed it," she said. "Creating the menu and ordering the staff around? Best part of my day."

But Beck couldn't help it—she had to know. "And seeing Val?" she asked.

Peyton looked at her for a long time, then shook her head. "Not yet, Mom."

Beck nodded, their connection so close and their communication so flawless, that she knew not to push. When Peyton closed the French door behind her, Beck turned to Josh, who'd been quietly taking in the conversation.

"Did you talk to him much today?" she asked.

"A little. He says he's doing well in Miami. Just got a promotion at the CPA firm."

Lovely snorted softly. "I still have a hard time wrapping my head around that Keys fisherman being an accountant. Although, I have to say, he looked more like one today with his short hair and tie. Still a handsome man, though."

"Toni thought so," Beck said softly.

Josh slid her a look, and she knew immediately the comment had bothered him. "I talked to her, Beck," he said. "Toni's a flirt and a party girl, but she doesn't have a mean bone in her body. As soon as I told her about his history with Peyton, she backed off."

"I know." She reached out and put her hand on his. "Something is bothering Peyton and you know that's going to bring out my inner Mama Bear. Toni was actually the life of the party today and I was happy to see her have such a good time."

He turned his hand and threaded their fingers. "I've got a little Papa Bear in me, too."

"Look, I'm going to make a better effort with her," Beck promised, and meant it. "I know she's very close to her mom and maybe not wild about me, but I swear, Josh, I'd like to change that."

He smiled and gave her fingers a squeeze, looking over her shoulder into the kitchen. "Thanks, Beck. And it looks like you're about to have your chance."

She sat up a little, vaguely aware that she was subconsciously "bracing" for Toni. She did that a lot around the young woman, who seemed to just suck the air out of every room she was in.

"Hello, hello, friends and fam!"

Like that. She burst onto the veranda with about ten times more energy than anyone else had left after a day like today. Of course, it helped that she was thirty and the three of them lounging out here were most certainly not.

"What a party, Beck!" She eased onto the bottom of Beck's chaise, smoothing the glove-tight dress that clung to a picture-perfect figure. "I can't believe this was the first time you did this at Coquina House!"

The compliment warmed, making Beck smile and wonder if Toni had made a similar promise to the one she just had. She sure seemed...enthusiastic toward Beck.

"Thank you, Toni," Beck said. "I have to give all the credit to Peyton, though. She's really the one that planned and executed. And cooked her heart out."

"This place is going to be a huge hit, I can tell." She crossed her legs and kept her focus on Beck in a way that seemed almost...well, more than usual. Most of the time, they exchanged a little small talk—and the subject was always Toni. "And you have real guests, I understand."

"Beta guests," Lovely interjected. "They aren't paying, so there's room for error."

"But still," Toni said, "are you ready for all that entails?"

Did she really care? Gosh, maybe Beck had misjudged her.

"I was just talking to Peyton," Toni continued. "Lots of work involved in running a B&B."

"No kidding," Lovely said, leaning into the conversation. "Beck knows I'm a little petrified but here we are, with customers expecting breakfast tomorrow. Clean towels, sheets, services..."

"I can handle it, Lovely," Beck assured her.

"But you're so busy with finishing the third floor," Toni said. "Peyton and I were just talking about that, too."

"That's sweet of you to worry, Toni."

"It really is," Josh added, a tinge of fatherly pride in his voice.

Toni leaned forward and looked hard at Beck. "You need help, and I need a job. What do you say?"

What? She sat up, not trusting herself to open her mouth and answer.

"Before you say a word, Beck, hear me out. Minimum wage is all I need. I'll get up really early, too."

Which would be ten or eleven for this woman. "Oh, Toni, I—"

"I know how to make beds and clean a bathroom. I can deliver room service. And those people might want errands run or...or...anything."

Think, Beck, think. "I doubt they'll be here that long, Toni."

"But then you'll have your next customer, and your next. And they *will* be paying." She put her hand on Beck's leg and squeezed. "Listen, you don't even have to pay me at first. Just let me help you guys out while you have these first guests, and if it works out? You can hire me. I'll literally intern as your staff."

"Toni, that's—"

"Amazing," Josh said, beaming at his daughter. "Antoinette Liliana Cross. I'm so proud of you."

"Thanks, Daddy." She grinned but her smile wavered. "I don't think I've convinced Beck, though."

Beck felt Josh's gaze on her and a slow heat roll up her chest.

Hadn't she *just* promised him she'd make an effort with Toni? And the young woman was offering her services for free?

"I can't let you work for free, Toni, so once we have—"

"Give me the little room on the second floor."

"Excuse me?"

"The, um, bird room?"

"Canary," Beck answered. "And it's the Canary Palm Room. They're all named after palm trees."

"Well, I'll stay there. So you will be giving me a great place to live, and you can cover my food, so—"

"Speaking of birds," Josh said with a laugh. "She eats like one."

Oh, yes. He loved this idea. But didn't he know that Toni was late for everything, and wasn't just a wannabe actress but kind of a drama queen? How was that help?

But Beck had *just* promised...

"I better consult my partner." She eased forward, looking past Josh to catch Lovely's eye, noting that her expression was...hopeful. "You like this idea?"

"I do," she said. "I think we need help, and Toni is offering to give that to us."

For nothing. *Why?* "You sure you don't want to work somewhere you can make more, or get tips?" Beck asked. "Waitresses get—"

"I'll get *experience*," she said, dragging out the word like she wanted nothing more than her first break in the hospitality industry.

"But you're moving to L.A., aren't you?" Beck asked.

"When the time's right. When I've lined up some real work. For now..." She pressed her hands together. "Please, Beck?"

She could feel Josh and Lovely looking at her, and could certainly see longing in Toni's beautiful brown eyes. What else could she do?

"Of course, Toni. You can start—"

"Tomorrow! I'll be here for breakfast. Six a.m. Or is that too early?"

Even Josh had to laugh at that.

"That sounds great," Beck said. "I better go tell Peyton she's off the hook for getting the scones in the oven. Now you can do that." If she knew what a scone was. And an oven.

Beck pushed off the chaise and slipped into the kitchen, instantly spying Peyton standing very still, staring out a window toward the dark night sky. Before she said a word, she saw Peyton's narrow shoulders shudder with a...

"Are you crying?"

She didn't turn but wiped her eyes in a dead giveaway move.

"Honey." Beck sailed across the kitchen, Toni forgotten. "I knew something was wrong. I knew it."

She turned and Beck bit her lip, her own heart shattering at the sight of Peyton's red-rimmed eyes.

"I'm going to kill him," Beck muttered. "I don't know what he did or said, but I'm going to kill him. And if this has anything to do with Toni—"

"It doesn't," she said.

"Good, because I just hired her."

"*What*?"

"I'll turn around and you can see the bruises from being backed into a corner. Not important," Beck waved her hand. "Please tell me what's wrong."

"Nothing."

Beck cocked her head and lifted her brows, silent.

"Really," Peyton said. "Nothing's wrong. Everything's right. Today my every dream came true and...I don't want it." She sobbed the last four words, her voice so thick, Beck wasn't sure she understood.

"What happened?"

"Val...oh, Mom, he all but proposed. I mean, he didn't, but he wants me back."

"That's wonderful." Beck reached for her. "Why are you crying?"

"He wants me in Miami. That's the only option."

Oh, not so wonderful. "That doesn't seem very much like...a compromise."

"It's not. He's really happy there, or at least he says he needs to be there, for family and work. But I need to be here for those things, too, and if I just walk away from everything I've done this past year, then who am I?" She wiped her nose and shuddered with another sob. "Just a desperate woman putting a man before my own needs."

"That's only one way to look at it. You really aren't ready to make that kind of commitment with him," Beck said. "Why don't you do long distance for a year or so? Miami's not that far away. Callie's there now, and we see her when she doesn't have her nose in a book."

"He didn't like the idea of long distance."

"Well, you don't like the idea of living in Miami." At Peyton's agonized look, Beck added, "Do you?"

"I don't...hate it," she whispered. "I still have feelings for him, Mom. Deep feelings that came flooding back the minute I saw him. But I also am so grounded here, and... and...I don't want to leave you and Lovely and Jessie."

"And we don't want you to leave." Beck didn't even want to think about life without Peyton around every day. She'd gotten plenty used to it when she lived in Atlanta and Peyton was in New York, but now that she'd had this dear daughter next to her for a year? Beck would be crushed to say goodbye.

But this was Peyton's life, and she had to let her live it.

"How did you two leave it?" she asked.

"We're going to spend the day together tomorrow, but what he wants is for me to go to Miami for a few weeks before my condo is ready, just to, you know..."

"Have a trial run," Beck finished.

"I could stay with Callie," she said, proving she'd given the idea serious consideration. "She has a pull-out couch, so I wouldn't be moving in with him or anything. Would you be mad if I went, Mom?"

"Mad? Oh, Peyton. I want you to be happy, as any

mother would." She took her hands. "I know you've changed, and I know you've built a life here, but I also know that being in a committed, forever relationship is your heart's desire. As is motherhood. And you adore Val. Might even love him."

"Definitely...might." She sighed, thinking about it, nodding, but then her eyes flashed. "Back up a second, though. Toni is going to work here? Seriously? She's never been on time for anything in her life. Have you lost your mind?"

"I lost something, and it felt like a battle. I don't know why she wants to, but—"

"Ohhh." Peyton inched back as realization dawned on her. "I know why. I know exactly why."

"Why...am I thinking I don't want to know this?" Beck asked.

"You'd figure it out in a minute. I'm surprised you haven't. She was out on the other patio for half an hour talking to Max Meadows. You don't think that wannabe starlet doesn't crave the attention of the manager to the Hollywood stars?"

Beck's mouth fell open. "Of course she does. And she never said a word."

"No, she'd rather let you think she's doing you a huge favor. Am I right?"

"So right."

Peyton shook her head. "She's probably not your best hire, Mom, but...I guess it would make Josh happy."

Beck's shoulders sank. "Only you would understand that."

"And only you would understand how impossible the decision that's facing me really is."

"Then don't make it tonight," Beck said, reaching to hug her. "Sleep on it and see how things go with Val tomorrow."

Beck held her a little tighter, already sensing that she might be losing this precious rock of strength and joy— and having her replaced by...someone not as precious. *Great*, she thought with a snort.

"Are you laughing?" Peyton asked.

"No, I'm just thinking of the irony of you and Toni switching places. Don't tell anyone I said this, but I feel like I'm getting cheated."

"You think I'm going, don't you, Mom?"

Beck leaned back and put a hand on Peyton's face. "I don't know. But whatever you decide, I'm here for you."

CHAPTER NINE
KENNY

*A*t least he didn't have to go to church alone.

That, Kenny decided as he pulled into a parking spot at Our Redeemer, was the real bright spot of meeting Heather here today. But last night after the wedding, he admitted to her that he really didn't love going there alone every week and didn't want to pressure Ava to go. So, of course, Heather suggested meeting him here today for the Sunday service.

And maybe that had been his not-so-secret goal all along.

He used the rearview mirror to watch the cars pulling in, waiting for the familiar SUV she'd driven down from Charleston. He let his mind drift back to yesterday's events—from the first time he'd seen her coming down the aisle as one of Jessie's attendants to late last night, when they'd hugged goodbye like friends and he'd high fived Marc and Maddie.

Every minute around Heather Monroe had been... too, too good.

He'd done a decent enough job of hiding just how happy he was to see her. Hadn't showered her with the compliments that echoed in his head like, *holy cow, you are beautiful.*

He hadn't touched her unless absolutely necessary, hadn't gotten caught staring at her, and hadn't stumbled over every other word because who could think straight looking into those blue eyes?

In fact, he'd just acted like the friend she wanted him to be.

And for that, he'd thank God as soon as he got into church.

He spotted her SUV pulling in and centered himself, taking a deep breath the way he used to when he'd be in an ambulance pulling up to an accident as an EMT. He wiped all other thoughts from his head except the job at hand. And today's job: never let her know how he felt. Her husband had died six months ago, and she was still tender and off limits.

He squinted into the morning sun as the SUV got closer, not sure what he was seeing. Was that Marc? Had she brought her son to church?

She certainly hadn't mentioned that last night. She only nodded with great understanding when he told her that Ava had gone to church once and was quiet and sad for the rest of the day. No surprise, Heather completely understood, since he'd shared enough about his late wife during their post-service coffees. She knew that Kenny had pulled away from his faith since his wife and son had died, too.

Because of Heather's interest in church, he'd started going again last fall when she'd asked him to "show her the ropes." And, oddly enough, he'd found an unexpected comfort. Heather found Jesus and never let go.

So, even after Heather and the kids went back to Charleston, Kenny had continued attending Sunday services at Our Redeemer. He didn't say much to anyone, hadn't joined any ministries, and stopped going to the Bible study Heather had convinced him to attend. He didn't tithe, didn't make friends, and frequently sat in the back row alone. But he did pray, and he and the Big Guy had reached a shaky truce.

She pulled into the empty spot next to him, flashing that stellar smile as she parked. Then she pointed a thumb toward Marc, who leaned forward to look past her and roll his eyes.

Okay, this was a story. And although part of him was disappointed they wouldn't be having their coffee alone after church, another part of him got a whole different kick out of seeing Marc. At fourteen, he was a few years older than his own son would be, had he lived through the fire that night.

He pressed down the familiar ache that came with the thought, and climbed out of his truck, coming around the front to greet them.

"Hey, Marc," he said, reaching out a hand to pat the kid's shoulder. "Nice to see you here."

Once more, he rolled his eyes. "I swore."

"So, this is, uh, punishment?" Kenny asked, scratching his chin to hide his smile.

"Basically," Marc said. "But when I heard you were going to be here, it was okay."

Heather looked up at Kenny with that warm, easy light in her eyes that he could bask in forever. "I don't want him to think of church as punishment," she said, "but he sure as heck wasn't spending the morning at the beach after that F-bomb exploded over breakfast."

"Mom, everyone says it."

"Not at *my* kitchen table." She started walking toward the church and Kenny easily kept up with her, exchanging a secret look with Marc, who really had to stop rolling his eyes.

"It's not so bad, kid," he said, putting a hand on the boy's shoulder.

"It's not a day at the beach."

He laughed as if he agreed, but a few minutes later, it was exactly where Kenny wanted to be. There wasn't a better place on earth than standing next to Heather Monroe when they stood to sing "How Great is Our God." When they greeted the people around them, many of the familiar faces lit up with recognition, asking where she'd been and taking a moment to meet Marc.

It all felt wonderfully like...home.

Was that Heather or church? He stopped questioning it after the singing ended, and just went for the ride. He thoroughly enjoyed a sermon about Daniel interpreting Nebuchadnezzar's dream that could not have been more boring for Marc, who only sneaked out his phone once. But even that earned a blistering look from his mother.

As they walked out, Marc fell behind them a bit, and Kenny leaned in to whisper, "I'm not sure the Old Testament hit its mark—or *Marc*—today."

She looked up at him, doubt in her eyes. "I know. I was hoping for Proverbs, not prophecy. Something he could relate to—but that's the story of my life with him."

"Heather." He put a comforting hand on her shoulder,

which was narrow but strong. "You're a great mother. Great."

"I'm struggling," she said softly. "He barely talks to me. And when he does...F-bombs." She glanced over her shoulder, then added, "Can you talk to him?"

"Me? About...what? Not swearing?"

"That's the least of my problems, Kenny. I think his friends are starting to drink, and it terrifies me."

"At fourteen?"

She gave a shiver. "I know. And he's falling a little behind in school, too. I don't think he wants that to happen, but he doesn't seem to have a compass like Maddie. And Ava's doing well. Do you talk to her about things like this? Drinking? School?"

"A little, but I have to be honest." He laughed softly. "Savannah does a lot of my dirty work, and Beck handles the rest. Ava just relates to women."

"I know." She sighed. "He needs a man in his life."

"Of course I'll talk to him," he said without hesitating. "But if he's struggling, are you sure it makes sense for you to come down here for a few weeks and leave the kids up there in school? Not that I'm second guessing your parenting, but—"

She held up her hand. "I know what you're saying, but..." She shut up as Marc joined them. "Tell you later."

"You want to get breakfast?" Kenny asked them.

Marc shrugged. "Sure. I can always eat."

And Kenny would try his best to help, but it'd been a long time since he was the parent of a boy.

What would he say to his young teenaged son about drinking and grades, if that kid were still alive?

He had no idea, but with the feeling of church still in his heart, he knew he wasn't completely alone.

MAN, the kid could eat. And eat. And finish Kenny's bacon.

They went to their usual after-church diner in Big Pine Key, which felt comfortable and familiar to Kenny, even though he hadn't come once since Heather left.

Marc was quiet, mostly, while Heather and Kenny chatted about yesterday's event, the family, Jessie's restaurant, and even the town. But when he'd finished eating everything on the table and three biscuits, Kenny knew he had to swing the conversation around to Marc.

"So, what did you decide about the baseball team?" Kenny asked him. "Didn't you tell me JV tryouts were in January?"

All he got was a signature shrug. "Yeah, no."

"You didn't make it?" He couldn't keep the shock out of his voice. "With that swing and your speed?"

Marc just gave a side-eye to his mother, who sipped her coffee as if that were the only way to keep from saying whatever she was thinking.

"I, um, didn't try out," he mumbled.

"Seriously?" Kenny inched forward, a little surprised at how disappointed he was. "You were so ready."

"None of my friends play sports."

"Then they're not the kind you want," Kenny said without thinking.

"I told him that," Heather finally chimed in. "But..."

"I can pick my own friends, Mom."

"Are they new friends?" Kenny asked.

"Yeah, a couple of transfer students. Just kids."

He assumed these were the troublemakers Heather had referenced. "So they don't play sports, that's cool. What do they do?"

"You know, Warzone."

He frowned, thinking. "Video game?" he guessed.

"The latest COD. That's *Call of Duty*? Please tell me you've played it. The game's been around forever."

"Yeah, I have." This time, Kenny shrugged. "Guys played at the fire station, but it really didn't do it for me. I'd rather be outside, throwing a ball." When Marc didn't answer, he narrowed his eyes. "And I could have sworn you would have, too."

"Well, maybe, but..." He huffed out a breath and glanced to his side at Heather.

"Mom thinks I'm a lost cause."

"I do not!" she exclaimed. "I'm just no fan of your friends."

He looked down then, and plucked at the last crumbs of biscuit.

"But you like these kids, right?" Kenny asked, sensing this was his opening.

"Yeah, you know, it's my first year of high school." He finally looked up and met Kenny's gaze with a little defiance in his eyes. "In the fall, we were down here after my dad died. I didn't make any friends. When I got back for this semester, I just...I didn't know anybody. I made a couple of friends who were new and..." He leaned back against the leather booth. "They thought baseball was lame."

Idiots. Kenny swallowed the insult and nodded. "What did they think was lame about it?"

"Practice every day after school."

"Prime COD time when parents are working," Kenny assumed.

"Prime," he agreed with a dry laugh.

"Marc, you are not playing video games while I'm gone," Heather said. "You're getting your grades up."

"How are those grades?" Kenny asked.

Marc shifted uncomfortably in his seat. "They're, you know. Not great."

Heather lifted a brow as if to say...*help.*

"So, do you care that your grades are bad?" he asked, hoping to kind of ease into the lecture rather than just hit the kid over the head with a "do better" message.

"Yeah, I care, but..."

"But what?" Kenny prodded.

He sighed again and kind of looked around like he'd rather pay the check than be parented by some dude. But Kenny had promised—and he'd prayed.

So, now what?

"If you study and do well, you're kind of going against the tide, is that right?"

Marc looked at him and nodded. "I don't want to be a geek, but I do want to get good grades. I don't know how to do both."

"You just do it," Kenny said. "You do what's right because...it's right."

"Easy for you to say," Marc fired back. "You're, like, a firefighter."

"I'm an EMT, not a firefighter. But mostly, I'm just a

guy who does construction, but if I don't do it right, the house will fall down."

Marc didn't smile at that, but swallowed hard, staring at Kenny. "I could still try and walk on the team."

Yes! Kenny managed not to react, but nod quietly. "So what's stopping you? You think you won't make it?"

"I think...I guess I care too much what people think. Certain people."

Ah, the friends. "I think 'certain people' might be a little jealous," Kenny said, "when they see how many girls go to the games."

Now that made Marc laugh. "They do, man."

In his peripheral vision, he saw Heather's eyes close at that, but he ignored it, finally getting somewhere. "Sometimes being different is hard, but in the long run, it's really good."

He shrugged. "I guess."

Kenny took a sip of cold coffee, searching his brain for some decent way to close this. A way to give him something to think about. Why hadn't that sermon given him something concrete? Nebuchadnezzar. Please.

But there was...Daniel.

"You remember that story in church? About the teenager who got sent to another country and helped the king?"

He tipped his head. "He kind of lost me on the giant metal statue and...no. I didn't get much out of that."

"It's not the best part of Daniel," Kenny agreed. "That kid—well, he was a prophet, technically—got taken from his home as a teenager and went to a totally strange place. Didn't know a soul, didn't understand the culture, was far away from everything he knew."

Heather leaned closer, her gaze on Kenny. "Kind of like high school."

"If high school isn't Babylon, I don't know what is," he said with a wry laugh. "But the thing is, Daniel broke the code. He did the right thing over and over again, when everybody around him didn't. He stuck to his guns and ate his food that everyone else thought was weird, and he got so strong and big, and was considered so smart, he ended up running the place."

Marc stared at him, silent, but it was the other set of eyes across the table that Kenny felt the most intently. Blue ones, full of...admiration.

And he couldn't remember the last time anything felt so good.

"Kenny's right," she said, a little breathlessly. "Daniel's the one who didn't get eaten by lions."

Marc glanced at her, then back to Kenny, still not saying anything.

"Anyway, what matters is..." Kenny put his elbows on the table, his hands fisted. "Walk on that team, kid. Go against the tide to do what feels right to you."

For a long time, Marc stayed silent, then swallowed. "I have to do it on Tuesday," he said softly. "That's the last day."

"Oh, I won't be there," Heather exclaimed.

"It's okay, Mom. I can...if I want to." He pushed his plate a little. "I'll think about it."

"So let's go throw some balls," Kenny said, pulling out his wallet to pay the bill. "And you know what? I think the batting cage is open today."

"Cool."

As they got up and headed to the car, Heather walked

next to him. She didn't say a word, but their hands brushed and she gave his fingers a grateful squeeze.

"Thank you," she whispered. "Not only did you help, you used the Bible."

"Pretty sure it was the girls who got him to consider my suggestions," he joked.

"Pretty sure it was..." She looked up at him with the warmest light in her eyes. "You."

And right then, he'd have waltzed into that lion's den with Daniel if she asked him to.

*N*ick hadn't been able to reach his agent the night before, but this morning he was on the phone with her while Savannah nursed Dylan in the rocker. It was early in Los Angeles, but Nick said that due to her husband's sickness, Eliza Whitney kept weird hours.

He'd been talking to her long enough for Dylan to finish, and for Savannah to start bracing for Max and Diana's arrival, since they'd promised to come to The Haven that day.

Just as she was about to get up, Nick came in from the veranda, his expression serious.

"Ben's in a coma," he said. "She's facing the worst imaginable decision."

"Oh, that's so sad."

On a heavy sigh, he sat in the chair across from the rocker, where he loved to settle in and watch Savannah nurse the baby. Usually, in that chair he looked content, but now he looked troubled. "The only happy marriage in Hollywood, and it ends like this."

He sat quiet for a moment, deep in thought as she rocked a sleeping Dylan, the silence comforting both of them.

"Life's so...unpredictable, isn't it?" he finally said.

She gave a soft laugh and looked down at the baby. "No kidding."

"Like...*Celebrity Wedding*."

"That is unexpected, too," she agreed. "What does Eliza say? Did you talk to her about it?"

"A bit. She's a little checked out, as you can imagine. But, yes, All Artists Reps is hinting that her job was really all about me, so..."

"They'll fire her?" She made a face.

"Right? I hate those people. But, yes, Sunshine Washington, the host of *Celebrity Wedding*, is her client and, yes, getting us on the show would be a huge feather in her cap."

"Do you know this Sunshine?"

"I've met Sunny, and I like her. She's talented and is much more than the pretty face on that show. She essentially calls the shots like a co-director." He ran his hand through his hair, making it adorably tousled. "Eliza said I could trust her—to a point. That was her advice, but like I said, her head isn't in the game so I didn't push for more."

She gave him a look of sympathy, her heart always softening when she witnessed this man's genuine goodness, especially for people he loved. "I know you want to help her, but..."

"But..." He grinned. "Then you'd be forced to marry me."

She laughed. "A dark fate indeed."

"Is it?" he asked, far too serious.

"Come on, Nick. I'm just being cautious. I never said I hated the idea of...it. I'm only iffy on the national TV part."

"That might make it fun and different," he said. "And, yes, it would help Eliza." He eyed her when she didn't answer. "Is it because I haven't officially proposed?"

"It's because...it's in three weeks. Don't you need time to think?"

"We've had a *year* to think, Savannah. All the time you were pregnant, then since he's been born, every day and every night. How much time do you need?"

She looked up at him, trying to see him—the man she loved—and not Nick Frye—the man she...

"I'm scared," she whispered, the truth of it suddenly harder than the hurricane she'd named her son after.

"Of what?"

"Of...getting hurt. Of making a mistake. Of wanting to leave. And, honestly, of your mother."

The last one made him chuckle. "Add it to the list of things we have in common. All of those, actually." He crouched down in front of her. "I'm scared of all of those things, Savannah. But...I love you. And I love Dylan. And I love us. And I love living here with you."

"Well, now I know what swooning feels like." She reached out her hand and touched his face. "I could be talked into this. You could convince me to...you know."

He chuckled. "You can't say the words 'marry me.'"

"I can't," she breathed the words. "They're so big."

"You say you love me. Why can't you say you'd marry me?"

"I do love you. And I think it more often than I say it."

He smiled and leaned closer. "*I* love you. I love *you*. I *love* you. Different emphasis, no acting. All true."

Wherever he put the emphasis, she melted. Didn't he see? "Nick, we're doing so well. We're going to jinx it."

"You definitely have a fear of jinxing, don't you?"

"I guess. Karma, fate, the universe, jinxing, whatever. All I know is my life has never been this perfect and... that...could blow it all to smithereens. Then I'll be miserable and alone."

"First of all, you'll never be alone." He looked down at Dylan. "Second, we make our own fate, Savannah. We take our own chances. We're in charge, and the future is ours."

"Are you trying to convince me or write Dylan's valedictorian speech?"

"I believe this. I've lived this way my whole life. I'm in charge."

She lifted a brow. "Not to be contrary or anything, but Diana is a master puppeteer, and you might have been her personal Pinocchio more than you realize."

"Don't think I don't know that. But I've manipulated her, too. She's here, isn't she? And, you may not believe this, but I'm always one step ahead of her, just like I am now."

She searched his face, a frown pulling. "I'm not following you. How are you one step ahead of her now?"

"She didn't come here to get me to marry you. Trust me, I know my mother."

"Then...why?"

"I really think she came to get me to *not* marry you." He finally pushed up and took a few steps back, crossing his arms and leaning against the railing with the gorgeous Gulf and blue sky as a backdrop. "She's assuming you will jump at the chance to marry me. But she's also assuming that I'm bored, ready to run, and missing the bright lights, big city, and major paychecks. And that marriage will freak me out."

"You've been married once." She made a face, thinking of his Hawaiian princess.

He just curled his lip. "That was a mistake. Don't compare that to us. But my mother knows how bad that was for me, and she's not counting on me *wanting* to get married."

He pushed off the railing and came down in front of her again, this time on one knee. "But I do want to marry you, Savannah Foster. I want to spend the rest of my life with you and Dylan, and maybe make a few more babies. And, damn it, I want their last name, and yours, to be Frye."

For a long moment, she couldn't speak. Strangled with emotions, she simply stared at him, so many thoughts jumbled in her head that she couldn't pick one to share. Plus, she was swooning again.

It couldn't be this easy, could it? Savannah's life was never easy.

"But...the TV show."

He shrugged. "Fast and fun. Let them do all the work and we'll just show up and look good."

"You really think your mother is using reverse psychology to break us up?"

"Oh, I know it and I can prove it."

"How?"

"By saying yes. And then, you watch how fast she tries to sabotage this." He looked skyward. "God only knows how she'll do it, but you can count on my mother to bring the drama and pain."

"Oh, yeah, that all sounds like so much fun."

"But if we know what she's up to, it could be." Still on his knee, he took her hand, bringing it to his lips. "Let's call her bluff, do the show, give me a chance to help Eliza if she needs it, clean my name up by giving my capricious fans something to cheer about, and at the end of it, we'll be Mr. and Mrs."

She'd never wanted that before, not like Peyton. And yet, right now? It sounded glorious.

She sighed. "Mr. and Mrs."

"Say yes, Savannah. Please, say yes."

Forget swooning. Her heart was officially skipping beats now. Much more of this and she'd have the vapors, whatever they were. She was living in a romance novel.

"Are you proposing, Nick?"

"Rehearsal. I want to do it right, with a fat, juicy, blinding, zillion carat Rock of Gibraltar, baby."

"That we could use for Dylan's college fund."

"We'll make them throw that in there, too. And a charity for...what's your favorite cause?"

"Single mothers who don't live in palaces or have literal Prince Charmings throwing cash prizes at them."

That made him smile. "We add that to the contract. The cost of the wedding—including the ring—has to be matched with a donation to..."

"Naomi Rising," she whispered. "It's an organization that helps single mothers find affordable housing. I found it when I was pregnant and researching, and I thought it was an amazing group."

His shoulders sank with a sigh. "I hate that you were worried about housing. I'm so sorry I put you in that situation."

"I put myself in it, but I came out okay," she assured him. "And millions of women don't. So if I can help..."

"You'll marry me on a reality show?"

She'd marry him on this porch with the guy named Guy from the town council officiating. She nodded slowly.

"Nicky! Nicky, where are you?" Diana's voice floated up from the first-floor deck. "Is anyone home? We're here!"

He stood, still holding her hand. "Let's go call her bluff."

"And see what drama and pain it causes." She handed over the baby so she could push out of the rocker.

He chuckled and laid a kiss on Dylan's sleeping head. "Did you hear that, French Frye? We're gonna be a real family."

Oh boy. He really *was* trying to make her faint.

SHE HAD TO ADMIT, Nick might have been right about Diana's bluff calling. She seemed a little stunned when they told her they'd do *Celebrity Wedding*, but recovered quickly. Max seemed even more stunned when Nick laid out his contractual requirements, including the donation.

After they made the announcement, Diana draped

herself on a chaise and held her arms out, silently demanding to hold the baby.

"You're ready to try again with such a pretty top?" Nick asked.

"I'll live on the edge, if someone will bring me a towel."

"Of course," Savannah said. "And how about something to drink? Tea? Coffee? We always have mimosas at The Haven."

"You do?" She lifted a brow.

"Mine's all OJ," she assured her, "but I can make yours however you like."

"Heavy on the champagne, which I hope to God is at least Veuve, and light on the OJ. Max drinks iced tea."

He was already on the phone, across the veranda, but gave a thumb's-up, used to easily managing two conversations at once.

"Nick keeps us in the orange label," Savannah assured her. "And light on the OJ is exactly how my mother drinks hers." Only Diana was so not Beck Foster.

"I'll get the drinks," Nick said as he eased the sleeping baby into his mother's arms. "And the towel, although he's conked out from his last feeding. You good, Diana?"

She nestled the baby closer and stared at Dylan as if she were trying so hard to soften. "I'm fine." When Nick left, she looked at Savannah. "He's such a carbon copy of Nicky, it's kind of eerie."

Not completely, but Savannah didn't want to cause any whitewater. "Do you have baby pictures?"

"Not with me."

"Any of you and his father? Because Nick really doesn't look like you."

Her eyes flashed. "His father is dead—"

Savannah gasped.

"To me," Diana finished.

Just then, Max came over and pulled out a chair from the table, setting his phone face-up in front of him. "The ball is officially rolling. Call's into the production company to start final negotiations. But it is a Sunday. Even the heathens in L.A. take that day off." He grinned. "Nice place, Savannah."

"Thanks, but Nick swooped in and saved the day by buying this house," she said.

"That's what my Nicky does," Diana said. "He's like Superman."

"Just," Max joked, winking at Savannah.

"Don't get comfy, Maximillian." Diana pointed at him. "You have more work to do. A lot."

"Your wish is my command, Diana."

"So where do you stand on the nanny hire?" Diana asked, pulling Savannah back to the moment. "I know you said you didn't have one, but—"

"No nanny." Savannah shook her head. "I've got a sister, a mother, a grandmother, a niece, and Nick. Trust me, this kid is already begging for alone time."

"You'll need a nanny," Diana said as if Savannah hadn't spoken. "I'll start looking for one."

Savannah blinked at her. "I don't want a nanny."

She angled her head and added a withering look. "Max, start the search, stat. Savannah, we will find the nanny, conduct the background check, and manage her employment status. And it will be a woman. You can trust Max, I assure you."

"Are you serious?"

"As a heart attack. Building Nick's entourage is what we do."

"His *entourage* is, uh, my family and friends."

"Not anymore," Max said on a chuckle, typing something into his phone.

Savannah dug for calm and cool. Found none, but kept digging anyway. "That's very kind of you, Diana. But we don't want a nanny."

She literally closed her eyes as if to silence Savannah. "And I think two security guards should be enough for this house, Max, don't you? One in front, one in back."

"So four total on twelve hour shifts," he said, tapping madly. "I can get that."

"No one hires a bodyguard like Max. I do not know where he finds these brutes but not a soul gets near Nick."

"I have my secret connections," Max said. "Armed and dangerous bodyguards are a specialty."

With every word, irritation straightened Savannah's spine. "Nick and I've discussed bodyguards, and since no one knows he's here—"

Slowly, Diana opened her eyes and leveled a gaze the same color as Nick's on Savannah. Yes, he had her eye color. But no other features, Savannah mused. "They will when production starts." She stroked Dylan's head. "And we can't let anything happen to this little angel, can we?"

"No one will see him unless we want them to."

She launched a brow north. "Someone out on...that boat?" She pointed to a cabin cruiser practically falling off the horizon it was so far away. "They could have a clear shot—"

"*What?*"

"With a telephoto lens," Max finished. "Stop riling, Diana."

She ignored the order and flattened Savannah with another look. "Do you want your child on the cover of the *National Enquirer*?"

God, no. "Are you saying there's going to be publicity before this...this reality show airs? That outsiders will know what we're doing here? I thought the whole thing only took two weeks."

Diana chuckled and shared a rich "can you believe this girl" look with Max. "I'm sorry," she said with faux apology dripping from her voice. "But, Savannah, *darling*. Do you have any clue, any at all, what it's like to live with an A-list celebrity?"

"I've been doing it for months."

Diana looked skyward. "When no one knows he's here. But once they do—and, yes, when you start filming a reality show, it will get out onto the blogs and podcasts —then your life will change. Expect helicopters, boats, paparazzi, lookiloos, and the occasional crazed idiot who thinks your baby is worth kidnapping."

Savannah inched back, but then she remembered... this woman was a master manipulator who didn't want her to marry Nick. But...was all that true?

"So who else do we need to hire, Max?" Diana asked. "Of course, you'll need a cook."

"We're doing our own cooking." And that wasn't about to change.

"For the crew who will be trouncing in and out of here day and night? Of course, they'll cater, but oh, God, the place will be a mess. So at least one housekeeper, but a house this size? I'd say two. And, just to make sure it all goes swimmingly, why don't we get Nicky a full-time assistant? You can borrow her, too, unless you want your own."

Savannah didn't dare open her mouth. Because she could not be responsible for what might come out. With white hot anger popping in her head, she pushed up slowly and reached for the baby.

"I'll take him now."

"You will not." She inched the baby in the other direction. "I'm just getting to know him."

"Diana." She ground out the word. "Give me my child. I'm taking him inside."

All Diana did was lean forward, holding Dylan tighter, fighting a smile. "Maybe the whole thing is too much for you, dear. It takes a certain kind of woman to meet the challenge that is Nick Frye."

And another kind to resist the urge to claw his mother's eyes out.

"The baby, Diana."

"Not too late to back out." She grinned maliciously. "I'll take the blame and we'll find a completely different way to save my son's tattered reputation."

For a long moment, she stared right back at the woman, feeling her heels quite literally dig in. So Nick was right. She was calling their bluff. When that didn't work, she was going to try and scare Savannah off.

She took a deep breath and tried to think of all the possible comebacks, which were *her* specialty.

But all she could hear in her head was...Nick's voice.

I want to marry you, Savannah Foster. I want to spend the rest of my life with you and Dylan and maybe a few more. And, damn it, I want their last name, and yours, to be Frye.

She would not let this woman steal her joy.

She deftly reached her hands around Dylan's little body and he stirred, fluttering his eyes open and looking at Savannah. For an instant they were connected, and she was even more sure of her decision.

"Diana." She eased the baby into her arms, letting him make his little cooing sound to add to the moment. "Nothing and no one is going to stop me from marrying Nick Frye. Not you, not a crew of bodyguards and cooks, not a TV show, and not your condescending comments. I'll go check on the champagne so we can toast to it."

Without waiting for her response, she walked inside, nearly colliding with Nick and the tray.

"What's wrong?" he asked instantly, searching her face. God, she loved that he knew her so well.

"You were right. She tried to call our bluff, and now she's threatening to bring an army of outsiders to cook, clean, protect, and destroy our lives."

He snorted, shaking his head. "We'll stop her."

"She's not taking no for an answer. Max is out there *building your entourage*."

"I have an entourage," he said without a second's hesitation.

"Right? I tried to tell her there's...Ava and Peyton and Lovely."

He laughed. "I have an idea. Let's get them all over here for the day and we'll shift the balance of power. And trust me, I will not let Max hire anyone for anything. I promise."

Dylan made a sweet little noise, half sigh, half toot in his diaper.

"My son agrees," he said, bending down to kiss his

head. And on the way back up, he landed one on Savannah's mouth. "Have I told you how happy I am that we're getting married?"

"Unless Dirty Diana tries to squash it."

"Oh, baby, she's just getting started. But we're strong, you and me and French Frye."

She sure hoped so. With that woman, they'd need to be.

CHAPTER ELEVEN

PEYTON

*V*al was pulling out all the stops. For one thing, he'd chosen the Coconut Key Marina for their rendezvous—Peyton didn't want to call it a "date." But their first "not a date" had been at this marina, too, she recalled as she parked and walked along the long, weathered dock to the slip number he'd texted her.

That first glorious Sunday afternoon, he'd taken her out in his trawler to teach her how to fish, and somehow they'd managed not to kiss. At the time, she was on vacation with her mother, and had left Greg McAllister, the man she thought she loved, back in New York. And Greg had cheated on her with a ski bunny.

She slowed her step and took a look around, listening to the soft clang of metal against masts and the steady slap of the water on the boat hulls. So much had changed since then. Peyton, in some ways, was a different woman.

But in other ways, she was still the same.

As she walked, she drifted back to those days, remembering how hard she'd fallen for Val from the moment he'd come into Jessie's restaurant kitchen and made crab jokes. He was attractive and funny and warm and all she'd wanted to do was melt into his arms.

"Yo, gorgeous. I'm right here unless you need more time to mullet over."

She turned at the sound of his voice, inching back at the sight of Val on the deck of a cabin cruiser.

Well, he was still attractive and funny and warm and all she wanted to do was melt into his arms. Like his bad fish jokes, some things never changed.

She smiled at him, pushing up her sunglasses to get a better look at the snazzy inboard that looked like it might be thirty feet long with all the bells and whistles.

"Nice boat, Captain."

"It's ours for the day." He came around the helm and jumped onto the dock, looking so much more like she remembered him than he had yesterday. In khaki shorts, a soft blue T-shirt, and sneakers, this was Val, the unassuming, sometimes silly, always sexy fisherman she'd crushed on so hard. And then it wasn't a crush...it was more.

"Seriously?" She walked to meet him, taking his hand without thinking because it felt so natural. "How'd you get this boat, and if you tell me this is CPA money, I'll be truly impressed."

"Not yet. But you remember my buddy Rich Brogan? We fished a lot together."

"Of course. He and Rhonda come into Coquina Café all the time."

"They gave me the keys to the Keys." He gestured toward the deck and drew her closer. "I thought we could island hop today." He leaned in and added, "A *trawl* down memory lane."

She laughed as he helped her on board. "Don't you have accounting jokes now?"

"Too busy working my assets off," he joked with a wink, then shook his head. "Just not the same, honestly."

"I would imagine you're surrounded by more serious people now."

He eyed her for a moment, inching back to take a fairly leisurely trip over her tank top and jeans shorts, all the way over her bare legs to her sneakers and back up. His gaze warmed her more than the blazing tropical sun.

Then he put his knuckle under her chin and lifted her face toward him. "Right now, I'm surrounded by the prettiest, sweetest girl who I've missed like crazy."

She let the compliment twirl around inside her, but couldn't help correcting him. "I think

woman is more accurate, Val, but I'll let it slide."

He didn't argue, scanning her face with those impossibly dark eyes. "Definitely a woman. And I definitely missed you."

She inched away, wanting to protect her heart. She checked out the boat, which was pristine and spacious, with a door that led to a downstairs cabin, and plenty of space for sunning, fishing, or just hanging out.

"Welcome aboard the R&R, so named for Rhonda and Rich." He gestured toward a cooler and a bag full of towels and sunscreen next to it. "We've got food, drink, and the whole day out there." He pointed toward the blue-gray of the Atlantic Ocean, then shifted to the right to a strait that separated Coconut Key from Summerland and Cudjoe. "We can head up to the tip of Big Torch, then cruise down around Sugarloaf or head toward Key West. Open water or between the islands. It's your call, my dear."

"I'll trust you to set the course, Val. You know the routes better than I do."

"All right. Let's thread the south side of the Keys, round Key West and spend the late afternoon on the Gulf. How about something cold to drink?"

And just like that, they slipped back to old times. The boat was fancier than his old fishing trawler, and it cruised at a much higher speed when they headed out to the ocean. Sipping a soda, Peyton took the co-captain's chair, feet up on the dash, head back to get the salty spray and sunshine.

A confident boater, Val kicked the speed up for a while, letting them feel the satisfying thump of the waves and leaving a huge white rooster tail of a wake behind them. They talked about nothing, waved to other boaters when they passed, and somehow, for what felt like an hour, thought about nothing but the goodness of the moment.

Maybe that was Val's plan. He knew she loved to "island hop" on a Sunday afternoon, soaking up the rays, and sometimes fishing for fun. When he slowed the motor and brought them to a rumbling standstill, she instantly recognized that they were off the coast of one of her favorite beaches, in a clean area perfect for swimming.

"I didn't bring a suit," she said, standing up to look at the clear teal water.

"That happened once before," he replied, making his way to the cooler.

"Oh, yeah." She gave a low laugh, feeling a blush. "I remember that day."

"A memory that's gotten me through some pretty long, lonely nights."

"Come on, Val." She joined him at the back of the boat, sliding onto a wide white leather bench. "Do you really expect me to think you're lonely in Miami? If you are, it's by choice."

He shrugged. "Fine, it's my choice. Doesn't mean I like it."

"You haven't dated anyone?" she asked, almost dreading the answer.

But he shook his head. "Nope. How about you?"

"Too busy, really." And not the least bit interested.

He flipped up a built-in table between the two benches and started setting out a beautiful lunch of salads and sides.

"Who did all this?" she asked.

"Rhonda Brogan," he replied. "She likes you and, well, wanted to help...reel you in." He winked. "I told them I was in the fight of my life trying to win you back."

She leaned back against the leather, still not quite able to get her head around any of this.

"You look confused," he said.

"Not sure if that's the right way to describe how I feel. I do have questions, though."

He raised his hands in surrender. "Ask me anything."

"How about...where have you been? I mean, if this is the fight of your life, why did you wait eight months? Why such spare and infrequent communications?"

He blew out a breath and snagged two beers from the cooler, offering her one. When she nodded, he twisted the top off and handed it to her, settling onto the bench across from her and leaning on the table.

He held up his bottle and tapped hers. "To truth. May we both tell it."

"Val," she said without taking a sip, "I don't have anything to hide. Do you?"

He took a long, deep drink before answering, then set the bottle on the table and leaned in. "I didn't know some things about myself, Pey. But I've been in therapy and now I do."

Therapy? He was such a guy's guy, a hands-on fisherman who made lame jokes and seemed so...together. He didn't strike her as the therapy type. Her ex, Greg? Oh yeah. He'd been in and out of it for years, probably because he loved the subject of himself better than any other topic. But not Val.

"Didn't expect me to be in therapy, did you?" he said with a laugh, obviously reading her expression despite her best efforts not to give away her thoughts.

"Honestly? No. But I've never heard anything but good things about it."

"I didn't know I needed it, and would never have gone, but Natalia, Marisa's sister, convinced me to go. It helped her a lot and she thought I might benefit, too."

"Did you?"

"So much," he answered with a second's hesitation. "It was a great, great help. And what I wanted to share is that my therapist, Saundra, made me realize that I'm an all-or-nothing kind of guy. Once you see something like that in your personality, it's all you can see. And it's so true. I'm not a toe-dipper, she told me. I never test waters...I dive in."

She took another sip of beer, considering that and all she knew about him. His therapist wasn't wrong.

"Marisa and I started dating in, like, ninth grade. But I knew from day one I'd marry her."

Her heart hitched a little, both for the fact that he'd loved someone else that strongly, and that he'd endured losing her.

"It was never going to be anything less. And when I went to college, I went whole hog, straight through B-school, and a second degree in accounting, heading directly to the best position in the largest firm in Miami."

She still couldn't believe the fisherman she'd dated for those few months was a CPA. She couldn't imagine him in an office, this man who belonged out on the ocean casting for anything he could catch.

"And after Marisa died and I decided to run away, I didn't just take a vacation or go backpack through Europe for a few months. I shut down my life, sold everything, and started over in a place where no one knew me. Built a commercial fishing business from scratch. I didn't just live in the Keys, I inhaled them. And...you."

All that was true, too. Their relationship had been... intense. Fast-paced and full-hearted. And she'd brought it to a screeching halt with an ultimatum.

"And I treated our separation the same way—all or nothing. I couldn't start talking to you frequently or come down here to visit. I knew it had to be everything or not anything."

"But when I told you *I* wanted everything, last year, before you left? You wanted nothing, not all."

"Not true," he replied. "But I knew I couldn't get to

that place with you until I worked out all my stuff with Marisa and our families."

She waited a beat, taking it all in. "What exactly does that mean, 'to work out your stuff'?"

He threaded his fingers through his hair, thinking for a moment. "When someone dies, especially someone so young, there's so much blame and guilt and anger and regret and...stuff." He lifted a shoulder. "That's why Natalia persuaded me to see a therapist. And it helped. A lot. Enough that I'm...ready."

"All or nothing ready?" she asked.

"I'm really trying to dial back on extreme decisions," he admitted. "That's why I asked you to come to Miami for a while." He leaned over the table and took one of her hands in both of his. "We didn't date long enough to make a lifetime commitment, and I don't think you asked me for one."

"I didn't. I just wanted you to know that was my end goal, and we should both be thinking like that."

"It's my end goal, too," he said. "And the old me would be on one knee convincing you we could do this, full steam ahead. I care that much about you, Peyton. Deeply. For real."

She inhaled softly at the words. "And the old me would have that wedding planned so fast, the invitations would have gone out unsealed. And I'd be pregnant before the end of the year."

For a long moment, he said nothing, but slowly rubbed his thumb over her knuckles.

"We've both changed," he finally whispered. "But when I look at you? The feelings I have for you are stronger than ever. Does that go both ways?"

"Both ways and back a few times," she said on a laugh. "At least based on the flight of butterflies I currently feel."

"Then come to Miami, Pey. I could find you a short-term rental or you could get—"

She held up her hand. "My sister Callie just transferred to UM and has an apartment near the university. I could stay with her for a little while."

He drew back, his eyes flickering in surprise. "Wow. You really are thinking about it?"

"Val." She squeezed his hand. "I really haven't been thinking about anything else. But I'm scared."

"It's not a big risk. A month in Miami? I'll be with you every minute I'm not working."

"But I'm starting culinary classes in Key West, and Jessie needs me at the café. I'm the assistant manager. When I'm not there, she has to be."

"Can she hire someone?"

"Actually, Heather, who knows how to run a café better than any of us, is staying in Coconut Key for a while. Not a month, but..."

"Perfect," he said. "And can you take cooking classes in Miami? They have a great culinary school. Jessie went there."

"But I'm enrolled in Key West."

He blew out a breath. "I can't leave my job or my family."

"Why can't we do long distance?" she asked.

"Because, eventually, one of us has to move."

For what felt like an eternity, they looked into each other's eyes. Peyton fell a little deeper, wrapped in the bittersweet mix of longing and uncertainty. "I don't know," she said.

"So," he finally said, opening up one of the food containers. "Stalemate."

"For the moment." She plucked out a fruit kabob and slid off a strawberry.

"Then let's have the best day of our lives," he said softly.

WHEN PEYTON PULLED into the drive between The Haven and the guest house she currently called home, the sun was just about touching down out on the Gulf. So, she was more than a little surprised to see all the cars. Jessie, Chuck, and Beau had left for their vacation, so she thought everyone had decided to forego the usual Sunday gathering at The Haven after yesterday's big party.

From the number of vehicles, it seemed no one got that memo. Hadn't Mom said she and Lovely were staying at the B&B all day to attend to their guests and train Toni? But there was Mom's car. Heather and the kids were staying at Jessie's house since Peyton was in the guest house, but her SUV was here, along with Josh's truck, parked next to Kenny's. And didn't Diana and Max arrive in that gray sedan?

Climbing out of her car, she let out a low moan, her body aching and warm from hours in the sun. The day with Val had been...spectacular. And emotional. And draining.

All she wanted to do was slip into the guest house,

take a shower, and maybe drown in a nice bottle of Merlot. Val was already on the road back to Miami and she was...not. She didn't want to socialize or fill Savannah in on "all the deets!"

She wanted to think about that last kiss and the look in Val's eyes. She wanted to think about some of the tender things he'd whispered, and the hope in her heart.

She wanted to think about Miami.

With a quick look at the long walkways that led to the main house, she decided to slip into the guest house unannounced. Inside, she grabbed a bottle of water from the fridge, stripped for a shower, and turned the faucet just as she heard Savannah's voice in the living room.

"Oh my God, I just realized you might not be alone."

Peyton let out a sigh, shutting off the water and grabbing her robe from the back of the door before going out there. "Sadly, I am."

"Sadly?" Savannah's eyes widened. "Were you seriously going to hide in here and not give me the deets?"

"Is she here, Sav?" Mom's voice floated from outside the front door.

"I see her car." And Lovely.

Peyton just started laughing and shaking her head.

"What? You wanted privacy?" Savannah teased. "You'll have to move for that." She took a few steps closer and reached out. "Oh, God, Peyton. Are you moving?"

Mom and Lovely came in just then.

"I thought you were back," Mom said, joining them.

"We're dying to know everything." Lovely finished the circle.

For a moment, all Peyton could do was look from one to the other. How could she even think about leaving this...this circle of love? She didn't want to live anywhere but right here, with her sister, mother, grandmother, and Jessie, who'd become like a beloved aunt to her.

But...*Val.*

"Why is everyone here?" she asked. "I thought we were taking a Sunday off."

"I needed back-up." Savannah headed around the counter to the small kitchenette to get a glass of water. "So Nick brought in the cavalry to fight Cruella de Vil."

"Diana?" Peyton guessed. At her sister's look, Peyton gestured to a chair. "Sounds like you need to go first."

"And fast. Before we're missed. I was up on the third-floor balcony feeding Dylan when I saw your car pull in."

Savannah launched into her tale and before long, they were gathered in the small living room like a coven of witches, brewing up some tidy gossip and news.

"So you're doing it?" Peyton asked, leaning forward. "You're going to marry him on live TV in a reality show?"

"I think I am, Pey." She looked at their mother and Lovely. "You all think it's the right thing to do, don't you?"

"I love the guy, Savannah," Mom said. "But with every man comes baggage. His is fame, fortune, and a frightening mother."

Lovely snorted. "I'll handle that woman. Beck's gonna keep her eye on Max."

"Or Toni will," Savannah said dryly. "Thank God she's glommed onto someone besides Nick."

"How'd she do with your very first breakfast?" Peyton asked. "I was so preoccupied I forgot to text and ask."

"She showed up for coffee at nine," Mom said dryly. "I managed our inaugural breakfast, which was fine. When Diana and Max came over here, we gave her a lesson in bed and sheet changing, but I'm pretty sure the old 'hospital corners' went over her head."

Peyton made a face. "How are you going to handle this?"

"She's not going to be here long," Mom said. "And it's important to Josh. Now, please, *please*, Peyton. What happened with Val?"

"He's on a mission to get me to Miami," she said. "No wedding, no ring, no promises, no

timeline. But, obviously, it's too soon for any of that."

"And you can't get it if you don't spend time together," Lovely said. "So he needs to move back here."

"He isn't going to," Peyton said. "His job, which pays very well, is in Miami. And his family is there. They need him and I really think he needs them." She let out a little groan. "We are at a deadlock."

"You can't do long distance for a while?" Mom asked.

Savannah snorted. "It's not the same, I assure you."

"He just hates that idea," Peyton said. "But he's really convinced we need to live in the same town for a while, at least until my condo is ready. And, God, you guys. I want to. Being with him is just..." She let out a noisy sigh. "He sure makes me feel things."

"What's stopping you?" Savannah asked, leaning closer. "Truth."

"Because I have a job here, and I was just about to start the culinary classes in Key West. And, damn it, I don't want to just fall into his arms—well, I do, but I don't want to simply...give up my life and my family." Her voice cracked. "I don't want to leave Coconut Key and you guys. It's that simple. Except...it's not simple at all. *Oof!*" She let out a noisy grunt.

"One problem at time, dear girl," Lovely said. "The classes in Key West are offered every three months, right? And as far as the café, you know Heather's staying for a few weeks and she can do your job while Jessie's away," Lovely said.

"I do know that," Peyton said. "She confided in me that she's looking to buy a house and move here, but just doesn't want her kids to know until she's sure."

"I bet Kenny's over the moon." Savannah lifted a brow when they all looked at her, making her laugh. "All right, all right. I love how y'all are acting like that isn't a romance about to bloom."

"She's been widowed for six months, Sav," Mom said. "She's not ready for anything like that. And I don't think she's told Kenny that she's thinking about moving here."

"Because if he knew he'd be even happier than he's been since she showed up," Peyton said.

Mom's eyes widened. "I know they're friends, but...am I missing something?"

"You're busy opening a B&B," Lovely said. "And he's your son, so maybe you don't notice his effort to not look at Heather every chance he has."

"And, whoa, he fails," Savannah joked. "Poor guy. He's a smitten kitten, but trying so hard not to let her know because she's so recent a widow. I have mad respect for that."

"Should I talk to him?" Mom asked.

"No!" They answered in perfect unison, then laughed at themselves.

"Let him figure it out, Mom," Savannah said.

"Not only are boys a little different, he's a grown man, and honestly, has only been 'your' son for less than a year," Peyton reminded her. "Unless he brings it up, of course."

"Yeah, you have your hands full with kid problems anyway," Savannah said. "I'm about to dive into the most unconventional wedding ever, and Peyton is..." She tipped her head. "Peyton's gonna go to Miami for a month."

Peyton stared at her sister. "I just said I..." But her voice trailed off. "You think I should go?"

"I think...love is kind of grand," Savannah said. "And I don't want you to miss out on one minute of it. But I sure don't want you to stay there, so you have to convince him to come back."

"I don't know, he's pretty set. But so am I, right here."

"You'll be three hours away," Savannah said. "Not three minutes like you are now, but you can force Callie to leave the library and meet us halfway in Islamorada once a week for sanity checks. You have to be back here for my wedding, though. And the dress fitting, because you and Callie and Ava are my bridesmaids."

"Yeah? Wow, thanks Savannah. And of course I'll come back." As the words slipped out, she pressed her fingers to her lips. "Did I just say that?"

Mom leaned closer, her eyes just a little misty. "Savannah's right, honey. You deserve love and a chance to find it. It's only a month. If you guys are truly meant to be together, then you'll figure something out."

Lovely nodded. "Sweet girl, if there's anything I can tell you, it's to have no regrets in life. In my seventy-four years, the only thing I regret is not doing something I should have." She looked at Mom and smiled. "I should have fought for my baby all those years ago, and since I didn't, I missed fifty-four years with her."

No regrets. Love is grand. You deserve love.

All the clichés rolled around in her head, pushing Peyton to do what she knew, deep in her heart, she wanted to do.

"Every week in Islamorada?" she whispered to Savannah. "You promise?"

"And I'll bring Dylan. And anyone else you want."

"I want...you all." She choked on a sob and reached for her mother. "I want you and I want him and I can't have both."

Mom inched back and put her hand on Peyton's face. "Do you love him?"

"I think I do."

"Then go. The answer will be clear soon enough."

"And then we can turn *Celebrity Wedding* on its head and have a double ring ceremony." Savannah grinned from behind her water bottle. "What? Just tell me that's not the best idea I've ever had."

But Peyton smiled because it kind of was. But first, she had to be sure. "I haven't even talked to Callie about it."

"I have," Mom said. "She found a two bedroom for sublet in her building, and she's already contacted the owner."

"That's our little overachiever," Savannah joked.

But Peyton didn't know how to respond to that. "Did everyone just figure I'd high tail it out of here the minute Val snapped his fingers?"

"Peyton." Lovely reached out to her. "He didn't snap his fingers. He's given this a lot of thought, and wants a real chance. You should take it."

"I hope you're right, Lovely. Okay, I'm going to call Val."

"And we're going to go back upstairs before Diana rearranges the furniture just to gaslight me," Savannah said.

"I'll be up in a bit," Peyton said.

When they left, she tapped Val's number and he answered on the first ring.

"Please tell me you're calling to say you changed your mind and you'll be in Miami tomorrow, Pey. Please."

"What if I am?"

"Then I'm the happiest guy in the world."

And then she knew she was doing the right thing.

CHAPTER TWELVE
BECK

*I*t didn't matter that her patrons were non-paying "beta" guests or that her only employee couldn't make a cup of coffee correctly, by the middle of the week, Beck knew she was born to run a B&B.

She rose early, warmed the scones, and sometimes slipped down to Coquina Café to meet Heather, who was opening for Jessie in the pre-dawn hours. They'd have a quick cup of coffee and Beck would gather up some fresh pastries, then head back to have the breakfast room ready and welcoming by the time Diana and Max came down.

Diana wasn't too early a riser, and Max was on the phone from dawn to dusk. He'd been in the throes of negotiations with the *Celebrity Wedding* producers, and had announced last night the deal was done.

Savannah Foster and Nick Frye would be married on live TV in less than three weeks.

"But it's going to be busy before that," Max told Beck as she refilled his coffee.

"We can handle it," she promised.

"Really? Could you handle more guests?"

Now that, she wasn't sure of. "What are you thinking?"

"I promised to help the production team nail down accommodations for some of the VIP production people," he told her. "They're getting the crew all in a few hotels, but they were forced to go to other islands in the Keys."

"Not surprised," Beck said. "Hotels are at a premium and hard to find here in February. But Coquina House only has two more rooms and they're not quite ready."

"Could they be?" He held up two fingers and rubbed them together in the universal "we'll pay anything" gesture. "I know how to motivate."

"There's no vanity in one of the bathrooms, or tile, and the paint isn't done," she said, just imagining what Kenny would say if she asked him to have the rooms done by the end of the week. "But there are a few other B&Bs and inns on Coconut Key. The best option would be a small resort in Summerland, and I know the owner. I'm sure you can find more on Big Pine or Big Torch, which are larger islands. And Key West is twenty-five miles away, but obviously will have many more options."

He shook his head, tapping his phone as he constantly did. "The director and AD—assistant director —want to be close, like right here. Five minutes from the set."

"The set?"

"The Haven, ground zero, the main set."

"Is that where the wedding will be?" Beck asked, realizing they hadn't talked about any of those details.

"Sunny Washington will make that decision, or advise the producers. She and her assistant are the other two that need a place close by in Coconut Key." He leaned forward. "Come on, Beck. Make that third floor ready for the director and AD. They'll pay. A lot."

If only she could. "My contractor is coming over today. He's also my son," she added with a smile.

"So get him to finish that vanity and tile and paint."

Josh was making the vanity by hand, and she knew it was just about done. But Kenny would need an installation team and—

"You know they do that kind of stuff in fifteen minutes on HGTV." He lifted his brows. "That sledge-hammer-wielding chick from Chicago is a client of my firm."

"They make it *look* like it takes fifteen minutes," Beck said. "But I think it's going to take a few more weeks to finish."

"Do it in a few days, Beck." He rubbed his fingers together again. "And we will make your contractor son very happy."

She laughed. "I'll talk to him. And I can call some friends who run nearby places to see if they have any unexpected vacancies."

"And Peyton is gone, right?"

She let out a soft grunt. "Don't remind me. But yeah, she's in Miami for...a while."

Or forever. In fact, that weekend she and Callie were moving into a sublease in the building, and they both sounded pretty darn happy.

"I know we agreed that Savannah and Nick's home was off limits except for filming," Max said. "And I get that. But that guest house? Actually perfect for Sunny and her assistant. Not technically in Savannah and Nick's house. Still close. Let's make that happen."

Too close, Beck thought. And they'd been promised a measure of privacy. "I don't know how she'd feel about that."

He inched closer. "Want in on a big secret, Beck? Savannah *wants* the show's host close. Having a relationship with Sunny will help everything go smoother. Director's important, sure. But Sunny isn't just the host—she calls all the shots. Trust me, it won't hurt for her to have a buddy in this woman."

But Savannah didn't want anyone breathing down her neck at every turn.

"I'll talk to her," she said.

"Why don't you let Nick do it?" Diana asked, swooping in like she owned the place, not Beck. And like she surely had been around the corner listening. "He understands the business." She stood in front of the window, her narrow shoulders square, her slender, toned body highlighted by purple leggings and a white T-shirt with a Lululemon logo. "We don't have to educate him on how to handle the powers that be."

Beck swallowed a retort and stood. "I still can't interest you in my coffee, Diana?"

"I told you already. It's Starbucks only for me." She groaned. "I still cannot believe the

closest Starbucks is in Key West. It might as well be Cuba."

"I picked up Starbucks brand coffee for you," Beck said brightly. "In light and dark, decaf and regular. With some flavored syrups. And I can make espresso." She was pretty darn proud of her coffee collection and the new machine she'd bought after living with one in The Haven.

Diana let her eyelids drift closed like the very idea of Beck's espresso sickened her.

"Don't even try, Beck," Max said. "Unless you have the capability to whip up a triple blond honey almond milk flat white with nonfat sugar-free vanilla and serve it in a venti to-go cup, you're wasting your time."

"*Oat* milk, not almond," Diana added, not a drop of irony in her voice. "You could get that flat white with almond in any decent coffee shop. But oat milk? Starbucks only. Savannah would know that. She used to work in one, before she roped my son."

It would seriously take a saint not to smack this woman. "Maybe I can buy some," Beck suggested with a tight smile, refusing to take Diana's bait.

But the other woman just shook her head. "No, it's fine. No one expects a homespun inn like this to have full service or the latest in coffee trends. But, please, God, tell me you found gooseberries." She tapped her smooth and glowing cheeks. "This face is craving vitamin C and manganese."

Beck doubted it was the vitamins or minerals that gave Diana the complexion of a woman half her age. But this time, she could reply in the positive...even if Coquina House was *homespun*.

"Toni got them yesterday." The two things that young woman could do well was drive and shop, and yesterday she'd finally found the rare fruit that Diana claimed she couldn't live without. Had to go all the way to Marathon, but it was worth it to say yes to this very demanding guest.

"I have them cut and prepared for you. Have a seat and relax."

"Relax?" Max snorted. "The 'r' word is not in her vocabulary."

"I'll relax when I'm dead," Diana shot back. "Which will be soon if I don't get to yoga, stat. Where is the closest studio, Beck?"

Good question. And the kind of thing a B&B owner should have at her fingertips. "I'll get that information for you, Diana."

"Never mind. Max, find me a spa with a yoga instructor we can hire by the hour."

He instantly started his finger tapping on the phone, then he frowned. "We? I'm not going."

"I don't want you. But someone needs to tell Savannah to be ready to leave in an hour. Will that give her enough time to..." She made little circles in front of her barely-there breasts. "Deflate or whatever she does?"

"Pump," Beck supplied. "But she doesn't do yoga."

"No kidding." Diana lifted a brow. "The camera adds ten pounds, Beck. Surely you know that. And Savannah, well..." She bit her lip and lifted a shoulder. "Those ten pounds should be going in the other direction ASAP, if you know what I mean."

What she knew was that her temper was rising at an alarming rate. "Savannah's perfect," she ground out.

"Spoken like her mother," Diana said. "But trust me. The fans on social media will not be so forgiving. She'll thank me for getting her in shape. We'll start with yoga, since it's so easy, then build up to some cardio, then weight training. Max, have you found a good trainer for her yet?"

"Wait a second," Beck said. "Savannah is gorgeous, and she's nursing a five-month-old baby. If she's carrying a few extra pounds, that makes her an ordinary human."

"And you think that legions of Nick Frye fans are going to be happy he settled for *ordinary*?" She practically spat the word.

Beck felt her back straighten. "First of all, he didn't settle. Second, there's nothing—I repeat *nothing*—wrong with my daughter."

"Ladies," Max said without looking up from his phone. "No fighting over the kids."

Diana let out a dramatic sigh. "He's right, of course. We shouldn't fight."

Beck didn't say a word, but she didn't back down either. Diana rounded the table and came closer, her flawless features set in a practiced look of sympathy.

"Rebecca," she said, whispering the name like it was an actual term of endearment. "I really don't think you know what's about to happen to your daughter. Her life is going to be an open book. Her every decision will be questioned. Her body, her face, her very humanity will be dragged all over the internet and back. She will be a hashtag and it might not be...lovely. And don't get me started on Dylan."

Beck blinked and stared at her as some blood drained from her head.

"Or she can back out now before the production company spends a dime."

"Diana!" This time Max looked up. "Are you out of your mind?"

"Max, this is about more than money! Savannah's happiness is at stake. And I can tell that this woman, her loving mother, cares about that."

But did Diana? And was she telling the truth, or just trying to get Beck on the "get them to stop this wedding" bandwagon she was secretly riding? Savannah had warned her not to fall for it, but this was—

Just then, she heard the kitchen sliders and Kenny's voice as he finished a call.

"Is that your contractor?" Max asked.

"It is."

"Let's see how much money it will take to move things along upstairs at lightning speed. We want the director and AD in this house where we'll have some control. And Sunny in The Haven, along with her assistant, Emily. There. Settled. Diana, eat your gooseberries and stop talking for five minutes."

Beck gave him a grateful look, happy he wasn't a mindless minion after all. Then she turned to get Kenny. And the gooseberries. And text a heads up on the yoga class to Savannah. *Who is perfect, damn it.*

A FEW HOURS LATER, Beck went up to the third floor to check on Kenny's progress. A tiler she'd never seen before was at work in one of the en suites, two men were cutting and nailing crown molding in the Coconut Room, and Kenny himself was painting the Foxtail Room.

"Is it my imagination or are things humming up here?" she asked as she poked her head in.

"Hey, that guy threw so much cash at me that I was able to call in a few men who want top dollar." He lowered the roller and pulled a bandana from his back pocket, swiping some perspiration. "Money talks, Beck."

"I guess it does. And the new timeline?"

He bent over to put the roller down and pull out his phone, tapping the screen. "I revised my schedule, based on the additional workforce and budget. I can have these two rooms ready to roll in...six days."

"I think you better make it five."

He laughed. "Okay, if I can bring in workers after hours, which will be double time, and I can find a final cleaning crew. And you get the rest of the furniture."

"Lovely and I are going to Islamorada to make our final selections and arrange delivery. And we get to see Peyton and Callie," she added as she stepped deeper into the room and checked out the paint job, which was flawless, of course. "You do great work, Kenny."

"I thought I was past this level of work once I had the GC license, but I know you want to get this done, so we will."

"Thank you. I hope it's not killing your social life or taking you away from Ava too much."

"She's fine. Did she tell you she's decided to sign up for the school play? Like we don't have enough drama around here," he added on a laugh.

"She told me she was thinking about it, but not for a part in the play, right? Doesn't she want to help backstage?"

He lifted a brow. "I think she's just saying that in case

she doesn't get cast. But whatever she does is great. The rehearsals will keep her busy, since she's not into sports in the least."

"You sound disappointed in that."

He waved it off. "Nah. Elise wasn't much for sports, either," he said. "But I have to say it was fun to take Marc to the batting cages on Sunday. Now that kid? He's born to play sports."

"Well, maybe you can take him when they—" She grimaced. "Never mind."

"When they what?" he urged.

Dang, she couldn't keep a secret. But maybe it wasn't. "I don't know if Heather has told you yet. I know she doesn't want her kids to know, but I'm not sure about you."

He frowned. "She did say she wanted to tell me something, but every time I've talked to her, one of her kids are there. Is everything okay?"

"Nothing serious. It's good, actually. She's looking to move here, and shopping for a house."

His eyes widened. "Here?" he croaked the word.

"Don't whisper a word to Ava."

"She'd text Maddie so fast, the WiFi would burn," he joked. But his voice wasn't light; it was taut with emotion.

And Beck could feel every single maternal cell stand up to take action.

"Do you think that's a bad idea?" she asked, casually sliding her hands in her pockets to act like she wasn't hanging on his every word.

"I don't...think I get an opinion," he said. "Ava will be over the moon. It's great for Maddie, and I'm crazy about her...son. I mean, he's a great kid."

"It's nice for you to help her out with him." She leaned against a stepladder, her whole being just wanting to settle in for a Mom Talk.

He shrugged. "We're all sort of like family now, right?"

"And that's why you're helping her?"

He eyed her for a minute, almost looking like he wanted to say something, but then he just nodded, bent over, and picked up the roller. "Uh, if you want it done in five days, Beck..."

"You're done talking."

"But not done working." He turned to the wall, pressing the roller against the last stroke. He slid it once, then brought it to a stop with a soft sigh. "And I'm good, Beck, if you're worried about anything."

"Oh, I know, I know," she assured him. "But sometimes, the mother in me..."

"That force is strong, no doubt about it," he said with a chuckle. "And don't think I don't appreciate it."

"But I didn't raise you."

He looked at her. "Even if you had, there does come a time to let go. Pretty sure forty's the official cut off."

"If you think I'm going to stop mothering my girls when they're forty—"

"I'm not one of your girls, Beck. And I'm...okay. I know where you're going, and you don't need to go there. I know what's right, and what's wrong. I know..." He swallowed. "I know my place." He waited a bit. "Which is painting right now, if you don't mind."

She smiled, message received. "Gotchya. And...wow. Janet Gallagher did such a great job on you," she whispered, suddenly hit hard by emotion. "God really knew what He was doing when that pastor called her about the teenage girl in the family way."

"He always knows what He's doing." He winked at her. "My mother taught me that before I could walk."

"Like I said, she did a great job." And Beck would have to learn that Kenny might be her biological son, but he wasn't her responsibility to mother. He was right though, the force was strong.

CHAPTER THIRTEEN

SAVANNAH

"*D*o I look fat?" Savannah turned in front of Nick, the black leggings she hadn't worn in forever, feeling like sausage skin.

He locked his hands behind his head and gave her a slow and painfully scrutinizing once over. "Take them off."

"Really? That bad?"

"Take them off, and that top, and get back in bed right now." He leaned forward and grinned. "Because you're too sexy for your own good, Foster."

She snorted a laugh. "Apparently your mother doesn't agree."

"My mother doesn't want you in that bed," he said dryly, dropping his hands and leaning forward. "Also, you don't have to do this. You know that, don't you?"

"She told my mother that the camera adds ten pounds. Is that true? Because..." She tapped her breasts and tummy. "These don't need any help."

He was up in a flash. "What they need is attention. *My* attention." He tried to kiss her, but she dodged.

"She's on her way over. Max found a trainer and yoga studio. We're taking a private class. No time for what you have in mind."

"Just say no, like the old drug slogan said. You don't have to do everything she wants."

She considered that, then shook her head. "It's a game now, Nick, and I'm gonna win."

"I know the feeling," he said, taking a few steps toward the crib to gaze at Dylan. "Let's never do that to him, okay?"

"Never."

"Let's not try to control him or live the lives we missed out on through him. Agree?"

"Completely. Is that what she's doing?" she wondered, heading back toward the bathroom to get her hair up in a ponytail.

"Yep. Wanted to be an actress, then found herself knocked up by some schmuck."

"Are you sure he's a schmuck?" Savannah asked. "Maybe he was wonderful before she drove him to schmuckitude."

He followed her, leaning against the door jamb with a wistful smile. "I met the guy. I'm sorry to say, I carry some serious schmuck genes."

As she brushed her hair, Savannah suddenly felt a glimmer of sympathy for the woman. "I know what it's like to wake up and find out you're pregnant. And I have to give her a measure of respect for raising you."

"You don't have to, but it's kind."

"I want to find a way to connect with her." She struggled to get the brush through her thick hair and finally gave up, grabbing a hair tie.

"You don't have to do that, either."

"Bond with your mother or put my hair up?" she asked as she snapped the tie in place and pulled her long hair to tighten it.

"Both." He came up behind her, wrapped his arms around her waist, and planted a kiss on her neck. "You don't have to connect with Diana Frye." He trailed kisses up to her earlobe, which always made her shiver and explode with goosebumps. "And I like it down." He tugged at the ponytail, loosening it. As he did he turned her around, and this time she didn't dodge the kiss.

She returned it with everything she had, lost, as always.

"But you know what I love?" he murmured into her mouth.

"Me, I hope."

"Duh." He drew back and looked at her, his blue gaze intense. "I love that you want to connect with her. That you want to win her over. It's sweet, you know."

"Not something I'm frequently accused of."

"But you are. Under all that sarcastic, hilarious, nickname-giving wit, there is a tender, kind, compassionate angel."

"Okay, you stopped being believable after tender."

He shrugged. "I see past your protective mask, Savannah."

He did. And that made her even weaker than the earlobe kisses.

"But be warned, babe." He tapped her on the nose. "Under her passive-aggressive, judgmental, control freak exterior lies a passive-aggressive, judgmental, control freak. Don't be disappointed when you try to get the gooey center and find concrete."

She sank a little in his arms. "Are you sure?"

"Yes. I gave up on that search a long time ago, and have been a happier man ever since." He kissed her forehead. "I don't want you to get hurt."

"I'm just playing her game," she said. "She wants us to not get married and is using every technique she can to make me quit. I won't."

"Is that all you're doing?"

She took a deep breath. "It's kind of scary when someone knows me as well as you do."

"And still loves you like a madman."

"Truly scary."

He tipped her chin up and lowered his face for another kiss, but Dylan started to cry, making him moan and step away. "How many years until that doesn't happen?" he asked.

"Eighteen," she said with a smile. "Come on, let's dress him in something cute and irresistible."

"Why? We're two guys home alone today. He's in a diaper-and-onesie kind of mood, and I feel him."

She laughed. "Because if anyone is going to find that gooey center in Diana—the one I truly believe is there—it'll be French Frye."

He started to argue, then stopped. "You might be right. Let's go with that sailor suit."

"It never misses."

"And the hat," he added. "And those stupidly adorable navy sneakers."

"Perfect." But then, everything about Nick was—including how well he knew her.

DIANA WAS a beast in the yoga studio, which really should have come as no surprise to Savannah. She was a pretzel. Made of rubber, fortified by iron, and able to do things with her body that shouldn't be legal at her age. Twists, turns, headstands, one-legged tree poses, and some horrifying thing called a *plow*.

By the end of the yoga lesson, Savannah was a mushy mess with wet hair plastered on her neck, her makeup smeared. Diana was barely glowing, a few damp red tendrils curled against her neck, her bony breastbone rising and falling like she was still taking deep *ujjayi* breaths.

"Let's use the sauna and sweat off a few more gallons," Diana suggested after they'd *namaste*'d the instructor and sat for a few minutes in the dark private studio.

"I don't think I have much sweat left, but..." She also had no ability to argue or will to live, so Savannah just shrugged.

"Perfect. And after that, I cannot, I will not, go one more minute without a trip to Starbucks. I understand the closest is in Key West, so you'll have to come with me. We're already closer than we were, right?"

They were only about fifteen miles from Key West now, but the traffic would be intense, and that drive just took longer in the middle of February when the roads were packed with tourists.

"I have to pump in a couple of hours," she said,

touching her tender breasts. "And I don't have any clothes, so I'd rather go home."

"It won't take long and I brought an extra outfit, so we can shower after the sauna and go."

In other words, *I call the shots.*

But the yoga class had wrung the fight out of her, so Savannah went along with the suggestion, only a little curious what "outfit" size two Diana would have that might fit Savannah. That might seal the deal.

But she'd underestimated her opponent, who offered Savannah a perfectly lovely loose beach coverup. It could easily be worn over the new leggings and sports bra ensemble that Diana purchased from the spa boutique while Savannah had been in the shower.

Fresh, clean, sauna'd, and still not too tender in the breasts, Savannah brushed out her just dried hair, dug out some lipstick from her bag, and headed to the lobby to meet Diana. Who seriously looked like the cover of a magazine in white leggings and a crisp striped tunic top.

"Ready?" she asked cheerfully, sliding her arm into Savannah's like they were the best of buds. "Now let's get that venti, please."

Diana drove a little like she lived life—as if anyone in her way needed to get out. It amused Savannah, who was just grateful they'd get to the small hotel on Duval Street where the Starbucks was located in a decent amount of time.

"I can't believe there's only one in this whole place," Diana griped.

"There's another one, but the GPS says it's currently closed."

"A *Starbucks*?" Her voice rose with disbelief. "Closed?"

"My guess? Fish are biting," Savannah said. "Welcome to the Keys, my friend."

With an exasperated sigh, she managed to get them just about to town, but that's where traffic came to a grinding halt.

"It's too far to walk," Savannah said, glancing at her GPS. "And with this traffic, it could take a while."

She threw Savannah a look. "Do you have to pump?"

"I'm fine, but we could be sitting in traffic a long time and, oh, look. There's a restaurant that serves coffee."

"I guarantee they don't have my triple blond honey oat milk flat white with nonfat sugar-free vanilla syrup." She pointed at two scooters that zipped right by between them and the next car, careening onto the main drag. "Now, that's the way to go."

Savannah gave a dry snort. "For the young and adventurous."

"Oh, Savannah. Pro tip for managing your future mother-in-law? There's one thing you don't want to do, ever."

"Suggest plain coffee?"

"Challenge me." Diana slid her own phone from the holder on the dash, madly thumbing the screen with the dexterity of a teenager. "Here we go. Closest scooter rentals are...one block west. And not only"—she grinned as she returned the phone—"for the young and adventurous. Which, by the way, I am. Let's go."

"You're—"

"Hang on." She threaded through traffic the minute one car moved, made a left turn that would have brought Savannah's niece, Ava, to tears, and whipped into a scooter rental lot.

She dumped the car in the corner, threw the door open, and climbed out. "What?" she said as she leaned into the back to get her Louis Vuitton bag. "Welcome to the Keys, right?"

She slammed the door and Savannah just sat there. "Right."

How many different ways could the woman test her?

On a sigh, she got out and followed Diana into the tiny hut where she rented two scooters and signed away both their lives on waivers.

Fifteen minutes later, a tiny scooter motor rumbled between Savannah's legs as she rolled out of the lot and onto Duval Street. She did her best to keep up with Evel Knievel, who laughed when she ran a stop sign, blew a kiss to a truck driver who whistled at her, and flipped off a little old lady who laid on her horn when Diana cut her off.

Somehow, they reached the Crown Plaza at the far end of Key West and pulled the deathmobiles into the lot.

"Fun, huh?" Diana asked, taking her helmet off with the flair of a Hell's Angel.

"If by fun you mean death-defying, then, yeah. A blast."

She shook her hair, looking surprisingly young and vibrant as she let out a giddy laugh. "I *loved* that! I needed that freedom. I could do that all day long. But now, coffee."

"Not just any coffee," Savannah said as she carefully unlatched her chin strap, not getting quite the kick from scootering that Diana did. "But a triple blond honey oat milk flat white with nonfat sugar-free vanilla."

"Spoken like a barista," Diana joked.

"And as such, you should know that if they don't like you? You just might get the high calorie vanilla in your coffee."

Diana sniffed like she didn't care, but Savannah suspected she did. Inside, they ordered and sat at a small table near the window.

"Your color's high," Diana observed. "You enjoyed our little adventure."

She snorted. "Define 'enjoy.' But, I'll hand it to you." She lifted her tea. "You're fearless."

"Don't be fooled. I'm scared to death of some things, but traffic and tourists aren't among them."

As Savannah opened the lid to sip the cold drink she'd gotten, she kept her gaze on Diana, admittedly a little fascinated by the woman.

"What are you afraid of?" she asked before taking a drink.

"Losing Nicky."

And Savannah choked enough to almost have iced peach green tea up her nose. "You're honest, I'll give you that."

"No, I'm not," she said dryly. "But I see no reason not to state the obvious."

"If you're afraid of losing him, why have you been so distant since he moved here?"

"I was pouting," she said, "for not getting my way with the Netflix show. Max finally had the answer, so here we are."

"Are you saying that if there hadn't been an opportunity to do *Celebrity Wedding*, that you wouldn't have come?" She heard her voice rise in disbelief.

"I don't know. Eventually." She sipped her drink and

looked around. "It's so different from L.A. here. I don't know what he sees in the place."

It didn't look that different to Savannah. There were people in beach clothes, tourists, no shortage of colorful weirdoes, and hot weather. But she wasn't in the mood to argue with Diana. On the contrary, they were alone, semi-secluded, and both a little buzzed from yoga, a sauna, and a wild ride through town.

What Savannah wanted was to crack this nut. No gooey center? Fine. But she still wanted to take off the shell.

"So, Diana," she said, putting her elbows up and leaning in. "Tell me about life as a single mom. I'm so intrigued by the women who are able to do it, and someone like you? Who rose above the stigma and hardship to such great heights..."

She rolled her eyes. "Please. I rose nowhere. Nick rose."

"Under your guidance."

"Which makes me a stage mother, not a star."

Savannah leaned closer. "Was that what you wanted? To be a star?"

She looked down, making Savannah think maybe she'd put a hairline fracture in that shell. "I wanted to be an actress," she said. "It was why I left a small town in Nebraska and moved to Los Angeles. I wanted to be..."

"What Nick is?" Savannah guessed.

She considered that, tilting her head in a practiced pose, every bit the actor that her son was. "I could have done all that he's done, and more."

"You couldn't do that as a single mother?"

"Not thirty years ago," she said. "But it's water under the bridge."

"So you gave up everything for him."

She shrugged. "It's what mothers do. And, I guess today, it's what fathers do, since Nick has made the same mistake with you."

"He wasn't happy in Hollywood," Savannah said. "He wanted to quit."

"Yes, Savannah, I know what he says. I know why he claims to have given up everything, why he's walked away from a dream career and left his life in shambles."

Shambles? It wasn't exactly...was it?

But Diana just leveled her with another look. "You really don't think it's you, do you?"

Savannah swallowed but her throat was tight. "I...I..."

Diana put her hand on Savannah's. "Please take it from a woman who was in the same situation. They can't separate the child from the mother at this point. Right now, you are the holy vessel that brought his baby to the world, after carrying him—and nearly losing him."

"I didn't, though."

She brushed that off and continued. "Today, you are the Madonna who nurses his baby, offering up your beautiful body to feed the child and then, I assume, to satisfy Nick's own form of hunger."

Blood drained from her head as she stared at the other woman.

"And that will last...for a while. It did with...his first one."

For a moment, she couldn't breathe. His first one—Nick's first wife, Kalani Pele—was rarely mentioned. But the Hawaiian beauty Instagram star was perfection from her three-foot-long hair down to the signature pineapple tattoo on her ankle.

"Not that she had his child," Diana added. "But she certainly had...something."

Savannah rooted around for a response, sipping her tea while she did, and willing herself not to be dragged into whatever new and hideous form of manipulation Diana had in store.

"I'm not worried," she finally said. "Nick and I are strong."

"Savannah." She crossed her arms and gave a look so smug, Savannah wanted to smack her. "Do you know nothing about men?"

"I know...enough."

"From what I understand, you should already be aware of the number one lesson. It's a fact of life, it never changes, and you will experience it, too." She leaned forward. "Men leave," she said, dragging out both words for impact.

"All of them?" Somehow, Savannah couldn't bring herself to believe that.

"Any one worth having. They leave. They...leave." The agony in her voice was actually heartbreaking.

Had Nick's father broken her that badly?

"So, is that what happened to you? With Nick's father?"

She just let her eyes close with a sniff, silent.

"What was he like?" Savannah pushed. "Nick hardly talks about him."

Finally, she opened her eyes. "Don't change the subject, but do take my advice and prepare yourself. Men leave."

"So you've said."

"And you think everything is so hunky dory right now, today, this minute. But when those things"—she waved in the general direction of Savannah's breasts—"are no longer necessary for Dylan, and that body doesn't hold any thrill for Nick? Guess what, babycakes? You'll be dumped as fast as the girl with the pineapple tattoo."

Savannah took a deep breath. "Why do you do this?" she asked on a tight whisper. "Why do you want me to doubt everything I know is true?"

"I'm sorry to burst your bubble," Diana said, sounding as far from "sorry" as any human ever did. "But you really should sign the prenup that Max is having sent over tomorrow."

What? Savannah blinked at her. "A prenup?"

"Oh, dear God, don't be so naïve. Of course, he's made sure you are well provided for and that Dylan can come and visit you many times a year, no matter where you or where he is."

"He...has? Or you have?"

"Lawyers. You're familiar with them, right? Your father's a lawyer. Your father...the man that...*left* your mother." She notched one incredibly perfect brow a little north. "As they do."

Savannah sat up straight, fury ricocheting through her whole body at the mention of her father. Probably because, damn it, she was *right*.

But if Diana had this much emotion on the subject, then maybe there was a soft center and maybe Savannah could find it.

"Can you tell me about his father?" she asked as sweetly as possible. "Because the only thing Nick has ever told me is that he was—is—a troubled man who lived in a trailer and drank a lot."

Diana picked up the coffee, then put it down as if drinking it might get in the way of her deep and heartfelt sigh. "That'll work."

Savannah let out a frustrated grunt. "Nothing more? This is the man who broke your heart? Who made you certain that men worth keeping always leave? You just don't strike me as someone who'd fall for a lowlife, Diana."

Her eyes flashed. "No one ever said he was a lowlife," she spat back. "And the trailer and drinking, well..." She blew out a breath. "I have no idea how he lives his life."

"But Nick told me..."

"Stop, Savannah," she ground out. "Just drop the subject."

"But I'd like to know about him. He's Dylan's grandfather. Is he still alive? Where does he live? Why didn't you marry him?" And shouldn't that history at least make her a little more sympathetic to Savannah's situation?

For a long time, Diana just stared at her. Then, she whispered, "You're challenging me again."

"Get used to it," Savannah muttered.

The other woman narrowed her eyes. "Do not push me, Savannah Foster. You have no idea what I'm capable of. None."

With that, she stood, pivoted, and waltzed out, tossing the coffee in the trash after barely taking two sips.

Nick was right. *Concrete.*

But even concrete could crack under extreme conditions.

CHAPTER FOURTEEN

KENNY

*W*hen he stepped inside Josh's woodworking shop to pick up the vanity Beck had ordered for the Coconut Room, all Kenny could hear was the high-pitched whine of an electric tool. The earthy smell of pine and oak permeated even the front showroom, where Josh had some of his work on display.

Walking past a row of gorgeously carved mirrors and one breathtaking mantle, he didn't bother to announce himself because whoever was working that saw or shaver wouldn't hear him.

So he just continued back to the shop, following the noise and woodsy aroma, coming around the corner to see Josh bent over a workbench, using a large electric jigsaw to create intricate carvings on a long piece of unpainted wood.

He wore plastic goggles and had earbuds in, his mouth moving. He muttered and cut, not stopping to even check his progress, which was a testament to his talent. It took a darn good woodworker to essentially sculpt freehand like that.

Fascinated, Kenny watched, feeling a little like he'd sneaked into Michelangelo's personal studio for a chance to watch the master at work.

Josh turned so his back was to Kenny, who really didn't want to call out now. If he even could be heard over the saw and whatever was playing in Josh's ears, the surprise might make him veer off and ruin his masterpiece.

So he watched, taking a moment to realize that Josh was working on a massive headboard, creating a pattern in the wood that mirrored a wicker basket, only the weaving was carved directly into the oak. He moved with a remarkable combination of power and grace, controlling the power tool like it was a pencil.

Suddenly the sound stopped, but Josh kept talking.

"Which is exactly the reason I can't say a thing to her. It could cost me everything."

Was he on the phone?

Then Josh straightened, laid down the tool. "You chicken shit worm, Cross."

Nope, those were the mutterings of a man to himself, and probably not something Josh wanted Kenny to hear. So he cleared his throat and took a few steps hoping it appeared that he'd just walked in.

"Hey, man, how's it going?" he called.

Josh turned, clearly surprised as he popped out his ear buds. "Oh, Kenny. Hey." He slid the goggles off and clicked the safety latch on the jigsaw. "I thought you said end of day for that vanity."

"I did, and unless you always work past six, we hit that an hour ago."

Josh whispered a soft curse.

"Time flies when you're woodworking," Kenny joked.

"No kidding. But don't worry, the vanity's ready and in the back. If you pull around to the loading dock, I'll help you get it in the truck."

Josh nodded to the headboard, which was even more stunning as he got closer. "That is a beauty."

"Thanks." He smiled at the king-sized headboard as if it were a person. For good reason. Even rough and unfinished, the personality of the piece came through with glorious lines and curves. "It's, uh, kind of a passion project."

"Not on commission?" Kenny blew out a soft whistle as he threaded between two workbenches, drawn to the stunning work. "Damn, buddy. You're gonna get a lot of money for that."

"I'm not planning to sell it."

"Really?" He reached his hand out. "May I?"

The other man laughed. "Sure. It's got a long way to go."

Kenny's fingers grazed the smooth curve of the top, then circled a sturdy newel. "Four-poster?"

"That was the plan, but..." He blew out a breath. "It's a labor of love." Then he snorted. "No pun intended."

Josh looked up, a little confused by the comment, which was made in that same self-muttering tone he'd used before. "Because it's a...bed?" he guessed.

Josh shook his head, his gaze shifting from the workbench to Kenny, a little uncertainty in his eyes. "Truth? I was kind of hoping to give it to Beck as a...a gift."

"Wow, that's some..." But there was something unsaid in that sentence, making him frown in question. "A birthday gift? Is it a surprise, because I won't say a word."

He crossed his arms and let out a sigh. "If she weren't your mother, I might be brutally honest right now."

"Technically, she isn't my mother," he said. "That job belonged to another great woman. But she's my friend, client, and biological mother, so don't say anything you don't want to." He searched Josh's face, seeing a little more...pain? Frustration? Something was etched into his features. "You, uh, need to unload?"

"It's probably not a bad idea," he said with a laugh. "Otherwise, I'm going to carve my frustrations so deeply into that wood, I'll wreck it."

Yeah, that was pain in his voice. "Well, I got a few minutes since Ava doesn't get home until seven-thirty tonight."

Josh smiled and notched his head toward the back. "I got two cold ones in the fridge."

"I'll pull the truck around."

A few minutes later, he parked in front of the small loading dock, where Josh sat on the end with a Heineken in each hand. Behind him in the garage-sized door, the bathroom vanity was draped in protective pads, waiting to go on the truck.

He jumped up on the dock and took the beer Kenny offered, holding it out. "Cheers, man, thanks."

Josh nodded, and they both took a pull, then Kenny dropped down to sit in the late afternoon shade. "I heard you griping about something while you were working," he said as an opening salvo. "Is this what my dearly departed father would have called 'girl problems'?"

Josh chuckled. "Man, I should be too old for that, right?"

So it was. "You and Beck sure seem...good," he ventured. "Am I misreading that?"

"Nope, not at all. We're good." He angled his head. "I'm waiting for great."

Ahh. "She's got her hands full with the B&B, and now this reality show, and always the girls."

"I'm familiar with the litany of excuses," Josh said. "I read them off to her every time she says she's sorry, she's busy, she needs time. And I'm like, well, maybe I shouldn't be making a, you know, bed."

Like a marriage bed, Kenny assumed, not needing to drive that home. "She's been through a lot," he said.

Josh nodded. "Sure has. I don't doubt that she needs time, space, and whatever else I'm willing to give her." He took another long drink, then looked at Josh. "Problem is, I don't want to give so much time or space that...time and space is all we have between us. But then I'm wondering if I'm just as guilty. I mean, if this was *it* for me, I think I'd be more...assertive. You know?"

"But sometimes space is the best thing you can give a woman," Kenny said. "And that bed," he added. "Cause it's stunning."

"But she might not like...sharing it." He said the last two words softly, as if he sensed that even saying that out loud was pushing his luck.

"I don't know," Kenny said. "She sure seems to depend on you for a lot."

"Dependence isn't..." He blew out a breath. "Love."

"Does she know you're struggling with all this?" he asked.

"I don't want to add to her burdens by pressuring her in any way. But the fact is..." He looked down at the bottle, peeling the label as he considered what he wanted to say next. "I gotta be real. Being with Beck has made me realize how much I *don't* want to spend this part of my life—the rest of it, I guess—alone. You ever feel that way?"

Kenny snorted. Since he met Heather? "Every damn day."

"Really? What's stopping you? Ava?"

"Nah, not Ava. I mean she wasn't a huge fan of Maggie when I was dating her, but, honestly? I wasn't a huge fan of Maggie's, either. It was pretty clear we weren't right for each other, but...she's not the one that has me..."

He closed his eyes. "Sorry. Spoke out of turn."

Josh studied him for a minute. "Then I might do the same thing," he said. "Is it Heather?"

He bit back a curse. "Is it obvious?" He gave an uncomfortable laugh. "Beck's danced around it, too, like she wanted to talk to me about it." He frowned at Josh. "She didn't put you up to this, did she?"

He laughed and held up a hand. "Absolutely not. And no, Kenny, it's not obvious, so don't worry that you've acted inappropriately because you haven't."

"But people are...talking."

"Only because...I don't know. It feels like you two belong together, in some weird way. Your kids are like siblings and you two go to church together and seem...aligned."

Each word hit Kenny a little harder. "Yeah, but there is one small thing." He took a deep drink and set the nearly empty bottle between them. "She's a literal grieving widow, and the last thing that woman needs is the complication of a relationship."

"Yeah, I get that." Josh huffed a breath. "Timing is everything, huh?"

Kenny smiled at him. "I think the cliché is 'waiting is the hardest part.'"

"Damn straight." Josh leaned back and looked at the sky. "And knowing when to stop waiting."

"And then what would you do?"

He considered that for a long time. "I don't know," he finally admitted. "But I don't want to sleep in that four-poster alone. I think that's why I'm taking so long to make the thing."

"Hoping she'll come around by the time you finish?"

"God, that's pathetic. Maybe it's time to finish it."

"The bed or...the relationship?" Kenny asked.

But Josh just stared at the bottle, silent.

"*Oof*." Kenny grunted. "You not being with Beck would be weird. Talk about two people who belong together."

"Yeah." He finished his beer and pushed up with a sly smile. "Glad we had this talk," he joked, then his expression grew serious. "Have you talked to Heather about it?"

Kenny got up, too. "Before the holidays. She made it clear she wanted to be friends and I assured her I didn't want anything more than that."

"So, you lied," Josh said, taking Kenny's bottle and tossing them both in a small recycle bin as they walked toward the vanity.

"No, I...yeah, I guess I did."

"Why?" He seemed genuinely interested.

"So she didn't run screaming from Coconut Key,

which must have worked since I understand she's thinking about moving here."

"And then what?" Josh asked.

"Then...I wait and wonder and try not to be obvious. How about you?"

Josh gave a tight smile. "Wait and wonder...or not."

With a nod of silent solidarity, they dropped the subject as Kenny took a look at the mahogany vanity, which was pure signature Josh Cross perfection, barely talking as they hoisted it into the back of Kenny's truck and secured it with ties.

When that was done, Kenny extended his hand to Josh. "Thanks, man."

Josh took his hand, shook it, then added a pat on the shoulder. "Don't wait too long," he said quietly. "I'm not an expert on women, obviously, but Heather isn't cut out to be alone and you two are just, well, like I said. Aligned."

"And you?"

"Me? I'll do what I have to do."

Kenny wasn't sure what that meant, but he thanked him again and hopped in the truck, the conversation fresh and strong in his head.

Aligned. What a perfect way to describe how he felt about Heather. And don't wait too long? Man, that was some advice he'd love to take...but should probably ignore.

And what the heck was keeping Beck from closing the deal on a guy as great as Josh?

He was still thinking about it when he pulled into the driveway of the three-bedroom rental, surprised to see

Ava sitting on the front porch, her hands pressed together.

She leapt up at the sight of his truck and came tearing toward him. He barely had it in park when she yanked his door open, her green eyes sparking like that bottle he'd just held in his hand for half an hour.

"Dad! Daddy! Daddy!" She threw her arms around him and squeezed.

"Yes?" He laughed into the question, always getting such a kick when this poor sweet motherless child showed joy.

"I got a part! I tried out and I got a part in *Mary Poppins*! A speaking role and dancing!"

He drew back, beaming at her. "Seriously? I thought you wanted to be a stagehand."

"You know I just said that in case I didn't get a part. But I'm Miss Lark! I get to wear this cool dress and carry a pretend dog across the stage and I'm in a whole bunch of dance numbers. And I sing! It's not a lead or anything, but still, I got it!"

"Ava!" He brought her in for another squeeze of pure pride. "That is so awesome. I'm so...wow. I'm so proud of you." And Elise would be screaming and dancing and making the costumes.

Suddenly his heart dropped so hard it nearly took his breath away. She should be standing here right now. She should be celebrating this little milestone in Ava's life.

He clamped his teeth over his bottom lip as a fresh wave of grief—shockingly fresh, like the way it was in the early days after Elise and Adam died—nearly knocked him over.

"Can you believe it?" She backed away and did a little jig of joy. "I'm gonna be on stage in the play!"

"Wow, A. I am so proud and happy for you. Come on, let's celebrate at Conchy Charlies."

"Really? It's a school night."

"We can go wild. Miss Lark, huh? Tell me all about her." He put his arm around her and pulled her in for one more hug because he didn't want her to see he was fighting back tears.

But the truth was...he might be no more ready than Heather was.

CHAPTER FIFTEEN
PEYTON

"What do you mean Savannah isn't coming?" Peyton shot Callie a look, tearing her gaze from the Key Largo traffic to make sure her sister knew how much she didn't like this news.

"Mom just texted that the production people are arriving today and Savannah couldn't leave The Haven." Callie thumbed a response into her phone. "But we get Mom and Lovely."

"Heather?"

"She's working at the Coquina Café to fill in for Jessie."

Peyton grunted. "Because I had to run off to Miami."

"No regrets." Callie pointed to her. "Remember, we had a deal, big sister."

Peyton smiled. "No regrets." They'd adopted it as their motto when Peyton had arrived with suitcases and high hopes and Callie announced they were moving to another apartment upstairs that had two bedrooms and more privacy. Val had come right over and helped them move Callie's stuff, which was minimal in the furnished Coral Gables units.

Callie had no qualms about the higher rent because, she told Peyton that first night, she was certain Peyton would love the city, love living with Callie, and definitely love Val.

She'd been right so far, but Callie's confidence that Peyton would be staying in the city didn't take into consideration one undeniable fact: she already desperately missed Coconut Key.

"Get in the left lane here, it's easier to get by that weird hotel entrance," Callie said.

"Do you ever not backseat drive?" she asked, but changed lanes dutifully.

"Does Savannah ever not make snarky comments? Does Mom ever choose not to hover and be maternal? Some things you can't change in a person, Pey. Oh, watch that truck."

At Peyton's look, she slapped her fingers over her lips. "Sorry. I'll go back to my paper. I really should finish it on the way down so I can study for a quiz I know we're going to get hit with in my philosophy class."

Peyton let her quietly tap the laptop, still marveling that Callie didn't get the least bit queasy while reading and writing in the car. But nothing fazed her. Yes, she'd been through a terrible time last fall. Callie had been grossly assaulted by a visiting professor at Emory University, and then the Atlanta PD didn't file charges thanks to the professor's wife, a powerful federal judge.

The situation, and fallout, had been so hard on her

twenty-year-old sister, but did Callie sit around and wait to heal? Never. She arranged to transfer from Emory to the University of Miami and resumed her education, dusting off her old dreams to be a lawyer and a judge and shifting them to a new one of becoming a prosecutor. Peyton had no doubt she would.

"You're amazing, Cal," she whispered, putting a hand on her much younger sister's arm. "I wish I had half your...gumption."

"Gumption?" She said it in a thick, fake southern accent. "What the blazes is that?"

"It's nerve. Fearlessness. Never letting life win when you want something."

She laughed softly. "First of all, I know what gumption is."

"Of course you do." After all, Callie was the genius in the family.

"But I don't think what I have is fearlessness as much as raw, blind determination. And I think you have it, too. You just also have that gene that makes you want to make everyone else happy more than you want to make yourself happy." She grinned. "That definitely comes from Mom's side of the family. Look what 'Aunt' Lovely did for fifty-four years. She sacrificed a lifetime with her own daughter to make other people happy. Yes, she thought that decision was best for Mom, which is why she did it."

Peyton considered that, weaving through the traffic, which was heavy even for a weekday. Her heart slipped a little, just thinking about all the tourists and the winter skies and crazy sunsets and the teal blues and bright greens bursting all over Coconut Key.

She drove a little faster, anxious to get to the halfway point, a restaurant in Islamorada, where she would soak up some time with Mom and Lovely. Yes, she'd miss Savannah, but she had so much catching up to do.

Had she only been gone a week? It felt like a month.

But the drive was only an hour and a half, and soon they were walking into The Hungry Tarpon and being led to a patio table right on that turquoise water she'd missed so much. Mom and Lovely were already there, and both of them jumped up with outstretched arms for a hug.

"You guys act like she's been gone forever," Callie joked as she hugged them, too, and they settled into seats. "I'm not exactly torturing her in Miami, you know."

Her mother smiled, reaching out both hands, her eyes an even deeper shade of green as they reflected the water and her love for her daughters.

"I know," Mom said. "We just got so used to her being there, but you look happy, Pey. You both do. How's life in Miami?"

As they ordered drinks and lunch, Callie and Peyton filled them in on the new apartment and Callie's classes, and Peyton confirmed that she was spending every possible minute with Val.

"Have you met his family yet?" Lovely asked as she squeezed lemon into her iced tea.

"Next week," Peyton said. "They're having a tradi-tional Cuban barbeque, which I'm really excited—and nervous—about."

"Don't be nervous," Mom said. "You'll talk about food, and you love Val, and you'll fit right in."

She lifted a brow. "Pretty sure they speak Spanish."

"When there's a guest?" Lovely shook her head. "They won't make you feel like that. How's Val?"

She sighed, then smiled. "He's amazing," she told them. "He's changed a lot in these last eight months. I really adored him when we were dating, but he was always a little, I don't know. Goofy?"

"Oh, yeah, the fish puns." Mom gave a playful cringe. "They get a little old."

"They were a cover," Peyton said. "He's much deeper than I realized, but he'd been too self-protective after what happened with his fiancée to get serious. It was easier for him to make jokes. He's really opening up to me."

"So you're glad you went up there?" Mom's voice was just a little tentative, like she was half hoping Peyton would say "Nah, I hate it. I'm coming home."

But Peyton couldn't say that. "Well, I love living with Callie and our apartment is walking distance from downtown Coral Gables. All these shops and restaurants, it's great. And Val is...well, he's perfect. It's all pretty darn wonderful."

With every word, Mom had to work to keep her smile. "That's so good, honey."

"But I miss you guys and the restaurant and, oh my God, I need a bite of baby Dylan!"

And Mom brightened again. "He's more beautiful every day. And Savannah sure could use the support."

"*Celebrity Wedding* is too much?" she guessed.

"They haven't really started yet, but the celebrity's mother?" Mom rolled her eyes. "Nightmare."

"Oh, tell me everything."

While they picked at fried conch apps—she'd missed those, too, because they just weren't the same in Miami—Peyton soaked up the news and gossip about Savannah's life. Diana Frye sounded like a piece of work, not to mention the whole "married live on national TV" gave Peyton hives just thinking about it.

"Do you really think Diana's end game is for the wedding to fail?" Peyton made a face. "God, I hope my in-laws are better than that. Does she hate Savannah or what?"

"I don't know what her game is," Mom mused. "Lovely thinks her issues are much deeper than just not liking Savannah."

They all turned to Peyton's grandmother, possibly the wisest woman any of them knew, giving her an expectant look.

"I think Diana is very troubled," she said quietly. "I don't think she's jealous of Savannah or threatened by her, and I don't think she's that dependent on the money that Nick's big career generated."

"Uh, she definitely likes money," Mom interjected. "Her clothes are ridiculously expensive, and she's a big spender."

"That's true, but I just don't think she's motivated by money," Lovely said. "I simply don't know what it is, but she can be the most passive-aggressive and nasty woman I've ever met."

"She reminds me of Olivia," Mom said.

Peyton and Callie nodded, thinking of the woman they'd grown up calling "Grandie" because they thought, as everyone did, she was their grandmother.

"Grandie had to control everything," Peyton mused.

"I feel her," Callie joked.

"Why?" Mom asked Lovely. "What motivated her to be so freakishly controlling and judgmental? Maybe figuring out the late, great Olivia Ames will help us dissect Diana Frye—and help Savannah manage her."

Lovely thought for a long time, sipping on her tea. "Olivia was always a little...high strung," she said, her green gaze moving beyond them to the water as she remembered. "But things got worse after her husband died."

"But her husband died and I was born in the same time frame," Mom said. "So maybe things got worse after you gave her your baby to raise."

"It can't be easy being a single mother," Callie said. "I would imagine you get a real 'it's you and me against the world' mindset, ready to kill anyone who threatens your baby."

Peyton smiled at her, marveling at how smart Callie was for just twenty years old.

"But Nick's father didn't die," Mom said. "He left them. I think. She doesn't provide a lot of details, and Nick doesn't like talking about him."

Lovely lifted a brow. "My guess is there's more to the story of the father than just her 'he left me and was a gutter drunk' angle," Lovely said. "I asked her about him the other day when we were alone with the baby and she was...cagey."

"Nick's met him, though," Peyton said. "And he told Savannah he was a cliché in a trailer park who'd left his mom and him high and dry when Nick was a baby."

Lovely looked out to the water, thinking. "If I had to

venture a guess, her control issues stem from the fear that someone was going to take her child. That's why Olivia left Coconut Key," she added. "To get Beck away from me, her real mother. Even now, Diana might have that deep-seated fear. And, of course, Savannah is taking him away, in some respects."

"No reason for her to be an absolute witch," Mom mused.

"It is if that's what drives Savannah in the other direction," Peyton said.

They all considered that for a moment, then the server came with their orders and the rest of lunch was just a long and delicious conversation about the family. They shared some pictures, including ones Jessie had sent to Mom from the "familymoon" over on Blackbird Beach, and talked about the amazing progress they were making at the B&B.

Oh, they were getting two more guests and Toni actually wasn't the worst maid to ever work in a B&B.

"Why do I find that hard to believe?" Peyton asked.

"She wants to impress Max Meadows," her mother said. "So his every wish is her command. And I think she's absolutely awestruck and captivated by Diana. And when she found out the director and producer were moving in to the third floor? I thought she'd cry."

"Doesn't she want them to think of her as an actress and not a B&B housekeeper?" Peyton asked.

"Are you kidding?" Callie answered. "In that business —in any business—networking is everything. I know what she's doing." She curled a lip. "It's the same thing I did when I was a little too nice to John Kepich and ended up with his tongue down my throat. I hope none of these men are creepy."

Lovely and Mom exchanged a look.

"Max seems perfectly nice, and we haven't met the others," Lovely said.

"If she should be scared of anyone, it's Diana," Mom joked. "Even Savannah loses her sense of humor around the woman."

Peyton let out a grunt. "Oh, I hate that. Poor Savannah. No one gets under her skin." Guilt wormed through her. She should be there to support her sister; Savannah needed her.

"And speaking of getting under skin," Mom said, pulling Peyton's attention back. "I can't help but think our Kenny is falling a little harder for Heather every single day."

"Ohhhh." Peyton's eyes grew wide. "That's right, Heather's there. Doing my job at the café."

"And so busy, trying to find time to look at houses because she is very serious about moving to Coconut Key."

"Perfect!" Callie said, elbowing Peyton. "She can *keep* doing your job, Pey, and you can move here permanently. What an awesome solution."

Peyton just looked at her, almost not able to speak, her heart was so torn in two directions. "But I like that job," she said. "And it sounds like it's a lot for her when she only has a few weeks to find a place to live, and Savannah needs me and…"

"Hey," Callie whispered as Peyton's voice trailed off. "Remember our motto."

"You're right, Cal." Peyton lifted her glass and looked

from one face she loved to the next. "I'll figure it out. Maybe I'll know more after I meet the family."

Because if the Sanchez clan wasn't as awesome as the Fosters, she might have to give up Val.

When she let out a little whimper-sigh, Callie leaned in and whispered, "No stinkin' regrets."

Right. No regrets.

CHAPTER SIXTEEN

NICK

*W*hen Sunny Washington's mother chose the name "Sunshine" for the statuesque goddess, she must have known what she was doing. She was warm, funny, brilliant, and Eliza had promised Nick that Sunny would have common sense on the set, which was critical.

After he'd introduced her to Savannah and taken Sunny and her assistant, Emily, for a tour around The Haven, they settled on the deck with tea and lemonade, while Dylan slept in his carrier under an umbrella.

"Have you seen Eliza?" Nick asked Sunny. "Any change with Ben?"

She shook her head. "Same. Failing."

"He's a great guy," Nick said.

"I've honestly never met him, since he was already sick when I started working with Eliza. But I've heard they had that rare thing in Hollywood—a terrific marriage." She leveled him with her espresso eyes, a few shades darker than her skin, crossing legs that went forever and kicking off a braided sandal to the floor. "Is that what you two will have?" she asked with a bit of a challenge in her voice.

"Absolutely," he assured her, looking at Savannah next to him. "She's stolen my heart and changed my life."

"Your life was pretty good," Sunny mused, maybe quietly looking for that crack in the foundation he knew she'd never find.

"It's better now."

Sunny shifted her attention to Savannah, openly scrutinizing her. "You must be quite a spectacular woman."

"She is," Nick chimed in, taking her hand before she could respond. "For one thing, she's endured a week of my mother while we waited for you to arrive."

"Ah, the famous Diana Frye." Sunny rolled her eyes. "Eliza warned me God threw the mold away after He created that one."

Savannah snorted. "Things we thank Him for."

"Did I miss anything terribly dramatic?" Sunny asked. "I am going to want a little emotional punch in this love story. Is Diana going to provide it?"

"Most likely," Nick said. "You missed the tearing up of the prenup."

She gasped, blinking at Savannah. "No! You tore it up?"

"I did," Nick said. "Stupidest thing I ever saw."

Savannah shook her head. "He has a bit of a dramatic flair, too. I'm fine with a prenup."

"We don't need it," Nick said. "This is forever."

"Ooh, I knew this was going to be a good episode," Sunny said, leaning forward. "Don't suppose I can get a re-enactment of the prenup tear?"

"Nope," Nick said. "We agreed to a proposal in the setting of my choice, some wedding dress shopping, cameras at the rehearsal dinner, and a live wedding ceremony. A limited number of sidebar interviews. That is all the film that will roll."

The other woman just nodded, silent for a moment, which Nick suspected was her way of lining up her own demands. This was a friendly tea-on-the-deck hour, but he knew this conversation would lay the groundwork for how the next two weeks would unfold.

So he waited for her, letting her start the game.

"Emily and I will stay in the guest house, so thank you very much for that," she said.

"Of course," he replied. "We're happy to have you." He and Savannah agreed it was smart to keep her close.

"And we'll turn it into production headquarters, so we can stay out of the main house unless we're filming."

"Perfect."

She sat up, shifting her gaze to the crystal blue waters and white sands of the Gulf, watching a seagull swoop into the water and emerge with a fish in its mouth. "You'll marry on the beach, of course, and have the reception here in this house. Are you okay with that?"

He looked at Savannah, giving her the chance to say no. "Once the house is on TV, we lose a measure of privacy," he told her. "We can have the wedding on the Atlantic side."

"We had talked about the B&B," she said.

"That beach isn't quite as clean and wide for filming," Sunny said, obviously having done her homework. "How about if I guarantee there are no long shots of the house, no location or address revealed, and we edit so you cannot know where it is? I can do that, you have my word."

Again, he checked with Savannah, who nodded. "I'd like it to be here, actually."

"Good, then it's settled." Sunny took another deep drink, then sat back. "I'm more than just a reality TV host, as you know. This show is my baby, and I only care about three things: staying on budget, staying on time, and staying on top of the ratings. That means, we shoot with minimal takes, we agree on what gets spent, and if we find drama behind the scenes, we get to use it."

"Drama..." Savannah frowned. "Like if we have an argument?"

"Like anything," she said. "Obviously Diana is a gold mine. But your family, Savannah?"

"They *are* gold," Nick said. "You won't get a lot of drama on that side of the family."

"I heard your parents are divorced, Savannah. Will both of them be here?"

Savannah's eyes flickered in surprise, but surely she'd known this woman would do research. "My mother and I are very close. And, yes, I suppose my father would come to my wedding, but don't expect fireworks."

"I don't, but if there's a soft underbelly to a family or event, we're not afraid of exposing it. If you are all hunky dory, sappy happy, well..." She shrugged. "We'll find a way to make that interesting. Who else? Your father, Nick?"

"My father?" Nick practically choked. "He could be dead for all I know."

"Really?" Sunny leaned forward, intrigued. "You don't have a relationship with him?"

"I met Oliver Jones one time, when I was seventeen. He reeked of booze, lived in a filthy trailer in Louisiana, and made it pretty damn clear he thought I owed *him* money."

He shuddered as he remembered how well Diana had made her point on that trip. *You want to know your dad, Nicky? Well, let's go meet him and you can see why he's not in the picture.* It took exactly twenty minutes in the guy's company to give up the childish fantasy of reconnecting and developing a relationship.

"But I'm glad I did meet him," he continued. "That day, when I left the trailer, I swore that if and when I had a child, I would be the opposite parent. I would be more than present, I would be his mentor, his hero, his friend. I vowed that I would be a father unlike any other, and that my son or daughter would know that when they needed anything, ever, I was who they'd turn to."

The words hung in the air as the three women looked at him.

"And that's why I'm here, in Coconut Key, with this amazing woman whom I love more than anyone or anything. That's how my father shaped me, but not the way he should have done it. Still, I'm grateful to him for being the schlump that he was. It made me a better man."

Next to him, Savannah sighed softly, and he turned to her, catching her wipe a tear. "Oh, Nick. I knew this, but... I never quite get over the impact of your story."

"Damn it!" Sunny exclaimed. "How can I get you to re-enact this? This? What's happening here?" She pointed her finger, wiggling it between Savannah and Nick. "*This* is what I'm looking for."

Nick shook his head. "You get a proposal, dress shopping, some interviews, a few shots of the rehearsal, and the ceremony. And that's it. Period. No ancient family drama."

"Fine," she agreed, turning all her personal force on Savannah. "What's your deepest fear about marrying Nick?"

Of course, his woman didn't flinch. "I'm not afraid of anything regarding this marriage," she answered instantly. "We are deeply in love and very excited about the future."

"But you're afraid of things regarding the wedding, then," Sunny suggested.

"Not of things going wrong, but now on TV? I guess I'm a little worried about being vulnerable."

"I understand," Sunny said. "Here's my advice: *be* vulnerable. The more honest and genuine you two can be, the more the viewers will fall in love with you. What else are you scared of?"

"Nick's mother," she cracked, making Sunny snort. "But you care about three things, and so do I."

"You want the wedding of your dreams, to look gorgeous, and to keep the baby off screen?" she guessed.

"No." Savannah turned to Dylan, sleeping in a carrier on the table. "He's too beautiful to keep off screen and obviously, he's a huge part of our story. He *is* our story, in some ways."

The other woman nodded. "Then what are the three things you care about?"

Savannah took a moment and grasped Nick's hand, as if seeking support. Not that she needed it, but he threaded their fingers and gave her an encouraging squeeze.

"Give her your demands, babe. This is the time."

She nodded. "I want to be sure my family and friends are not excluded or pushed aside for extras. They are very much a part of our lives."

"Fine, no problem. Next?"

"I want to be protected at all times, all of us. No strangers in this house who haven't been vetted and bonded, and *no one* in our private quarters upstairs, ever."

"That's entirely doable. And your last demand?"

"When Dylan's had enough, he's had enough," Savannah said. "Nick and I make that call and no one—and I do mean *no one*—can argue with us about it."

Sunny nodded a few times, in complete agreement. "Dylan's needs come before everything," she said. "We also employ top security with FBI background checks, and will make sure the entire third floor is off limits to anyone and everyone. I give you my personal word of honor."

"Good," Savannah said. "Because I will hold you to that."

"Anything else?" Sunny asked.

"Well, yes. One more." Savannah took a deep breath and looked at Nick. "This ceremony has to be real and legitimate. It has to count in the eyes of the law, God, and...each other."

"I swear it is real, legal, and you can write your own vows."

Nick couldn't help smiling at Savannah. "Isn't she amazing, Sunny? Isn't this woman just the most beautiful and genuine and remarkable human you've ever met?"

"She certainly is," Sunny agreed with just a touch of tease in her voice. "She certainly has charmed a prince."

"The only prince in this place is His Royal Highness Dylan Foster," Nick said.

"As it should be," Sunny said, pushing up to stand. "All right, then. We have work to do. A few days of prep, then we dive into filming, editing, and the wedding. Come on, Em, let's put together a final production calendar, give the crew the go signal so they can fly out in the next few days. Oh, the proposal location. You said you know what you want to do, Nick. What is it?"

"A surprise."

Her eyes widened. "I hope it's screen worthy."

"It most certainly is. And I'll tell you privately."

"I don't get to know?" Savannah asked.

"What part of surprise don't you understand?" Sunny teased. "I gotta have *some* drama with you two, otherwise I'm going to kill my production budget trying to manufacture it. But I can. Oh and remember, I am the last word and control everything. You want something, you come to me."

She gave Nick a wave. "Come with us to production headquarters and tell me your ideas for the proposal, then Em and I will start a production schedule." She stretched and gazed at the Gulf. "This is going to be an amazing show. Amazing. And, yes, it all comes down to one day where nothing can go wrong, but I haven't had a miss yet and I don't intend to."

As she and Emily headed down the stairs, Nick stood to follow, but first he leaned over to give Savannah a kiss.

She dipped back, narrowing her eyes. "You thought about the proposal, huh?"

"Many times."

As he was stepping away, Savannah snagged his arm. "She's looking for drama. You picked that up, didn't you?"

"She's not going to find it."

"With your mother?"

He winked. "She's accepted her fate," he assured her. "Have you accepted yours?"

"I guess...I'm going to be Mrs. Nicholas Frye."

He smiled. "And I'm going to be the happiest man alive."

CHAPTER SEVENTEEN
BECK

*I*t was close to six when Lovely and Beck got back to Coquina Court after the day in Islamorada, both of them wiped out. At seventy-four, Lovely had a good excuse. But Beck shouldn't be quite this tired, she mused as she pulled her car into the lot, noticing that Max's car was not there.

Thank God she didn't have to put on a happy face for him. Diana, maybe, but God willing, they were both gone. She really just needed some alone time. Something was pressing on her heart and she'd been so busy, she hadn't had time to really consider what it might be.

"What's wrong, Beckie?" Lovely asked, her gaze searching Beck's face.

"I don't know," she said honestly. "I'm just a little... blue. Maybe seeing Peyton so happy—not that I'm blue about that—but I have a hunch she's Miami-bound."

"Maybe," Lovely agreed, still inspecting Beck's face. "But you've been unusually quiet for most of the way home. And that was the fifth heavy sigh in the last forty minutes."

"Over my allotment, huh?" Beck teased. "Long day, Lovely."

But such a good one. After lunch with Callie and Peyton, they'd shopped some more, and the car was loaded with some fun, decorative purchases that would finish off the upstairs, and the beds were ordered. If necessary, they could take more guests next week, thanks to Kenny and the crew.

"Something's eating at you," Lovely said. "I can always tell."

"I'm...emotional," she admitted. "I shouldn't be dependent on my daughters for my happiness. They have to live their lives, and if Peyton's is in Miami? Well, it's not far, and I want her to be happy."

"Are you sure that's all?"

She wasn't sure of anything, to be honest. "It's enough. And this reality show wedding, the world's most demanding guests, and..."

And Josh. The minute she landed on that, her heart hitched. So maybe it was Josh that was at the root of her restlessness, she thought, but kept that last one out.

"At least we have Toni," Lovely said brightly as they climbed out of the car and grabbed some of the bags of pillows and small picture frames.

"Yeah, Toni." Not the most stellar employee, but her working here made Josh really happy, and surely she wouldn't last long.

As they trudged up the steps to the veranda, Beck frowned at the sight of some dishes at the outdoor tables. "The workers are almost done and Kenny promised me they wouldn't eat here anymore. And why didn't Toni clean—"

"Uh, Beck." Next to her, Lovely peered through the French doors into the kitchen. "Brace yourself, honey."

"Why?" She pushed open the door, which was unlocked, and gasped at the hot mess that was the kitchen.

"What the..." Beck peered at the counter, covered with dishes, a pile of dirty sheets and towels, and empty bottles of water.

"She just left it?" Lovely's voice rose at the sight. "Toni said she'd have this place spotless while we were in Islamorada."

Beck pulled out her phone to call her ace employee, blood pressure rising as she tapped Toni's name in the contacts.

"Hey, Beck," she answered in a happy sing-song voice. "What up, boss?"

What up? "Toni, the kitchen is—"

"A wreck, I know. But customers always come first, right, isn't that the saying?"

No, but Beck didn't want to argue semantics. "Why weren't the sheets washed or the breakfast dishes put away and...is that macaroni and cheese on the stove?" Her voice rose in horror at the sight of something orange and coagulated on her beautiful gas range.

"Oh, shoot, I meant to put that away. I made lunch for myself. Oh, good news. Kenny said they are just about done upstairs. There were no workers in the house today."

"But the doors were unlocked."

"My bad." She let out a little giggle, then exclaimed,

"Hey! Wait for me, you guys. Oh, sorry, Beck. I'm with Max and Diana in Key West. Max is nuts, you know that? You're nuts, Maxie!"

"What are you *doing*?" Beck demanded through gritted teeth.

"Bar hopping," she trilled out the words. "This place is wild. Oh, Beck, you're not mad, are you? I mean, I thought you wanted me to take care of our guests, so I am taking care of them. They wanted to see Key West and..." She lowered her voice. "Diana can really be a drip, you know? Max begged me to come along for fun. How could I say no?"

"Because you're being paid to clean and keep the B&B perfect, not go bar hopping with the guests."

"But you said full service. Oh my God, no! Seriously?" She let out a hoot. "Max is getting one of those buggy carriages pulled by a lunatic on a bicycle! I gotta go. Look, it's gonna be a late night here for us, so I won't worry about coming down too early. Our only guests will be sleeping it off, I promise. I gotta go, Beck!"

And she was gone, leaving Beck holding the phone and a scream that welled up from deep inside.

"I'll get these in the wash," Lovely said, already scooping up the pile of dirty sheets.

"You will not." Beck put down her phone. "I can do the laundry and the kitchen. You must be dead tired from today."

"I'm tired, but not dead." Lovely lifted a brow. "But that girl might be if she walked in the door right now."

Beck put her hands on the counter for stability, closing her eyes, a little surprised at how much her lids stung. Was she going to cry? No. That was crazy.

"Beckie!" Lovely was next to her in a minute, both arms wrapped around her. "It's just a little laundry and dishes. I can help you make the beds when the sheets are done. Ava said she can keep the dogs as long as I need her to, so I'll just text her. No worries."

Beck shook her head, no longer able to keep it in. "I'm a little overwhelmed," she admitted. "Not completely. Just a little."

"You're whelmed," Lovely said, stroking her back. "I always wondered why you could be overwhelmed and underwhelmed, but not whelmed."

The joke almost made Beck smile, but the world and her heart and everything was just too much. She blinked and a tear fell.

"How about we throw the sheets in and have a mimosa?" Lovely suggested.

"Oh, I'd love—Josh! Shoot! What time is it? He's making me dinner tonight and wanted to hear all about the day with Peyton." She dropped her head back and let out a grunt. "I can't do it."

"Then cancel, dear girl. It's just Josh. He'll understand."

The words weighed heavy on her heart. "That's the problem," she whispered. "It's *just* Josh. He *always* understands. And, really, doesn't he deserve better than that?"

Lovely frowned, shaking her head. "I don't quite follow."

Beck sighed—number six—the truth bubbling up and leaving her mouth with a bad, metallic taste. "I have to...make a decision about him."

Lovely bit her lower lip, silent.

"It's been a year," Beck continued. "He's been the best

friend a woman could want. A soft place to fall, a broad shoulder to lean on, a truly great man."

"He is, and you know I love him like a son."

"I know and maybe that's why..." She swallowed. "Lovely, I just can't bring myself to go...over the edge with him. I know you think I need to forgive Dan first."

"Eh." She shrugged. "After that stunt he pulled that almost broke up Savannah and Nick? He can stay unforgiven for a while."

"And my daughters tell me Josh is a keeper, just in case I didn't know that. But they agree that I've been badly hurt and am very self-protective."

"Josh would never hurt you."

"I know that." And her mother's defense of him was probably why it had taken Beck so long to admit this. "But after seeing Peyton today, something clicked. I don't know what it was. Maybe her happiness at being with a man who sends her over the moon. And watching Savannah fall so hard in love. Or maybe just the realization that I'm so much older than my daughters and I shouldn't be out hunting that feeling at all."

"Are you?" Lovely asked.

"No, not really. I'm too busy. But, when I'm with Josh..." She just couldn't put it into words.

Lovely took Beck's hand and squeezed. "Something's missing."

"Yes." She breathed out the confession. "Whatever it is that's keeping me from falling...in bed, in love, in... forever. It's not there. But I feel like he's given me a year of patience and understanding and friendship and...and... brotherhood?" Her voice rose. "I think that's what it is.

I've known Josh since he was skateboarding down Coquina Court. He's like my big brother."

The minute she said the words, it felt like a fog lifted. Like...that was what had been hanging over her head for weeks. Months. As long as the B&B was being renovated, she had a perfect reason to keep him at arm's length. But with it done, and the girls more or less settled, and her divorce long in the rearview mirror...she was running out of excuses.

"I've seen you kiss," Lovely said. "No one should kiss their brother like that."

"Oh, it's not that there's no attraction. He's wonderful and I have felt plenty of...desire. But..." She pressed her fingers to her lips, not even wanting to say what she was thinking. Lovely adored Josh and she might rightfully take his side—not that there were sides to take.

"What?" Lovely urged. "Please tell me all of it."

"Sometimes," Beck whispered, "I wonder if the desire is just for...all I'm missing. The longing for that sort of... magic. Like I'm in love with the idea of finding it, of getting swept away again, of riding that rollercoaster that I haven't ridden since I was in college with Dan. And Josh was just...a rebound after Dan. Yes, I adore him and he's got a good, good heart, but..." With each word, her heart hurt more. "Oh, why can't I just give in and love him?"

"Because you don't," Lovely said. "Not that way. And I do love Josh like a son, but you are my daughter. So, here's my advice."

Beck held up her hand, already knowing what was coming. "Tell him."

"Tonight," Lovely added.

Beck let out a soft moan. "I don't want to. I'd rather

stay here and do laundry and remake the beds and get breakfast ready and maybe have a root canal and a pap smear at the same time."

Lovely narrowed her eyes. "You have to tell him, Beckie."

She sighed. "I know, I know."

"Then I'll call Heather, who can be here in ten minutes to help. You, go get dressed, and do the right thing, Beckie. Talk to the man. He may talk you out of it. He may feel the same. He may seduce your right into his bed and make you realize how wrong you are. But until you address this head on..." Lovely stroked her cheek. "You're going to keep sighing out sadness, and I don't like that."

She blinked and another tear escaped as she folded her little mother in her arms and squeezed her, overwhelmed. Not just whelmed, but definitely overwhelmed.

IT DIDN'T HELP that dinner was perfect. Didn't make things easier for Beck when Josh grilled steaks with a side of buttery mushrooms, poured a lovely merlot, and didn't just listen to her description of every detail of the day—he asked insightful questions.

How did Peyton look, had she met Val's family, was Callie fitting in at UM, did they get the best deal on the mattress they'd ordered for the Coconut Room? All the things, mundane and critical, that highlighted Josh's good heart and caring ways.

And he looked particularly nice, too. Faded jeans and an indigo T-shirt that not only made him look strong and tanned, but brought out the blue in his eyes. And those eyes were intense tonight, leveled on her when he asked questions and when he listened to the answers. They sparked with humor when she told him about Lovely making friends in the stores, and warmed when he brought nightcaps to their favorite spot on his dock to watch the moonrise.

She didn't tell him about Toni's latest antics, but she would have—if her employee wasn't also his daughter. And if she didn't have way more important things to talk about tonight.

"So, Beck," he said after they sat in a companionable silence with no sound but the soft splash of water against the dock posts and a breeze whispering through the palm fronds.

"So, Josh," she echoed, eyeing him.

"We need to talk."

She sat up a little straighter, the tone and words surprising her, even though they were exactly the ones she was about to use. "We do? We...are, aren't we?"

He smiled. "About something very serious, and something we've been dancing around for a while."

"Oh." She took a sip of wine and set the glass on the table between them, her heart kicking up a notch. Was it ultimatum time for him? Was he going to force her into a do or die moment with their relationship? Or maybe this was about Toni, and she needed to come clean with how upset she was.

"What's on your mind?" she asked, trying for casual.

"You," he said simply. "And us."

Oh, dear. She almost reached for the wine, but turned

in her seat a little to look at him instead. "That does sound serious."

"I've been giving it a lot of thought," he said, adding a soft chuckle. "Which would be the understatement of the year."

"You're good with understatement," she said. "It's one of your strong suits. One of many."

He gave a tight smile. "I've been working on something. A surprise, a gift for you."

"Really?"

He nodded and took a drink, looking out to the canal as he set the glass down, silent for a few long heartbeats. "But I'm having second thoughts."

And that beating heart dropped like a rock. "About... me? About giving it to me? About..." She clamped her mouth shut, knowing that Josh would just let her babble, and whatever he had to say was more important right then.

"I don't want to be alone in this life, Beck. I want a partner. I want a best friend. I want a wife," he finished.

Oh, God. This was a proposal? On the very night she came over to tell him this wasn't going past friendship? That some kind of magic was missing? She had no idea what to say, except...would it be no? Would she actually turn down a proposal?

For what felt like a lifetime, she looked at his profile as he stared straight ahead, noticing, not for the first time, how handsome he was. How the angle of his jaw sort of hollowed out his cheeks and how straight and strong his nose was. Even his ear was kind of perfect.

Was this her mind, gearing up to say...yes?

Well, would that be so bad? No, maybe it wouldn't. Maybe "magic" was a foolish thing to look for in a man when he was perfect in every other way. Maybe this was what she'd been waiting for all along. Maybe marriage was the magic she was missing. Of course! This was strong and steady Josh. Her rock, her shoulder, her soft place to—

"So that just makes this conversation all the more difficult to have," he finally said, turning to her.

Wait. *What?* She blinked, not following. "How so?"

He had nothing but pain in his eyes. Not the look of a man who was about to drop to one knee and pop the question.

"I think we should...change the parameters of our relationship."

Her heart slipped around for a bit. "Change the... what...what does that mean?"

"Oh, God, Beck." He reached for her hand. "I hate to see that look on your face. I don't want to disappoint you. I really don't want to hurt you. I love you, you know that. But..."

She drew her hand back, her throat tight. "Are you breaking up with me?"

"I guess the answer would be yes, if we were ever 'officially' together, but this relationship is—"

"You don't think all that kissing and laughing and making out was..." She closed her eyes and took a breath, trying to remember that *this* was her goal tonight. But he beat her to it. So pride be damned, they both wanted the same thing.

Or did they?

Now, she took a drink. A deep and long one, nearly draining the glass.

"Beck. You might not realize it, but I think this is what you want, too."

Oh, she realized it all right. She'd had a whole speech ready about being friends and like brother and sister and something about needing...magic.

But if she told him that, she'd just sound like a fool and he might not ever believe her. She wasn't sure she believed it herself, because something inside her was cracking a little.

"I think," she said, rooting for the right words in a head that had suddenly gone blank. "That I don't know what I want." Truer words were never spoken.

"Well, I know what I want," he said. "I've known that from the day I walked into Jessie's restaurant and saw you and your pretty blond hair and heard that musical laugh I remembered from when we were kids. That first night, when we had dinner and you told us about your divorce, I knew...ooh, boy. Dangerous territory. A broken woman who'd come here to put her life back together didn't need Josh hitting on her."

She let her eyes drift closed, taking a breath. "For one thing, Josh, I didn't come here to put my life back together. I never expected to stay."

"But you did."

"And for another, you were one of the reasons I did." Maybe she'd never realized that before, but it was true.

"Then, Beck, why have you kept me at arm's length for a year? Why have I spent a year on hold, waiting and wondering and being kind of pathetically patient?"

"You're not pathetic."

"You're not committed," he countered. "And I think it's

best if we recognize that and move on, as friends, which we will be forever."

Holy...*friends*. Friends. Yes, it was what she thought she wanted but...did she? And maybe she could beg, which would be beyond ironic, and he might fold. Josh loved her; she believed that. But what if six weeks or six months or six *years* from now, she craved...*magic*?

For a few long seconds, neither of them said a thing, the unspoken words hanging as loudly as the ones he'd spoken. The fact was, Josh was ending their relationship. And it hurt.

Which was stupid and selfish and prideful and embarrassing, especially considering her plans for the night...to do the same. Or at least *talk* about it.

Why would it bother her? Did it matter who was the dumper and who was the dumpee? Or maybe she wasn't going to break up with him. Maybe she'd have stared at his handsome profile and climbed into his lap and kissed until they finally, finally went inside to his bedroom.

"Beck?" He whispered into the long silence. "What are you thinking?"

"I'm thinking...where do we go from here?"

"Well, I'm not going anywhere," he said. "And neither are you. We continue as we have been—here for each other, supportive, enjoying our life in paradise."

"Without the kissing," she said with a wistful laugh.

"Without the...hope," he replied. "I just can't hold out for it anymore."

She looked at him. "So this is because I've been unable to...commit?" Or was it because they hadn't had sex? Or could she even separate the two?

"This is because we both should be free to find whatever it is we're looking for. I know that I want permanence and certainty. And all the stuff that comes with that."

Like sex and marriage, she thought.

"But I don't know what you want, Beck."

"Neither do I," she admitted.

"So you should be free to figure that out." He took her hand and held it tightly in his. "That's what I want for you."

And, honestly, that's what she wanted, too. It just hurt to get it. "Thanks, Josh."

They didn't bother to finish the wine, but headed back into the house. Like always, he walked her to her car and opened the door for her. They didn't kiss but he gave her a hug and pressed his lips to her hair, then stood in his driveway and watched her drive away, as always.

But tonight, on the way home, instead of playing a song for the short drive back to Coquina House, maybe humming along after a nice night with her rock-solid Josh, Beck cried. Hard, and from a hurting heart. She hadn't cried like that for...well, almost a year.

CHAPTER EIGHTEEN

A Cuban barbeque, Peyton discovered very early on, wasn't quite like any of the backyard parties she'd been to in her life. For one thing, the food was insane, in quantity and quality. No hot dogs and burgers for this crew. The featured dish was a whole pig cooked in the ground, and the dozens of sides were exploding with layers of flavor and heat and textures she'd never even imagined. High energy music played just loud enough to be heard over the constant chatter in two languages. But it was the warmth and color of the people that just blew Peyton away.

Val's "family" included friends, neighbors, cousins, and a few people who may have walked in off the street, so there was no way she could remember everyone's names.

She had help from Val and Abuelita, the tiny, white-haired grandmother who might be "sick" but cooked like her purpose on earth was to feed everyone in the neighborhood. Val's grandfather, Papi, was in charge of the pig, while Val's mother kept producing side dishes and his father poured rum drinks that were not for the average day drinker.

"So, what do you think?" Val hooked his arm around Peyton's neck and eased her closer, tapping his red Solo cup to hers. "Could you get used to the big Cuban family?"

When he asked her questions like that—which he did all the time—Peyton's whole body tensed in anticipation, a mix of uncertainty and excitement for what he might be implying.

"It's a wonderful family," she said. "Your grandmother is a hoot and Papi gave me a pepper that blew my head off."

"That means he likes you." Then his eyes widened. "Wait. A habanero? 'Cause you have to work up to that, Pey."

"It's fine. He had me wash it down with a drink." She lifted her cup. "A very strong drink."

He laughed. "Then he really likes you. Which comes as no surprise to me."

"Even though I don't speak a word of Spanish?"

He shrugged. "That doesn't matter to us. My family just wants me to be happy."

"Are you?"

He looked into her eyes. "As happy as I've been in—"

"Hey, Val." A dark-haired woman, around thirty, came up to them, reaching out to him. "Good to see you."

"Natalia!" He seemed surprised to see her, instantly letting go of Peyton to hug her back. "I had no idea you'd be here. Are you back in Miami now?"

"I'm here to help my mother get settled in a new

house. Trying to navigate the divorced parents and not take sides." She smiled at Peyton.

"Been there, walked that tightrope," Peyton said, extending her hand.

"This is Peyton, Natalia," Val said with an emphasis that made Peyton suspect he'd talked about her to this woman.

"Ohhh!" Her eyes flashed with interest as she shook Peyton's hand. "Natalia Vega. I'm Val's..." They shared a look as if they didn't quite know how to describe their relationship. "Almost sister-in-law," she finished, then jabbed his arm with her elbow. "You were right, she's gorgeous. Now go get me a drink from Papi. Tell him to have mercy with the rum."

He laughed, but as he inched away, he narrowed his eyes. "Be nice to her, Natalia. I'd like to keep her."

And with that, he was gone, and Peyton faced the sister of the woman who was supposed to marry Val, but succumbed to leukemia. What could she possibly say? But Natalia's dark eyes were warm, and her smile seemed natural.

"Listen," Natalia said. "You got big shoes to fill, but we're rooting for you."

The bluntness, and the sentiment, surprised her. "Thanks. I'm so sorry about your sister. What a tragedy."

She closed her eyes. "Marisa was my favorite human on earth," she said. "But Val's a close second. We all want him to be happy. And he's told me a lot about you. I understand you cook."

"I'm learning."

"And you want to get married."

She blinked, not sure how to answer that. "Doesn't...everyone?"

She shrugged and took a deep breath, glancing around. "It won't be easy with some, but it'll be a breeze with others. Filling those shoes, I mean. There's only one thing you have to do to win every one of these people over, even Abuelita who might seem like a sweet little Cuban lady but is judging you *so hard* right now."

"She is?"

"Don't look," she joked.

"What's the one thing?" Peyton asked.

"Don't let her know you have a weakness."

"What if I let her know I have a decent plantain recipe?"

Her eyes popped. "That could go one of two ways. She might steal it, or kill you. She's unpredictable."

Peyton laughed, at ease immediately. "Did Val tell you that I love living in the Keys?" she asked, wanting to know if he'd shared one of their biggest obstacles with his friends and family.

"Val loved it down there," she said, sounding a little vague. "But he *belongs* here." Now that wasn't vague.

"But I belong there," Peyton countered.

Natalia tipped her head, her dark hair falling over one shoulder. "Then you'll have to move. Or lose him. Just don't keep him hanging, Peyton. He's ready for love and we all want him to find it."

The irony of that statement almost made her laugh. Eight months ago, Peyton had essentially said the same thing to him, and he took off for Miami.

Val came back with a drink, looking curious about the conversation. "So, Nat, what do you think of my new girlfriend?" No mincing words in this family, that was for sure.

"She's awesome, and I'm going to go arrange a plantain cook-off with Abuelita," she said with a wink. "If she survives that, she can obviously handle anything. Thanks for the drink and great to meet you, Peyton."

She stepped away as quickly as she'd come.

"She's a piece of work, that one," Val said, picking up his own drink.

"She's...honest."

He lifted his brows in question. "What did she tell you?"

"That I need to turn my life upside down for yours," she said on a sigh, the rum maybe making her a little too open.

"Just be, Peyton," he said.

"What do you mean?"

"I mean, life's short and unpredictable. Let go of where you belong for the rest of today and just be here. Open up your heart and your mouth and your mind to my life and see how it all feels."

She looked up at him, not at all sure how to answer.

"Starting now." He jutted his chin over her shoulder, and she turned to see Papi coming her way with another hot pepper and a challenge in his eyes.

Val was right. She had to open up and feel this family and live this day. So she did, and by the end of it, she could have sworn she loved them all.

But something burned in her stomach, and she had a feeling it wasn't the habanero she ate that day. It was the fear of letting go of her life so she could live his.

LATE THAT NIGHT, when Peyton heard Callie's keys in the apartment door, she realized just how much she'd been anticipating her sister coming home from a study session at the library.

Peyton *had* to talk to her. To someone in her family. She just needed to say her decision out loud and make sure it was right.

It felt right, down to her toes. But she needed validation.

"Oh, you're home from the barbeque?" Callie asked when she stepped into the living room and saw Peyton curled on the sofa in her PJ's. "Did you bring me some pig?"

"Pork. It's in the fridge with plantains which, I sadly admit, are better than mine. I have a lot to learn about Cuban cooking."

As Callie dropped her overloaded backpack on a chair, she eyed Peyton with interest. "You do, huh?"

"But I'm a quick study in the kitchen."

Still looking at her as if she sensed Peyton was holding something back, Callie eased onto the sofa. "So how was it?"

How could she describe the day and evening in one word? Amazing? Perfect? Life-changing? "Good," she said simply.

"His family?"

Peyton smiled. "I loved his family," she said. "They're warm and vibrant and loving and funny and...exactly what you'd expect would produce a gorgeous goofball like Val."

Callie stared at her, her dark eyes wide and wondering. "And..."

"And?" She shrugged. "They liked me, too."

"Not that I ever doubted that, but I know you were worried about fitting in."

"I think I'll fit right in."

Callie's brows shot up. "That sounds...promising." She leaned closer, searching Peyton's face. "Have you made a decision about anything?"

"I have." Peyton gnawed on her lower lip, holding her sister's gaze. "I love that man," she said softly. "And I want to be with him, Callie. More than I want...anything else. I think I want to move here and give this a chance to be forever."

"Oh, wow." She dropped on a grunt of surprise and relief. "Wow. This is...huge. You're going to move here? Live with..."

"You," she said. "If I can."

"Are you kidding? This is a dream come true for me. Does Val know?"

"I haven't made any formal announcements to him or anyone." She'd only really made the decision in the last few hours, sitting alone, still humming from the perfect day with Val and his family.

"Anyone like Mom?" she guessed.

"I want to wait until after Savannah's wedding. It's so soon that I just don't want to put a damper on Mom's mood. So when we go down there for the dress fitting, don't say a word."

Callie looked at her for a long time, her eyes damp with rare tears. "I'm so happy for you, Pey. And for me! And Val." She reached out to hug Peyton, but stopped just in time to frown in doubt. "Why don't you seem happier?"

"I *am* happy," she insisted. "I'm actually quite certain of this decision because it feels right in my heart." She picked up her bottle of Pellegrino and took a drink, but the bubbly non-taste reminded her of...Savannah and home and Mom and the Keys and Jessie and...all that she had to give up. "I just wish I could have both. I want Val. I want to give Val every chance to be the man I spend the rest of my life with. But he cannot leave Miami."

"But it's not like he wants you to live in Alaska, Pey. You're living with me and you know we'll be down there a lot, every holiday and—"

"Not every holiday. Don't forget the Cuban family. They're going to want Val home for the big ones. But after today, that doesn't seem so bad."

"Really? They were that great?"

Peyton smiled, remembering the dancing and the laughter and the life of that party. "You know what they reminded me of? Remember Christmas at Aunt Judy's? With all the cousins?"

"Good times," Callie said.

"It was like that, and I loved it. Honestly? I almost wish I hadn't liked his family so much—the decision would be easier."

"It'll be fine," Callie promised her. "You'll split your time on holidays, and spend plenty of weekends in Coconut Key. It's what married people do."

"And we're not married," Peyton added. "But Val said he wants to get engaged in six months, maybe less."

"Wow, that's fast."

"It doesn't feel fast," Peyton said. "But it does feel

right. I just..." She made a face. "Mom's going to be upset."

"You used to live in New York, Peyton. She was fine."

"That was before Coconut Key. It was different. We got so close this past year, and I connected with that island so much."

Callie tipped her head. "You can't marry an island."

"And this is why you're the family genius."

Callie snorted and popped up. "Gimme those plantains, please. And tell me there was some great dessert."

"There's homemade flan and tres leches cake."

"*Ay caramba!*" Callie joked as she whipped open the refrigerator door. "I'm going to love this new arrangement."

Peyton smiled and took another drink. "Just do not tell Mom, Callie. Let me do that in my own good time."

"Promise."

She didn't know what time would ever be good, though, and that made her heart a little heavy.

CHAPTER NINETEEN

SAVANNAH

*W*hen Sunny Washington gave an order, minions scurried. It was, Savannah decided, quite a beautiful thing to behold. And right now, the tall, commanding goddess was firing orders at everyone—including the director, Brian Barnes—like a general in charge. Savannah thought he'd be the boss, but not even close.

At Sunny's order, cameras were moved. Lights were changed. Mics were tested. Plants were adjusted. And right now, the living room of The Haven looked like, well, a television set, which was exactly what Sunny wanted.

"Now we're ready for you," Sunny said, turning her blinding smile and impossibly dark gaze on Savannah. The woman had vision and style and some of the most beautiful waist-length braids Savannah had ever seen. Today they were partially tied up with a bright orange scarf/ribbon. "We're going to talk, nice and natural, you and me."

She leaned forward. "He's not going to walk in here and pop the question, is he?"

Sunny laughed. "No, hun, he's long gone and waiting for you."

"Where?"

"It's a surprise." She lifted a shapely brow. "We want you surprised, Savannah. We want to catch all the emotion and have it be as real as possible. With cameras."

The minute she said that, three different stationary cameras came to life, and then a fourth—a handheld thing that looked about the size of the one her dad used to use to take family videos before cell phones were invented—got low and close enough for the camera operator to get a shot up her nostril.

"So, Savannah," Sunny said with the enthusiasm of a girlfriend over brunch. "It's your engagement day. How do you feel?"

"Nervous," she replied, accidentally glancing at the handheld camera that got even closer.

"Don't look at Hector," Sunny said. "Right here." She pointed her two fingers at her eyes. "Let's try that again." She waited a beat, then asked. "How you feelin', girl?"

"Nervous and excited." And really trying not to look at Hector.

"Certain you're doing the right thing?"

She thought for a moment. Oh, Sunny meant the wedding. "Of course."

"Tell us about your doubts."

"I don't have any."

Sunny held up her hand and let out an exasperated sigh. "Do better, Savannah."

She blinked. "I don't have any doubts," she insisted.

Sunny leaned in, closing the space between them. "We need to get inside your head and heart, girl. We need to know your every dark and questionable thought, and the bright ones, too. We need to know if saying yes to a famous movie star is a childhood dream or your worst nightmare. We need to feel you, honey, right down in our bones. Or you know what's going to happen?"

She shook her head, not sure she wanted to.

She held up her hand, her thumb pressing on an imaginary remote.

"Fast forward?" Savannah guessed.

"Worse. They'll switch right to last season's episode of *Magic Man* and be really, really mad that Nick Frye decided to marry that bore instead of make more of his great magic detective show."

"Oh."

Sunny dropped back, satisfied she'd made her point. "Come on, sweetie. Dig deep and show us some *feels*. All you have to do is be as honest as you can. And then be more honest. Also, vulnerable. And beautiful. Some powder, here, please."

"Okay. Feels. Honesty. Digging deep." She closed her eyes as the makeup person slipped over and puffed her with powder. Someone held a fan a few feet away, far enough that her hair didn't blow, but close enough to make sure not a single bead of perspiration emerged... even though they wanted her to sweat.

All right. She could do this. She took a deep breath, centered herself, then looked up—and instead of seeing Sunny Washington, she saw...her mother. There was imaginary Beck Foster, tenderhearted and caring, asking her how she was feeling.

"How am I feeling? Like those scones I ate are going to make a second appearance."

Someone chuckled, and it kicked up her confidence.

"Like I stepped into someone else's life and her shoes are too tight and her dress doesn't fit, but oh my God, her man is hot."

Sunny laughed and she leaned back, getting comfortable.

"'Cause let's be honest. I am not the girl who gets a 'guy who looks like Nick,' as that famous song goes. But, here I am. Sadie, Sadie, soon to be married lady."

"Yes, you are. Tell us more," Sunny urged. "What was your first thought when you woke up this morning?"

Just how honest should she be? Enough that they didn't go back to *Magic Man* and demand he return to the show. She wanted Nick Frye in Coconut Key, with her, as her husband.

"My first thought was that a year ago, I wouldn't have thought this could be possible," she said softly, seeing her mother again. "I was pregnant, scared, lost, lonely, and the future looked bleak."

"How did that change?" Sunny asked.

"Well, first of all, my family wrapped me in love, so I wasn't so lost or lonely. Then, the minute I told Nick Frye the news, everything changed. Everything. He took fatherhood more seriously than I'd ever dreamed a man of his...stature or celebrity...ever would. And not only that, he wanted to know everything about me."

"He didn't know you?" Sunny acted surprised, or at least Savannah assumed it was an act. She'd been around long enough to know that Savannah and Nick were strangers when they conceived Dylan.

"He didn't know me at all," Savannah admitted, then she laughed. "You want honest? Okay, folks, here's your soft underbelly."

Sunny's eyes flashed like Savannah was finally about to deliver...the juice.

"You can judge me for what happened, and"—Savannah shrugged—"I can't do anything about that. But I know his fans are confused about why Nick would leave his show and live a different life." She leaned forward. "Because he is the most real and loving man on earth. And that's the beauty of our story. Nick didn't have to be a father or follow me here or marry me. He chose to love me, and Dylan. And that's why he's so amazing. Yes, he's a great actor and easy on the eyes, but it's his heart I've fallen in love with. One that his adoring fans might not even know he has. He's a gem." She blinked, a little surprised her eyes were misting up. "And I can't wait to be his wife."

"And cut!" Brian stood and high fived Sunny, who beamed at Savannah.

"Now that's what I'm talking about!" Sunny power fisted the air. "You're going to make him even more beloved than he already is and that is exactly why viewers watch *Celebrity Wedding*. Now let's get on that boat."

"A boat?"

"Oh, crap. You didn't hear that," Sunny said with a wink.

But she had, and suddenly, she knew exactly where Nick was going to propose to her. And she was so there for it.

THE LAST TIME Savannah stepped aboard the seventy-five-foot yacht called *The Legend*, it had been her thirtieth birthday. She'd been seven months pregnant, and it was exactly the second time in her life she'd been with the baby's father, who'd orchestrated the birthday surprise. Oh, and she'd been carried in on a "litter" like Cleopatra since she'd been on doctor-order bedrest after a life-threatening boating accident. So, Nick had arranged for her to be held aloft by four hot dudes who refused to let her feet touch the ground.

Today she stepped on board by herself, no less excited for what the day held. She looked to the upper deck, greeting the audience for today's shoot with a little wave. Mom raised a mimosa, looking quite glam in a cream-colored pantsuit with spaghetti straps. Gah, it had been days since she'd seen her mother, and all Savannah wanted to do was fly up there.

Lovely was next to her, and—

"Jessie! You're back!" Savannah had been so wrapped up in the days of pre-production and rehearsals and planning that she'd forgotten the familymoon on the Gulf Coast was over.

"Wouldn't miss your big day, Sav." She stood next to Chuck and little Beau, currently crawling all over Savannah's niece, Ava. Heather was there, holding Dylan, and...*ugh*.

Well, of *course* Diana was here. Max had come over the night before and said goodbye, called back to Hollywood for a client emergency. Sadly, Diana didn't go with him, though she'd kept a fairly low profile since the crew had arrived and production had gotten into full swing.

But where was Nick?

Glancing around, she started toward the wide stairs to take her up to that deck, but Emily snagged her sleeve.

"Let's get you into hair and makeup, and wardrobe," she said, guiding her toward one of the many staterooms.

"But I want to see my baby. He's up there."

"He's fine. We're on a budget and only have this thing for a few hours."

"Well, can someone at least get my mom down here?" she asked. "I haven't talked to her for days."

"Mom stays upstairs, come on."

Disappointment kicked, along with a little frustration. Yes, she was getting engaged "for the cameras" but this was also a big, big day and she wanted to share it with her mother.

With a sad look and a wave up to the gang, she followed Emily to a luxurious stateroom and submitted to three people who painted her face, styled her hair, glued lashes on her eyes, and dressed her in a dress only one shade darker than raspberry sherbet and just as sickeningly sweet.

"I'm not really a fuchsia person," she told the wardrobe woman as she stood in front of a full-length mirror and squinted through the fake lashes at the silk mini dress. "Unless this was my sixth birthday party, then this would be perfect for pin the tail on the donkey."

"You said pink, and Diana brought this on board this morning. We thought you wanted it."

Diana brought it? "Excuse me?"

"It's a Stella McCartney design."

"I don't care what it is, I hate it." Twice as much now that she knew where it came from. "And it's my engagement."

The woman sighed. "It's actually quite attractive on you and...honestly, it's all we have."

"You're kidding."

"Diana said she'd handle wardrobe."

Of course she did. But this dress was dreadful. "Where's Sunny?"

Emily, hovering in the corner and never more than ten feet away, glanced at her tablet. "She's upstairs with the crew. It doesn't look bad, Savannah."

"Why does Diana get a say in what I'm going to wear?"

"She said you wanted pink," Emily said.

"No." Savannah felt tension expand across her chest and mix with the anger that woman always kicked into high gear. "I wanted soft pink, something elegant and not..." She glanced in the mirror again, a little horrified that the entire hem was actually fringe. *Fringe?*

Why did she want Savannah to look ridiculous?

"I'm not wearing this," she said. "I'll get engaged in the jeans and T-shirt I had on when we got here."

The wardrobe woman gasped. And Emily was on the phone in a split second, explaining the situation, all of them glancing at each other like Savannah was some kind of prima donna. Normally, she could go with any flow. But, please. This *dress*.

"Sunny said you have to just make it work," Emily told her as she hung up. "We can't take the time to go all the way back for another outfit. Just do your—"

"No!" Tears welled up and the false eyelash lady looked a little horrified. "I won't just make it work. This is my—"

"Savannah?"

"Mom!" She practically flew into her mother's arms. "Look at this! It's all they have for me to wear."

She stepped back and did a slow up and down, biting her lip to keep from laughing.

"It's not funny." Tears spilled over. "This whole thing is just stupid! Bad idea. Bad. I told the world how I had a one-night stand, too, because I was trying to make them like Nick." She took a breath, wiping her hands on the dress which probably added sweat streaks to its ugliness. "It's like I ate Barbie's closet and threw up."

Around her, the others laughed nervously, but Mom just shook her head and then turned to them. "Out. All of you."

She spoke with the same authority as Sunny, and they obeyed as if their fearless leader had called the shots.

When they were alone in the room, Mom put her hands on Savannah's shoulders and gave a squeeze. "Relax, honey," she whispered.

"I can't. I don't know why. I feel like I'm losing myself," she said. "Like my life is happening around me and I'm not in it to experience it. Does that make sense?"

"No, but I can understand the stress," Mom assured her. "And, wow, speaking of missing moments. Wait until you see what they filmed earlier."

"What?"

She made a mushy face. "Nick asked me for permission to marry you."

"He did?" Savannah's heart shifted around under the bright pink fabric.

"He got all choked up and said that you were the light of his life and that he didn't even know who he was until he met you."

"Really?" Now she was definitely going to cry. "What did you say?"

"Oh, I said I'd think about it," she deadpanned, then laughed. "I cried my fool head off. That man loves you so much. And you found it, baby girl. You found...*it.*"

There was something sad in her voice that made Savannah frown. "It?"

"You know...the magic. The missing ingredient. The thing...that...makes life worth living." Her voice cracked slightly. "I just think of it as magic."

Yeah, definite sadness. "Mom? What's wrong?"

"Nothing, nothing. Except that dress. Oh, my God, no, Savannah."

"Right? I can't, Mom. I can't do this. Not in this dress, maybe not at all." Stress strangled her. "I just want to get married with my family and friends, not the whole stinkin' world. How can I possibly—"

A hard knock on the door cut her off. "Savannah! The light is perfect. We need you *now*."

"Yikes. The Sun Goddess has spoken," Savannah whispered. "Mom, we have to—"

Her mother shook her head and cleared her throat before calling, "Sunny, give us five minutes and Savannah will be ready to say yes!"

"In this dress?" she moaned.

"Savannah." Mom took her hands and squeezed, her gaze direct and determined. "That man loves you in a way many women, myself included, dream about. He is real. He is kind. He is committed. And he is going to be your husband. You've agreed to this and if you stay the course, you'll be married and starting your happily ever after in no time. Trust your instincts, and don't fold under pressure."

"Okay," she whispered. "But...the dress—"

"Is revolting. But mine's awesome." Mom turned around and offered the zipper of her gorgeous silk pantsuit. "Strip me, honey. Let's get you into this and I'll wear that. Take a lot of pictures of me, and we'll laugh about this for the rest of our lives."

Savannah suddenly felt all the stress melt away. "Oh my God, Mom." She leaned over and rested her head on the narrow shoulder that had held her up for thirty years. "I love you so much."

Ten minutes later, Nick was on one knee, professing his love. And then they cut because the light wasn't right. Then he was on the other knee, but the ring was in the wrong pocket. Then Savannah forgot the lines they'd written. The light was wrong for the next try and on the fifth take, Dylan squawked so loud everyone laughed.

But the final proposal was as flawless as the diamond he slid onto her ring finger. As he rose to his feet, the kiss they shared was bathed in sunshine and love and so many high hopes. Nothing—no dress, no stress, no mother-in-law, no silly reality show—could get in the way of their happiness.

CHAPTER TWENTY
KENNY

*K*enny arrived early at Coquina House, but Beck had told him that all of the B&B guests would be out, and he'd be free to work on the punch list for a few unfinished items. He trotted up the back steps, not surprised to see that Beck's veranda looked as cheery as ever, especially since she'd added two more tables and umbrellas to accommodate any guests who wanted to gaze at the ocean while they enjoyed their scones and coffee.

The TV people had been here over a week now, so the B&B was officially in business. That gave him a real jolt of pride when he considered how integral a role he'd played in helping Beck and Lovely make their dreams come true.

But when he looked through the French door to the kitchen—that he'd remodeled from top to bottom with his own two hands—he caught sight of Beck pushing a vacuum toward the breakfast room, her hair tied up, her expression anything but...dreamy.

As he inched the door open, he saw a mess of dirty

dishes and pots and pans on the counter, and some linens that needed to be folded.

A B&B was hard work, for sure, but didn't she have help?

"Knock knock," he said, raising his voice to be louder than the vacuum but not so booming that it scared her.

"Oh, oh, Kenny!" She flipped off the vacuum, and swiped one hand over her cheek, visibly getting a hold of herself. "I forgot you were coming to work on that sink stopper."

"And the outlet that isn't turning on," he reminded her, coming into the kitchen. "Still a good time?"

"Perfect, yes." She brushed back some hair then fluttered her hands in front of her face, uncharacteristically nervous. "It gets so hot when you work this hard."

He nodded, and didn't mention that the AC he'd personally installed was blowing out and keeping things a cool and comfortable seventy-two degrees.

"Where's Toni? I thought all this manual stuff was going to be her job."

She let out a huge sigh, shaking her head. "She had an audition in Fort Lauderdale and left last night. I'm not entirely sure she'll be back."

"Seriously?"

"I think when Max disappeared, so did the thrill of working as a hotel maid. The *Celebrity Wedding* people are too busy to give her career advice, so she headed back up to South Florida until the wedding." She leaned the vacuum handle against the wall and came into the kitchen to meet him halfway. "But I've got this covered."

For a moment, he studied her face, which just didn't look as bright and happy as he was used to.

"Everything okay, Beck?"

"Yes. Kind of. No." She pushed that hair back again. "You caught me at a bad time."

He almost offered to zip out and avoid whatever emotion was wracking her, but this was Beck, and if he'd learned anything from his biological mother, it was that she didn't run from people having breakdowns. And neither should he.

"You want to talk about it?" he asked.

"More than anything," she replied on a whispered sigh. "The only daughter close by is wrapped up in filming a TV show about her wedding. The other two are...busy. Lovely..." She closed her eyes and let out a groan. "I told Lovely but..."

"Told her what?" he asked. "Is there a problem with the B&B? I can help you."

She smiled at him, her eyes still misty. "The B&B is perfect," she said. "I currently have real guests and I love what I'm doing. I don't mind cleaning and doing laundry, honestly. I kind of like it." She gave a laugh. "It's what I trained for."

"And the building and renovations?"

"Your work is exquisite, Kenny. I couldn't be more proud of how this place looks."

Well, something was wrecking her. "Is it the wedding stress? Diana? She can be a—"

"It's Josh."

Oh. He inched back, his whole conversation from Josh's shop last week coming back to him. "What happened?" Did he present the bed and she turned him down?

"He ended our relationship," she admitted, pulling out a chair at the table and easing into it.

"Seriously? He didn't...I thought he...really?" He shook his head, definitely not seeing that coming. "I knew he wanted..." Shoot. He had no right to repeat what Josh told him. But the man had said he was ready to make a decision.

"You knew he wanted what?" she asked, then held up her hand. "Never mind. I know what he wanted. He told me. And I respect that completely. He's a man who is just happier in a long-term, committed relationship with a ring and the same last name."

"And you're not?" He sat down in another chair. "Did he...ask you?"

"No. The only proposal this week was Nick and Savannah, on *The Legend*. Did you hear about it?"

He looked skyward. "In great detail from my daughter, who announced that she would be marrying a movie star, too."

"Ava had such fun that day," Beck said. "Nick helped her rehearse her lines for the school play. I'm sorry you missed it."

"I had a meeting with a new client," he told her. "I've got three renos lined up, Beck. One in Coconut Key and two on Big Pine."

"Kenny! That's awesome. You're going to be the busiest GC around when you show pictures of this place."

"That's how I got the jobs, but wait a second. Get back to...Josh. Are you okay?" He leaned forward. "I'm not used to you not smiling."

She closed her eyes and let her shoulders sink. "I'm fine.

I know it's best, and right. I think it's just that everyone is so busy right now and involved with the wedding, and Jessie's all in love with her new-old husband." She smiled, trying to make light of the situation, but he could see she was hurting.

"I admit I'm confused," Kenny said. "Josh wanted to go the distance and you..."

"I think we both know I'm not ready for that. Well, I can't say I'm not ready, I just..." She bit her lip. "We both know we're better off as friends, but he came out and said it first, and I got my ego hurt. And of course, I'm second guessing the whole thing, thinking maybe I was wrong and that he is the...magic one."

He lifted a brow, letting that ask his question for him. What the hell is a *magic one*?

"I know it's silly at my age," she said. "But I think I'm holding out for something that doesn't exist. After all those years of marriage ending in such a brutal way...and seeing Jessie and Savannah and even Peyton all falling in love, I just..." She gave a tight smile. "It's wrong, isn't it? Looking for magic at my age?"

"You're what? Fifty-six?" He shook his head. "Not wrong at all. God made us to connect to another person, but I recognize that you don't want to make a mistake."

"With Josh?" She rolled her eyes. "What's wrong with me? I mean, if it isn't there with a guy like him, who is utterly wonderful, then what on earth am I looking for? And why can't I just be satisfied that I don't have it?"

He searched her face for a long time, wanting so much to give wise counsel to this woman who had so frequently offered it to him.

"I guess it has to be perfect the second time around," he said. "And you're wisely cautious. And Josh *is* a great guy, which is why you do *not* want to hurt him. But if it wasn't exactly perfect and what you wanted down to your soul, then you're both doing the right thing."

"I know." She reached over and put a hand on his arm. "Thank you. I'm just having a little pity party here."

"I'm no stranger to those," he assured her. "I used to hold them on a daily basis. Sometimes more."

"But you're not deep in grief anymore, Kenny. Maybe you're even ready for some magic yourself, huh?"

He blew out a breath, looking into Beck's eyes, always finding comfort there, and the knowledge that he could trust this woman who gave birth to him and handed him to Janet and Jim Gallagher. He loved her for that, and always would.

"Let's not pretend we don't both know I found it and am...avoiding it as much as possible."

"Ooh." She made a face, knowing exactly who he meant. "And everyone, including your own conscience, is telling you to give her a wide berth, and go find someone else."

"I think even you tried when I was painting upstairs a while ago, and I shut you up."

"You didn't shut me up, but you didn't want to talk about it. Do you now?"

He considered that, looking down at the table for a moment. "There's nothing to talk about," he finally said. "What will be will be, right?"

"It will be if you...make it happen."

"I thought it best to...she already told me she..." He rooted around for how to explain all that was going on inside of him. "I'll wait for her," he finally said. "I don't actually think I have a choice."

"What do you mean?"

"I can't look at another woman after meeting her." The admission felt so good, he almost laughed out loud. "Talk about...magic."

Beck's eyes filled. "Tell her, Kenny."

"No, no, that's not—"

"Yes. She needs to know."

"It'll scare the crap out of her, Beck. She's still mourning Drew and the timing is wrong and I can't..." He gave her a look of disbelief. "You think I should? Why?"

"Because she should know that you feel that way. If it's too soon, and it might be, she'll tell you. But if you have a shot, you should know it. Don't make the mistake Josh and I did, dancing around uncertainty for a year." She inched closer. "Don't you want to tell her?"

"Part of me does," he said. "The other part is scared it'll make her run screaming back to Charleston and never return."

"But I told you she's moving here. She's got a buyer for her restaurant up there, too. Have you heard?"

He shook his head. "She's never told me any of this herself. So, for all I know, it's a rumor."

"Not at all. In fact, she's going back to a house for a third time this afternoon and she's close to making an offer."

He sat up. "Without knowing whether or not the house is structurally sound? I can't let her do that."

Beck laughed softly. "Then text her and meet her there. I'm sure she'd love your help on making the decision."

He started to reach for his phone, but stopped as

doubts suddenly appeared. "Maybe if she wanted me, she'd have asked."

Beck lifted a brow. "Maybe she's avoiding her feelings for you, too."

Was that possible? "But it's too soon."

"It's soon," Beck conceded. "But there's no law that says she has to wait a year for you."

"Everyone says—"

"What do you say?"

"I say I wouldn't want her to put an offer on a house I haven't checked out." He tapped the phone. "And if she doesn't want me there, she'll tell me."

Beck smiled. "I think she'll want you there. In fact, I think she'll be over the moon."

"Two amazing mothers." He looked up from the phone and smiled. "Who gets that in one lifetime?"

"You." She patted his hand. "And thank you for talking to me. I needed a son, and you showed up."

HE WASN'T ENTIRELY sure he'd make any heartfelt confessions when he arrived at the address on Ibis Way, but Kenny would, at the very least, make sure the stilt house on a wide canal had structural integrity. He hadn't come here to bare his soul, but the more time he spent with Heather, the better his chances of knowing what she was thinking...if anything.

From the look on Heather's face when he found her in the driveway, looking up at the house, the only thing she was thinking about was how much money she'd have to spend on this house.

She pulled back some long blond hair blowing in the breeze and greeted him with that glorious smile.

"This was unbelievably kind of you, Kenny," she said. "I know you're so busy. And I know I should have told you I was house hunting."

"I heard through the grapevine," he said. "I understand you didn't want to risk me slipping and telling Ava."

"No, I didn't, but I also didn't..."

Want to get his hopes up, he assumed. "It's fine, Heather."

She reached for him. "I wasn't keeping it from you," she said. "I just wanted to...be sure."

"Be sure you were moving here?"

"Be sure..." She swallowed. "Of how I felt about... things. I had to pray and think and...be sure."

"And are you?" he asked.

"Nope, but I'm just letting God lead me and I will go where He says."

Right then, he could have sworn he was having this conversation with his late wife, a woman who'd let her entire life be led by God. A woman he missed, but who he knew would completely approve of the one in front of him.

"That's a good plan, Heather. For both of us."

For a long moment, he just looked at her, and though they were silent, he felt like a million words were hanging between them. This attraction was mutual, and just knowing that fact, Kenny felt like...like he could do *anything*.

"Just take it slow," he finally said. "And I'm here...for you."

She broke into a wide smile. "Thanks. You want to see the house?"

"Sure," he assured her. "Is your broker here?"

"He's running late, but I know the code to get in and he said I could go up. Come on!"

Feeling lighter than he had in years, he followed her toward the house. On the way, he scanned the white stucco, which wasn't large or new, but even at first glance, he could tell it was well maintained.

"It's nice," he told her. "And a primo location on the canal."

"And I'm paying for a primo location," she said, gesturing him to the stairs that led up to the door. "Which is either a complete waste of money or a fantastic investment."

"Here? The latter. Come on, let's look."

It didn't take long for him to do a routine, top level inspection of the three-bedroom house, and everything he found was cosmetic.

"Your biggest expense is going to be the AC unit," he told her as he came up from the first level to meet her on the upstairs patio. "It needs to be replaced."

"What does that cost?"

"A couple thousand, so I'd negotiate down for it."

"And that second bathroom?" She grimaced. "That tile is heinous."

"I can replace that for you. And the bedroom carpets have seen better days, but I can handle those, too."

She sighed with relief. "You're wonderful, you know that?"

"But negotiate for that, Heather. I made a list." He held up his phone. "All told, the house needs about two thousand in general repairs. You should get that taken off the asking price, or at least use this list as a negotiating tool."

"Gosh, I would have never known that. Oh..." She turned at the sound of tires on the shell driveway. "That must be the broker." She reached out and put her hands on his arm, squeezing with just enough desperation to break his heart. "Will you stay and help me talk to him? I've never attempted a purchase this big all alone. I have no idea what to say."

As if he could say no to that. To anything she wanted. "Of course."

When she headed out to greet the broker, he stood stone still, putting his hand over the spot on his arm that was still warm from her fingertips. Closing his eyes, he did the most natural thing in the world...he prayed.

God, help me through this.

It was what his late wife, Elise, would call a bullet prayer, and she'd promised they were always answered.

If God thought he meant "help me through this contract negotiation," then, yes, he'd answered the prayer. Heather had been quiet and let him take the lead with the broker, which he did with ease and confidence. He knew houses, and he understood how this sale should work.

By the time they walked the man down to the driveway to send him off to make an offer that was fair— and substantially lower than the broker originally intended—Heather was glowing.

"I have no idea how to thank you for that," she said, reaching for his hand as the broker's car pulled out. "You got my offer down by ten percent, and I had no idea you could put all those contingencies in."

He shook his head. "It's my business, and you don't have to thank me."

"How about I make you dinner this weekend? I can cook more than just a mean scone, you know."

He blinked at her, trying to pretend it was the light behind her that blinded him. "Dinner is..." Intimate and perfect. "Not necessary."

"I want to."

"Okay, sure. And I, uh, can bring Ava." Since that would make it not a date.

"You can, but why don't you give her a break from an evening with adults, Kenny?"

So...it was a date? Dang, he should know. He had to know. "I can do that," he said, "but, Heather...you don't have to make me dinner if you don't want to."

Why was he arguing with her? Because he had to know. He couldn't go into this hoping for the impossible. Staring at her, he shot another bullet toward the sky.

Come on, God. Make it clear to me, one way or the other. Tell me what to do, whatever is Your will, and I'll follow.

"Kenny." She took his hand and threaded her fingers through it. "I want to." She added a little pressure. "I'm going to be living here, in Coconut Key. And we'll be..."

"Friends," he finished for her.

She smiled. "At the very least."

He gave her hand a squeeze of his own. "That's good, Heather. That's...enough."

"For now," she whispered.

Message received. For a long moment, he tried to breathe, but his chest was tight. Probably because his heart was swelling with hope and warmth and an emotion he hadn't felt in a long, long time.

As he drove off, he said one more prayer.

Watch over this, Father. Guide me every step of the way.

Well, if nothing else, Heather had brought a lost man back to prayer, which was huge progress from where he'd been for the last six years since his wife and son died. Six months ago, he'd have scoffed at the idea of ever saying a prayer again. Or of falling in love...again.

Now, he believed in both.

CHAPTER TWENTY-ONE

BECK

*L*ovely leaned over from one tufted white silk chair to the next, inching closer to Beck. "Big moment, isn't it?"

"So big." She lifted the bubbly mimosa that had been served when they arrived, but didn't dare take a drink, per instructions from the crew. "They said we couldn't drink, but we can toast until she finds the dress. Those last three just weren't right."

"Yes, we can toast." Lovely lifted her glass. "To the glorious day of wedding dress shopping with your three daughters and one granddaughter..."

As if on cue, a cascade of laughter came from behind the large dressing room wall.

"And my dearest, darling mother," Beck added, dinging Lovely's flute. "Without you, I'd—"

"Savannah!" Diana's shrill note made them both cringe. "You can't consider anything so fitted. It doesn't work with your, uh, curves."

"And your co-mother-in-law," Lovely whispered.

"If Savannah lets her live." Beck narrowed her eyes. "She isn't even supposed to be here."

"But she is."

"Pure white, Savannah?" Diana's voice rose. "With a five-month-old baby? You'll be the laughingstock of the internet."

Beck put the drink down. "I better go back there."

"And cross the great and powerful Sunny Washington?" Lovely's eyes widened. "You stay right where you are. Savannah can handle that woman better than anyone."

"Can she?"

They heard Diana's voice again, then silence.

"Listen, Cruella," Savannah said from behind the wall. "You need to step out of here, stat."

Beck's eyes widened at Savannah's command, but Lovely snorted. "Told ya."

With a noisy huff, Diana flounced back into the "showroom," rounding the stage where Savannah would stand and look in the mirror, weaving through the cameras being set up. Checking that none were on, she dropped onto the third white satin chair, grabbed Beck's mimosa, and knocked it back in one long and really unladylike gulp.

"Your daughter drives me to drink," she said when she finished, sliding a sideways look at Beck while snapping her fingers at one of the dress shop employees for a refill.

"And if she could join you, I'm sure she would," Beck said. "You need to lay off the body shaming comments, Diana."

"She needs to lay off the scones."

Ire shot through Beck, bubbling up like the champagne she'd been denied. "What is wrong with you?" Beck hissed. "What do you have against Savannah, who is a fantastic mother, a beautiful woman, and will be a dream wife for your son?"

"Dream wife?" she scoffed. "He had a dream *life* and she stole it."

"Are you *serious*?" Beck leaned forward, pushed by the shockingly strong urge to punch this woman's lights out.

"She was a barista, he was a star."

"And you showed up here promoting a wedding that's happening in less than a week," Beck fired back. "So let her have it and quit picking on her because you are—"

Lovely put her hand on Beck's arm, squeezing hard. "Beckie. Stop. They're rolling."

Beck and Diana both whipped around to see the red light of a handheld camera. Instantly, Diana stood, squared her shoulders, and smiled down at Beck.

"I'll be back in a little while, my friend. We're so close to my favorite place in Key West, I think I'll take a quick run over there." She leaned all the way down to whisper, "You have fun picking out your daughter's virginal, skintight wedding dress."

She strode out, leaving them speechless and happy to see her go.

"Don't worry." Emily rushed over with champagne in one hand, orange juice in the other, and her ever-present tablet under her arm. "We won't use that." She poured and smiled at Beck. "And you can drink that in two minutes, because we're all set up for Savannah to come out."

Beck smiled her thanks and glanced at Lovely. "That woman."

"I know. The worst."

But a few minutes later, Diana was forgotten when Savannah stepped out in an off-the-shoulder white lace dress fit for a princess. Her face was a little flushed, likely from the run-in with Diana.

But when she walked up to the center stage, Beck knew that color and the light in her eyes hadn't been caused by Diana. She'd found The Dress.

Looking at Beck in the mirror, she broke into a wide smile. "What do you think, Momma?"

"I think..." She wiped a tear before it fell. "You're perfect."

"For a *cow*," Savannah joked, mimicking Diana, but then she laughed as she smoothed her hands over her waist, which was enviably narrow. "This is it. This is the dress."

Just then, Callie, Peyton, and Ava stepped out in turquoise dresses, the exact color of the water around Coconut Key.

"And there are my gorgeous bridesmaids."

Beck sucked in a breath at the sight of the three of them, each dress so different, yet so spectacular. Callie chose a clean column strapless dress, while Peyton wore one with a little more flounce and spaghetti straps. Ava's was totally perfect for a sixteen-year-old, with a youthful skirt and lace cap sleeves.

For a moment, Beck just gazed at all of them, then slowly rose, completely forgetting the cameras and crew, reaching out her arms to all of them.

Savannah carefully stepped down and joined a group

hug that mixed laughter and tears and kisses on the cheek.

"And our grandmother!" Savannah called, stepping out to widen the circle to let Lovely join them.

"This..." Beck's voice was thick with emotion. "This is all that matters to me. My daughters. My mother. My incredible family."

"We know, Momma," Peyton whispered, her eyes brimming. "I feel the same way. And now I have to give it all up."

They all inched back at her words, staring at her in stunned silence.

"I mean, if I stay in Miami."

"*If?*" Savannah rolled her eyes. "You're a goner, sister, and I predict that in less than a year, we'll be in another dress shop somewhere, and you'll be the one wearing white and—oh my God, Mom, why are you weeping?"

"Weeping?" She wiped her cheeks. "I'm just emotional."

Savannah tipped her head. "You do realize that every tear is being captured on film and now *you* will be the laughingstock of the internet."

She tried to laugh at that, but it came out like a sob, a sound she'd heard in her throat way too frequently lately.

"I'm a mess," she admitted, looking up to see a camera sticking into their small group like a sixth head. "My babies are all grown up!" she added with fake brightness.

"You can cut that," Savannah said to Hector, ever present with his handheld cam. "In fact, could this little interlude be saved for Foster family posterity and not the world?"

Sunny swooped in from the sidelines. "No promises

on that footage," she said. "But we got what we need for now. You all can take a break and we'll do pick-up interviews, starting with..." She turned, looking for Emily, who stepped right up.

"We're done with Callie, Peyton, and Beck," she said, checking her tablet.

"Great. Let's do Lovely and Ava," Sunny announced, pointing at the white chairs. "Then we'll shoot B-roll and do final pick-ups with Savannah back at the house. Someone find Diana."

"Oh, joy," Savannah said.

"Where did she go?" Callie asked.

"To hell, one can hope," Lovely muttered, cracking them all up.

"She said she was going to her favorite place," Beck said.

"I know where she is." Savannah stepped out of the group. "I'll change and go get her."

"You're not going alone," Beck said. "Callie and Peyton and I are done shooting. We can go with you."

"Because y'all care so much about her?"

"Because we don't want you to kill her...alone."

"How do you know where she went?" Beck asked as the four of them stepped onto a Key West side street, not far from Duval.

"There's a Starbucks nearby and she's an addict. This way." Savannah pointed toward Mallory Square, which was already getting crowded in anticipation of the stunning sunsets that could be viewed every evening at dusk.

"Why is she such a wretched woman?" Beck mused as they strode down the street.

"Good question. I keep thinking if I knew that, I could crack the code with her. But better question, Mom. Why does everything make you cry lately?"

Beck slowed her step, looking from one to the other. Why hide it any longer? They hadn't had a family event recently, but the rehearsal dinner was next up on the schedule, then the wedding day. They'd see she wasn't with Josh.

"I broke up with...no, let's be honest. Josh broke up with me."

They all stopped dead cold mid-step, staring at her.

"And you didn't tell us?" they asked in perfect sister-like unison.

"I didn't tell anyone but Lovely. Oh, and Kenny."

"Kenny?" Savannah choked. "The long-lost son given up for adoption is on the first-to-know list now?"

"Mom, how could you keep this from me?" Peyton asked, her voice tight.

"Well, you've been with Val and—"

"It's not important who she told." Callie ushered them all off the street before they got run over. "What's important is how you're doing."

Beck sighed, the sun suddenly too, too hot. "How far is Starbucks? I don't want to talk out here."

"Right down the road," Savannah said. "But let's go here." She pointed to a small bar with a huge wooden toucan holding a margarita. "Diana can wait. We're here for you, now. Come on."

They stepped into a classic Key West dive, which was dark and cool and not very crowded. And the minute Beck held a margarita—not unlike the one the toucan was drinking—she knew she'd made the right decision.

"I've kept this in for days," she admitted, taking a sip without even toasting. "And honestly, this wasn't how I envisioned ending the dress shopping day."

"This wasn't how I envisioned you splitting with Josh," Savannah said. "I honestly thought that man would wait around to be your lap dog forever."

"He doesn't want to wait around or be anyone's lap dog," Beck said. "And I totally respect that, and him for being honest."

"What happened?" Callie asked. "Are you two cool with each other, or did you fight?"

"No fight, and we're fine. But, I'm...a little dazed. I honestly planned to tell him something similar, or at least be totally honest with him about why I couldn't go the distance, as Kenny put it."

Savannah rolled her eyes. "I still can't believe you told him before me."

"Get over it," Callie said. "I still can't believe *he* broke up with *you*."

Peyton nodded. "Did *not* see that coming, Mom."

Beck stirred the drink, thinking about their reaction. "So you're surprised who initiated the break up, but not that it happened?" Beck asked.

Savannah glanced at Peyton next to her. "Are you?"

"I've known you've been holding back for a while, Mom," Peyton said. "But I honestly thought you were holding all the cards."

"Well, apparently I dropped them."

"My opinion?" Callie squeezed a lime into her water.

"I just never got you two, although he's a great guy. Really nice and all, but…"

"No wow factor," Savannah chimed in.

"Not that a woman my age needs a wow factor," Beck said, feeling some heat crawl up her cheeks that wasn't from the tequila. After all, these were her daughters.

But all three of them were staring at her.

"You need a wow factor," Peyton agreed. "No matter your age. And I love Josh, I seriously do. He's been like an uncle—"

"Which would make him like a brother," Beck whispered. "And I don't want…that."

"But I'm still surprised he did it." Savannah swiped her fingers down her glass. "Defensive move, I'm guessing. He smelled the end was near?"

Beck shrugged. "We're coming up on a year since I moved here. A year that he and I have been, well, I guess you call it dating. Talking and sharing and laughing and…"

"Not sure I want to know this," Callie whispered.

"No, not that. And I think the fact that nothing physical happened between us was really at the root of this. I don't blame him for getting impatient, but I just couldn't…" Her voice trailed off, then she smiled and admitted the absolute truth. "I really, really like him. But I just keep thinking I want…magic. I know that's crazy at my age, but—"

"Stop that," Savannah interjected. "As a woman currently drowning in magic, I say hold out for it. Best feeling in the world. Right, Pey?"

"Mhmmm." She sipped through her straw.

"I kind of agree," Callie jumped in for her. "I know I'm

the baby and have never been in love, but after what Dad did to you? You deserve to be up on a pedestal and adored."

"She *has* been," Peyton said.

Beck couldn't argue. "He's been nothing but good to me, which makes it harder."

Savannah turned to Callie. "Nice to see you've finally converted to Team Mom."

Beck reached across the table to give Callie's hand a squeeze. "You don't need to be on any team, sweetheart. I love that you support both your parents." She shifted her gaze to Peyton, who was looking at her drink. "Pey?" Beck asked. "You certainly believe in the magic, right?"

She looked up, surprising Beck with tears in her eyes. "Yes," she said softly.

Callie sighed. "Come on, Peyton."

And for that, she got a vile look from her oldest sister.

"What?" Beck asked. "What's going on with you two?"

Callie didn't say a word, but stared at her sister, a palpable thickness in the air.

Savannah looked from one to the other, then at Beck. "Methinks there's trouble in Miami."

"No trouble," Callie and Peyton said at exactly the same time.

Then Peyton tipped her head. "You promised."

"I'm sorry," Callie said. "I hate secrets and from the look on your face, so do you."

"So do we all," Savannah said. "Spill, Peyote, or I'll do that with this drink on your head."

She let her eyes shut for a moment, then opened them and looked at Beck.

And before she said a word, Beck knew. She put her

hand on Peyton's back and added light pressure. "It's fine," she whispered. "If you found the magic, then I'm happy."

Peyton just stared at her, eyes filling until she blinked and a tear fell.

"You did find the magic, right, Pey?" Beck asked.

"I did, Momma. And I want to stay with him."

"Peyton!" Beck choked her name. "Why wouldn't you tell me that? I'm so, so happy for you!"

"But...it's been amazing living in Coconut Key and working at the café and all our Thursday girls' nights and Sunday feasts and..." She looked from one to the other. "I've never been so torn in my whole life."

"Don't look at me," Savannah said. "I love it here so much I wrecked Nick's career to stay."

And Peyton crumbled with a sob.

"No, no," Savannah insisted, reaching out to her sister. "That doesn't mean it was the only way. And he doesn't have the family that Val has. And Miami isn't three thousand miles away, it's a few hours away. Weekly lunches, weekends, holidays..." She looked at Beck and Callie. "Help me out here, kids."

"I told her all that," Callie said.

But Beck just kept her arm around Peyton, totally understanding how torn she was. "Talk to me, baby girl."

"I don't want to hurt you, Mom," she whispered. "You've been so good to me. I was so lost in New York, and you brought me here—"

"Uh, *you* brought *me* here," Beck corrected. "And I was the one drowning in my own tears a year ago." She smiled and squeezed harder. "Honey, if you've found what everyone is looking for—and I have no doubt you have—then you grab that with both hands and hold on. Nothing makes me happier than you being happy. It's just a fact of motherhood."

"Which is something that *you*," Savannah added softly, pointing at Peyton, "deserve to experience. You're going to be the best mom of all of us."

Peyton managed a smile.

"Are you happy?" Beck asked.

She laughed softly. "Ask Callie."

"She's over the freaking moon," Callie said. "And so am I, because we Foster girls are going to live together until the next wedding. And I may move in with them after that. Who knows?"

"I will drink to that," Beck said, lifting her glass. "And to all of you finding some—"

"Holy crap," Savannah muttered, looking out the window over Beck's shoulder.

They all turned in time to see Diana whiz by on a scooter.

"Headed to Starbucks," Savannah said, gathering her purse to get up. "I better go talk to her. You guys better go back to the dress shop."

"What are you going to say to her?" Beck asked.

"I won. You lost. Suck it." She grinned. "Only really nice."

"You need backup?" Peyton asked.

"I'm good." She grinned at Beck. "And, hey, I got one perfect mom," she said. "I can handle the she-devil of a mother-in-law. She is not sabotaging this wedding, no matter what."

As Savannah walked out, Callie leaned in. "You know,

it's not the ten things you expect to go wrong, but the one you never saw coming."

Beck stared at her youngest daughter, knowing that she was not just beautiful, but wise beyond her years. "Then let's brace for the unexpected, huh?"

CHAPTER TWENTY-TWO

NICK

*W*hen Nick stepped out to the veranda during the rehearsal dinner, he took a moment to scan, and appreciate, the group gathered. With the exception of Sunny and two camera operators who were left doing pick-ups, the people chatting, laughing, and enjoying the buffet were some of his favorite and closest in the world. And they all looked pretty dang happy—except his mother, of course, who barely smiled, looked at her phone a lot, and seemed more interested in scrutinizing the buffet than talking to strangers.

Well, she'd gambled and lost. Tomorrow evening, as the sun dropped into the Gulf, he and Savannah would walk down an elaborate set on the beach, and say their vows in front of their friends, family, and millions of strangers watching it live. So who could blame Diana, who'd done her level best to force him to run, for being a little sullen?

No one else was unhappy, that was for sure.

Starting with Savannah, who looked radiant, holding

Dylan and chatting with Beck and Jessie, laughing as they fawned over the baby.

Maddie and Ava were playing with little Beau, while Chuck stood nearby, talking to Josh. Next to them, Peyton and her boyfriend, Val, were deep in conversation with Callie.

On the other side of the deck, Kenny was explaining something that looked like swinging an invisible bat to Marc, while Heather watched, beaming at both of them. Lovely had been put on "Dan Duty," assigned to making small talk with Savannah's father who'd arrived with little fanfare and had done his best to be civil to Nick. Obviously, the older attorney's lousy attempt at getting Nick to sign some kind of legal document had been a dismal failure, like the prenup.

Savannah and Nick had giggled late into the night at the fact that they'd sat her father with his mother at the wedding, laughingly nicknaming that table the "axis of evil."

No manipulative parents could break them up. No long-distance separation, no unconventional romance, no baby crying in the middle of the night, no unseen force from nature or people could separate Nick Frye and Savannah Foster, and just that thought made his smile stretch wider.

"You certainly look happy." Sunny sidled up next to him, scrutinizing his expression.

"Just counting my blessings, as they say."

"People still say that?" she scoffed. "*Oof*. My friend, you have been out of Hollywood too long."

"I couldn't disagree more." He lifted his mostly untouched drink in a mock toast. "I don't miss the drama, the trauma, or most of the people out there. Sorry."

She made a tight face, nodding. "Well, speaking of drama..."

"Yeah?"

She perused the gathering on the deck. "We just haven't had enough of it, if I'm going to be perfectly honest. And that, as you know, does not make for good TV."

"But it makes for a great life," he replied. "I mean, look at this, Sunny. I have it all. An incredible woman at my side for the rest of my life, a healthy child and hopes for more, and an amazing extended family. I couldn't be happier. Sorry, if that isn't going to lift the ratings."

"I'm sorry...too."

He glanced at her, the strange note in her voice catching his attention. "You aren't happy with the final product?"

"The product isn't final until you and Savannah say, 'I do,'" she reminded him. "We might still salvage this one." She gave a regretful smile he couldn't quite interpret.

"Still *salvage* it? That bad, huh?" He wished he cared about the ratings and the audience reaction, but, honestly? He didn't. He'd met his half of the bargain. Netflix was happy enough. Eliza had held on to her job. His mother could show her face at the spa again. And he was done with it all.

"I'm afraid I hoped for a little more emotional punch," she admitted. "Everyone is so...content."

"I know." He chuckled. "Sorry that sucks but, hey, it's a wedding. We should be happy, right?"

She shot him a look that he could have sworn was

sympathy. But she was the one who needed sympathy, in his opinion. Didn't these Hollywood people see how much better this life was than that one? It reminded him how much he missed Eliza, the only person in that whole cesspool who understood what was important. But her husband was literally on life support, so coming for the wedding was out of the question.

"Well, I got a little friction with Beck and Diana," Sunny continued, glancing around as if she could somehow find more excitement. "And Savannah's snark is going to get big laughs." She gazed out to the deck, taking a deep breath. "But I'm really sorry that's not quite enough."

"I'm the one who should be sorry then," he said, then chuckled. "Except I'm not."

She took a deep breath and gave him another enigmatic smile just as one of her crew came up the stairs and signaled for her attention.

"Looks like you're needed in the editing booth," he said.

She nodded slowly and put her hand on his shoulder. "Just remember, Nick. It's business, okay?"

He frowned as she walked away, puzzled by the exchange.

Catching Savannah's eye, he debated whether or not to share his low-key sense of unease. But one look at that smile and he couldn't do anything that would make it disappear.

"Hey, gorgeous." He walked to her and put his arm around her. Looking down, he thumbed Dylan's bald little head, getting a gummy smile that never failed to thrill. "And baby gorgeous."

She laughed and took a few steps away with him. "Having fun?"

"As if you have to ask. But..." He rocked his drink, the ice having watered down the scotch since he barely sipped it. "I think I'll just get some of Lovely's lemonade, which is better than this."

"I'd like some, too." As he led her toward the bar set up at the top of the stairs, she leaned in and whispered, "I think I know why they say the rehearsal dinner can be the best part of the wedding. A party with no stress."

"Not the best for Sunny," he said on a sigh. "She claims we just don't have enough drama."

"Well, where's Diana? She's always good for—"

"Right behind you," he warned under his breath, making her bite her lip and widen her eyes.

Just then, Hector, the most intrusive of the camera operators, came jogging up the stairs, his trusty handheld out as if he could smell a candid exchange that might get juicy.

"I thought we were done with all this," Nick said to him.

"Done?" Hector snorted. "Sunny says we're just getting started."

Nick scowled, looking for Sunny and catching a glimpse of her, halfway down the stairs talking to some man, and pointing up to the deck.

He groaned, leaning into Savannah. "Can't they just pull the cameras and let us have a private party?"

"Just hang in there, Nick." Savannah stroked the baby's head.

"But she's looking for drama."

"She isn't going to get it." She stood on her tiptoes and kissed his cheek. "Relax."

"I am, I just..." He looked into her eyes. "I want to marry you so damn bad."

She smiled. "Now how is that not drama? Can you repeat that for..." She turned, looking for Hector, but his camera was trained on the man coming up the stairs.

"Who's that?" Savannah whispered.

"No clue." The older man, fifty or maybe sixty, started up the stairs, dark eyes scanning the crowd, seemingly unaware of Hector and his handheld.

"Are you sure you don't know him?" Savannah asked under her breath. "He seems...familiar."

He certainly did, but Nick was sure they'd never met. Despite his age, he moved as though he were an athlete in excellent shape, with strong, memorable, and yes, familiar, features. His hair was dark gold with some silver at the temples, his eyes brown and warm. His face had a few lines that showed a life well-lived, but with enough definition that Hector's camera probably loved him.

Some of the conversations paused as he reached the top of the stairs and came to a stop, his gaze landing on Nick. As it did, his strong jaw loosened a bit and those dark eyes widened.

"Hello..." Nick took a tentative step forward, wondering why Sunny didn't come flying up the stairs to make an introduction. She obviously knew who he was.

"You must be Nick," the other man said, his deep voice clipped and vaguely accented. Not British, but...Australian?

As soon as he spoke, he heard Diana gasp, the intake

of her breath just soft and shocked enough to make the hairs on the back of Nick's neck rise.

"I'm afraid we haven't met." Nick extended his hand.

But the other man didn't move. "Bloody hell," the man murmured, staring at Nick. "It's even more shocking in person."

He was used to people reacting at the sight of him in person, but this wasn't just a run of the mill fan happy to meet an actor they liked. This seemed more like...a moment of recognition.

"Do I know you?" Nick asked, a thump starting in his head as his pulse ratcheted up for no good reason.

"Not yet." He angled his head in a way that also reminded him of...someone. Who? "It's a bit of a tale, I must say."

"Well, I'd rather you didn't tell it." Diana's voice, icy and low and threatening, cut through the sudden silence that had descended over the deck.

Nick turned to her, getting a jolt from the look on her face. Bloodless, shocked, and horrified, she stared at the man. One of the other camera operators took a few steps closer, but she didn't even seem to notice the lens pointed at her face.

"Hello...Diana," the new arrival said, giving her a mirthless smile. "It's been quite a while, hasn't it? Thirty... four years or so?"

She knew this man before he was born? Like everyone else, Nick looked from one to the other, waiting for an explanation. But the two of them just gave each other challenging looks.

"What are you doing here?" Diana demanded through grit teeth. "How?"

"How? Why don't we start with *who*?" Nick suggested, trying to lighten a mood that was not getting any lighter.

Diana took a visible breath and squared her shoulders like a soldier headed into battle. A battle she wasn't going to come out of alive.

"Nick, this is Oliver Bradshaw. Your father."

What?

The word in his head was echoed by half the people out there, and underscored by audible gasps.

His...*father?*

Nick shook his head a little, knowing without a shadow of a doubt that this was not his father, who was named Oliver *Jones.* He'd met that man, years ago. That man had been short and sunken, dark and drunk. He'd been sloppy and pushy and foul. He wanted money, which Diana gave him when they left—he'd *seen the cash* pass from her hands to his—and remembered that he, at seventeen, had felt relief to be done with the man.

Diana told him to forget the embarrassing mess of a man who lived in a trailer.

But Nick never really had. He'd had *nightmares* about the man. So he was certain of one thing—this wasn't his father.

Except...it was like looking in a mirror, thirty years in the future. But how was that possible?

"I met my father," Nick finally said, vaguely aware of the eyes and cameras, and the way Savannah came closer to him, but he was unable to do anything but stare at the man, and then slide an accusing look to Diana. "Didn't I?"

She just swallowed and his blood began to simmer.

"*Didn't I?*" he repeated. "It was just after my seventeenth birthday, when my TV show hit number one in the ratings and the movie studios were calling. I wanted to meet my father and you told me that he wanted to 'worm his way into my bank account.' But I begged you to let me meet him."

She bit her lip. "You wouldn't let it *go*."

"So you took me to Louisiana. To that trailer park. To that man named Oliver...*Jones*." He inched a centimeter closer to his mother, a little dizzy as blood hummed in his veins. "You told me *he* was my father."

"We've never met." Oliver swiped his thick golden hair back with his fingers, a gesture that was so deeply familiar, it took Nick's breath away. He'd seen the same move a hundred times—watching himself in a mirror or on a screen.

Reeling, Nick narrowed his eyes at Diana. "You better start talking, and fast."

Hector and the other camera operators stepped closer, and well behind the new arrival's back, Nick caught a glimpse of Sunny's face. She had her hand pressed to her lips, her dark eyes on fire with...*drama*.

But he couldn't deal with her or the crew or the family or anything else until he knew the truth.

"Diana," he ground out. "What the hell is going on?"

Finally, she eased into the closest chair, pressing a hand to her chest, her gaze locked on the man at the top of the stairs.

Nick felt Savannah's fingers close around his own. "You want me to get everyone to leave?" she whispered. "So you can talk?"

"I want...answers," he said. "I don't care who's here."

Sunny took a few steps closer, making a little circular

motion with her hand, indication that the cameras were rolling, and they were not about to stop.

Nick took a deep breath and let his eyes close. "Diana, who did I meet in that Louisiana trailer park?"

"That was..." She groaned a little, dropping her head into her hands. "I actually don't remember his name. An actor I hired to play the part."

Savannah gasped. "You *what*?"

"Why would you do that?" Nick asked, taking a step backwards as if that truth was just too much for him. No one could be that low. No one. Except...her.

A sudden heat rolled over him, and for the first time in his life, he felt what he would describe as hate. For his own mother.

"You wouldn't stop talking about meeting him!" she exclaimed as if that explained everything. "You were obsessed. And I...I couldn't take a chance on you knowing the truth." She shook her head as if regret rocked her.

"The truth is so bad?" He looked at the man, who appeared as perplexed by that as anyone, but nothing like the stinking drunk she'd made him believe was his father. Why? Why would she lie?

He knew the answer, of course. Because she kept control over him that way—as long as she was the only family he had, a man who valued and treasured family would never leave her. But now he had another family... and a father.

"And why didn't *you* tell me?" he asked Oliver, a little afraid that whatever the answer, it would make him despise his father as much as he did his mother.

But the man's expression softened as he stepped closer. "I didn't know you existed for many, many years. I left Los Angeles after a month-long rugby tournament there, quite, uh, enamored with the beautiful aspiring actress I'd met." He lifted his brown eyes in Diana's direction. "I tried repeatedly to contact her, which wasn't that easy back in 1987. After many attempts and letters and transcontinental telephone calls that were never picked up, I gave up."

"She never told you she was pregnant?" Nick asked. What the hell was wrong with her?

From her seat, Diana groaned, dropping her head in her hands to hide her face. "Do we have to do this now?"

"Would you rather wait thirty-four more years?" Nick demanded. "I want answers. Every single honest answer." He turned to Oliver. "When did you find out? How?"

For a moment, the man didn't speak, still studying Nick as if he just couldn't stare at him enough. "To be honest, I eventually forgot about her. Shortly after, I met the woman who would be my wife of thirty-two years. A dalliance as a young athlete on the road with his team was forgotten. But then, a few years ago, my wife passed away."

"And you went looking for that actress?" he guessed.

"No, but I *was* lonely. So, I discovered American television." He gave a wistful smile. "Couldn't help noticing the main character of *Magic Man* reminded me of, well, a young version of myself. Then I saw your name, read a bit about you, saw your birthday, did the math. *Then* I searched out the old flame."

"You've been in contact?" he asked his mother as another shockwave hit, but she shook her head vehemently.

"No, no," Oliver said. "I never reached out to her. It was you I wanted to meet."

"And you chose today?" But even as he asked the question, he knew it hadn't been Diana who dropped this bomb, but Sunny...in search of drama.

"I actually started following your career as sort of a rabid fan might," he admitted sheepishly. "Discovered these, uh, chat boards where fans congregate."

Nick had heard of them, but never wanted to actually look at one.

"And someone recently posted a search for a man named Oliver...and I contacted her." He turned in the general direction of Sunny. "They told me this would be the only way to meet you, but..." He angled his head. "I was assured it would not be filmed."

"Live," Sunny jumped in. "We assured you it wouldn't be *live*."

Nick held up a hand, still trying to process this. "Why wouldn't you just contact me directly?"

He let out a breath. "I read an interview once where you said you despised your father and refused to talk about him. I had no idea Diana hadn't told you the truth." He gave a dry laugh. "I was honestly miffed and maybe... scared. But the fact is..." He took a step closer and finally reached for Nick's hand to shake it. "I couldn't be happier to meet you...son." His eyes filled. "Just couldn't be more delighted. And a bit overcome, truth be told."

Time stood at a complete stop for that moment, as Oliver's strong hand closed over Nick's. And then it was like a dam broke, both of them closing the space and wrapping their arms around each other, giving sound pats on the back, both sort of vibrating with emotion.

"This is my..." Nick eased back. "My fiancée, Savannah," he said. "And our son, Dylan."

Diana's chair scraped the deck as she got up, and another camera followed her.

"Leave me the hell alone!" she snapped at Hector.

But Nick didn't care about her, not now. Maybe not ever again. Because...holy hell. He had a father who was right this moment shaking hands with Savannah.

Her eyes glistened with unshed tears as she greeted Oliver. "Welcome and wow. It's wonderful to meet you, Mr. Bradshaw."

"Just Oliver, please. And..." His smile grew as he looked at the baby in her arms. "Dylan? Why, hello, young one. I hope we'll be good mates." He reached a tentative hand toward Dylan's head. "How I've longed... for this." He stroked the baby's head and looked up at Nick. "Margaret and I never had children, so this is..." He swallowed and took a second to compose himself. "This is quite something."

"Well..." Savannah took a step closer. "Now you have a son, a daughter-in-law, and a grandson."

"Then this just became one of the best days of my life," Oliver whispered.

And just like that, a low-grade hum of excitement rolled through the small crowd as everyone seemed unable to stop themselves from getting closer. A cascade of congratulations, introductions, handshakes and hellos practically exploded, and during it all Nick still couldn't quite process what was happening.

Savannah stayed close, holding his hand, her attention on him as much as the people who were all meeting and greeting.

"Are you okay?" she whispered.

"I can't believe it," he murmured to her, holding her gaze which seemed to gleam with joy. "He's my father. That other man was..." He stole a glance over his shoulder, but his mother was long gone.

"Do you want me to find her?" Savannah asked.

"No. I never want to speak to her again."

"She's probably spinning a tale that makes her look good to the cameras."

"As if I care," he said, looking over her shoulder to catch the moment that Oliver shook Lovely's hand.

"You do care, Nick. That's one of the things I love about you."

"But she kept us apart on purpose," he said, reeling every time he thought of it. "Why would she do that? Who is truly that evil?"

"Maybe she thought he'd take you away," Savannah said. "I'm sure Australia seemed far and scary. I know I had that fear, and it's what kept me from telling you about the baby for months."

"But you also had a moral compass that said you couldn't do that to me. But she..." He took a deep breath. "I'm not letting her steal another moment of my life." He pulled her close as he watched the first exchange between Beck and Oliver, the two of them sharing a warm smile. "And this moment? This one is right up there with the day I first laid eyes on you."

CHAPTER TWENTY-THREE

*S*he hadn't planned to spend the night before her wedding with the groom, but under the circumstances, Savannah couldn't bear to follow convention and not sleep with Nick. Not after his world was rocked. But they'd stayed up to the wee hours getting to know one endlessly fascinating, funny, and wonderfully honest retired advertising executive named Oliver Bradshaw.

It seemed they simply couldn't run out of topics—at least Nick and Oliver couldn't. Savannah had tried to keep up, but exhaustion won out and she'd slipped into her own bed, cuddling with Nick around four a.m. when he joined her. Even then, he was still kind of pulsating with emotion over the day's revelation.

But now, the man who would be her husband before sunset was sound asleep next to her, his chest rising and falling with the steady breaths of someone who was profoundly content. Just beyond him, in the crib they couldn't quite bear to put in the next room, Dylan looked like a teeny-tiny replica of his daddy, snoozing just as blissfully.

If only Savannah could feel that way.

But a restless anxiety had tapped her awake just before dawn, nudging her with a sense that she needed to do something, but she didn't know what. Well, get married, for one thing. But the wedding preparations didn't start for many hours, so she should really just close her eyes and enjoy the peace.

But nothing felt peaceful. Something wasn't right. Was it because she'd slept here when tradition said she shouldn't have?

Was it just this new and unexpected arrival? Despite the strange circumstances, there was nothing not to like about Oliver. For one thing, it was truly like looking into the future and seeing Nick in thirty years. Yes, Nick had his mother's blue eyes, but that was where the resemblance stopped, at least once you saw the other side of that gene pool.

A former semi-pro rugby player from Sydney, Oliver was every bit as handsome as his son, with a sharp wit and a brilliant mind. His love of sports kept him fit and looking much younger than his sixty-one years, but it was his deeply ingrained aura of *goodness* that really reminded Savannah of Nick.

He'd shared much of his life's story with them, which included owning a well-known Australian ad agency that he sold to a much larger entity, making him quite wealthy. He'd also enjoyed a long and happy—although childless—marriage to Margaret, a woman he loved very much and still mourned, two-and-a-half years after her death from cancer.

It was clear that the idea of having a son brought Oliver great joy, but nothing compared to when he'd held Dylan for the first time. He couldn't hide his tears, deeply moved by the power of being a grandparent. He just never had any idea a torrid affair he'd had with a pretty actress he'd met in a Brentwood bar while "pub-hopping with some mates" had resulted in a son.

And that, Savannah realized with a start, was what *really* nagged at her this morning. *Diana.*

Was she going to be held accountable for her decisions? Was she going to apologize for not only keeping a man from his son, but for literally creating a *fake* father with the sole intention of making Nick hate him? Was she going to explain herself or hide from this situation or dig her heels in and claim she had only been protecting her son?

Because that last one would actually have a ring of truth to Savannah, who knew all too well the fear that someone could take your baby far away.

With another quick check on her two sleeping men, Savannah slipped out of bed, snagging her phone in one hand and the baby monitor in the other. Silently, she left the room and padded downstairs to the main floor and kitchen, already imagining that first taste of her one allotted cup of coffee.

No, that wasn't her imagination. That was the actual aroma, so Oliver must have already gotten up and discovered the coffee bar in the kitchen. She spotted him immediately, alone on the deck which had been completely cleaned by the crew the night before.

This morning, in the dawn's early light, Nick's father stood at the railing, looking out over the silver blue water of the Gulf, lost in thought as he sipped his coffee.

Was he angry at Diana, too? They'd had so many other things to talk about last night, so many lost years to catch up on, that subject had been left off the table. With the exception of him telling them when and how he'd met Diana, Oliver had made an almost concerted effort to keep her name out of the conversation. But they couldn't do that forever, and she was curious where he stood on making Diana pay for her misdeeds.

After getting her coffee, she stepped out the French doors to join him.

"Good morning," she called.

He turned and smiled, beckoning her closer as he stepped toward the table. "Oh, hello. I hope you'll join me as I soak in the horizon."

"It's pretty, isn't it?"

He looked again toward the water. "Stunning. I've got a place in Wollongong, a beach town an hour or so from Sydney. The water's gorgeous there, too, but quite different. This is so serene, and still."

"Until there's a hurricane," she joked as they both sat down. "Did you sleep well?"

He lifted one of his broad shoulders. "Bit of jet lag, I'm afraid. And shock." He laughed softly. "Okay, I didn't sleep a wink. I keep thinking about...the moment I saw Dylan."

"Dylan? Not Nick?"

"Well, to be honest, I knew what Nick Frye looked like. I've heard his voice and seen him on the television. And I won't lie, I spent far too many hours studying him once I...realized the truth." He sighed and covered his thoughts by sipping his coffee. "But seeing Dylan? That was..." He broke into the hugest grin. "A moment I'll never forget. Your sweet mother captured it with her camera, did you know?"

"She did?"

"Yes, she showed the pictures to me before she left. Rebecca, right? That's your mother? I apologize because I met quite a few people in a very short bit of time."

Savannah nodded. "Beck Foster, yes." She picked up her phone but didn't have anything new from Mom. "She got a picture when you held him?"

"She did," he said. "When she showed it to me, she said, 'No feeling like it in the world, is there?' and I had to agree." His gray eyes danced at the memory. "She's lovely."

"Yes, she is. And..." Savannah had to say something, or they'd sit out there and make small talk instead of...big talk. "What about Diana?"

He notched a brow. "What about her?"

"Do you think *she's* lovely?"

He snorted. "I did the night I met her," he admitted. "All my rugby blokes were after her, but she liked me. And she liked me the whole time we spent together until I flew back to Sydney. Then..." He gave a sad smile. "I realized she'd been a better actress than I'd given her credit for."

"But now you know the truth. Can you ever forgive her?"

"Certainly," he said without a nanosecond of hesitation. Then he frowned. "You look surprised."

"Gobsmacked," she agreed. "Because I think Nick

wants to strangle her and send her packing, if she hasn't gone already."

"Oh, she hasn't gone," he said. "The television producer woke me with a request to do an interview with the two of us."

Savannah gasped. "Seriously?"

"They wanted to film early this morning so they'd have time to edit it and air it as part of the show."

"And she's doing that?" For some reason, Savannah found that hard to believe. Although it would give Diana a chance to tell her side and at least try to salvage her reputation so people wouldn't see her as the villainess they all knew she was.

"I hope so," he said. "I would very much like a chance to ease her mind and, as you say, forgive her."

"How can you?" she asked.

For a long moment, he didn't answer, but took another sip of coffee. "You're looking at a man who held his dying wife's hand for the last time," he finally said. "Who closed her eyes after she breathed her final breath, and kissed her forehead goodbye forever."

A lump grew in her throat. "I'm so sorry."

"I learned a lot from the experience," he said. "One is that life is far, far too short to hold grudges. And the other is that whatever road led me to Margaret, it was the right one. We had a wonderful marriage." A smile pulled as he looked off, remembering. "We laughed as much as we did anything, and took every day as an adventure." Finally, he turned to her. "How can I resent Diana for what she did? If she would have told me she was pregnant, my life would have been completely different. I would have known Nick, yes, but might never have met

Margaret. Certainly wouldn't have married her, because I would have insisted on marrying Diana."

Her heart melted a little. Yep, this is where Nick got all his goodness.

"So, when she comes here, we can have a nice little conversation, long overdue, and she can be off the hook."

Just then, she heard the familiar squeak of Dylan's morning wake-up call, coming from the monitor.

"Oh, I'm being paged." She stood slowly, still studying this man who she somehow sensed was going to be a big part of her life. "Thank you for your honesty, Oliver. I'm glad you took the chance to come here and meet us all."

He lifted his cup. "As am I. And, young lady, if you and Nick have a life together that's anything like the one I had with my Margaret, you will both be lucky indeed."

"I already feel very, very lucky."

BUT THAT WAS the last time that day Savannah felt anything other than stress. Diana never showed for the interview, and no one had any idea where she was. Beck said she'd used the guest key code and had been at the B&B overnight, but wasn't in her room this morning, although all her belongings were. So, she hadn't packed up and gone home.

Throughout the day, Savannah was separated from Nick, constantly being filmed, and the *Celebrity Wedding* crew always wanted her in four different places at once. As icing on the wedding cake, darling Dylan chose today to develop colic or start teething or had gas or just wanted to scream his fool head off no matter how much he ate or was walked.

By mid-afternoon, Savannah wanted to cry as much as Dylan, who'd been whisked off to be cared for by her sisters or mother—she wasn't sure—while they filmed her in "the beauty chair" they'd set up in the dining room, which was also known as hair and makeup. She had false eyelashes on her left eye, half her hair in a partial up-do, and nail tips applied to one hand when Sunny blasted in with Nick.

For the first time in hours, Savannah's heart felt lighter. "Hey," she said, starting to stand up, only to be stopped by the hairdresser's hand on her shoulder.

"Hey." His expression was dark, far more than it should be for a man getting married in a few hours. "We got an issue."

"We do?" She brushed off the hairdresser and leaned forward, searching his expression, and Sunny's. "What's up?"

"Diana's still MIA," he said. "She's not answering my texts or calls. We have to decide if we're going to take a chance and go on without her, which, obviously, I don't care, but..."

But something in his voice said he cared very much.

"We'll do what you want, Nick," she said.

"It's not that easy." Sunny stepped in. "We have a cutoff for a live show, since the first ninety minutes is taped. Well, there will be a live introduction from the beach, then we cut to edited package. But at seven-twenty-five on the nose, we're live. So, if we decide to can the show and run an old one, which we can do, we have to make that decision..." She looked at her watch. "In ninety minutes. Two hours, tops."

"Why would we do that?" She looked at Nick. "Oh, you don't want to get married without her."

He snorted. "I don't trust her, Savannah. For all I know she could blow in during the live show and wreck it."

"Or make it more interesting," Sunny muttered. "Obviously, we're willing to take that chance. But Nick..." She glanced at him.

"Can we talk alone?" Savannah asked, pushing out of the chair. "Completely alone, with no cameras, nothing?"

Sunny's eyes shuttered as she nodded. "Two minutes. We are coming down to the wire and once it's go time, it's *go* time."

Savannah reached for Nick, a little surprised to feel his hand seemed clammy. "Nick Frye," she whispered as they walked out to the covered veranda and closed the door. "Are you nervous to be marrying me?"

He let out a little groan and led her to the railing, the slight breeze lifting the half of her hair that wasn't clipped up.

"No," he said simply. "I'm nervous that my mother is going to do something outrageous, or, should I say, even more outrageous." His voice was tight. "I'm really having a hard time forgiving her."

"Oliver isn't," she said. "Have you talked to him about it?"

He shook his head. "We're avoiding the subject of the woman who denied us a lifetime of being father and son."

"Then you should talk to my mother and Lovely," she

replied. "They found it in their hearts to forgive Olivia and make the best of the years they do have left as mother and daughter. You'll have plenty of time to forge a relationship with him. And you *should* talk to him about it. He might change your mind."

"I doubt that," he said. "He's just a great guy. But…"

Savannah reached for his hand. "But what?"

"I don't know. Something feels wrong in my gut. Where is she? What's she up to? Should I get married without her? Should I ever speak to her again? Should I be worried about her? Or should I just hate her? She's ruining this wedding, one way or another."

She stepped closer and put her hands on his handsome face. "Listen to me."

His lips lifted. "Very hard to take you seriously with one set of eyelashes."

But she didn't smile, only added pressure to his cheeks. "She's only ruining this if you let her," she whispered. "But this is what you need to remember. You have a soft heart in that big old strong chest of yours. You're a family man, Nick Frye, and the people that you love are your number one priority. She, for better or worse, is on that list. If you want to reconcile, forgive, have it out and move on, or whatever, before we marry, then you should. Sunny can live with it."

"No, no. I want to marry you. I don't want her to destroy that. I want her…" He swallowed. "I really wanted her to be happy for me." She could see the admission pained him, but she totally understood.

Not that Diana would ever be happy for anyone, but Savannah's heart broke for this man she loved so very much.

"Where could she be?" he asked.

Savannah thought about that, narrowing her eyes as something Diana said floated through her memory.

I loved that! I needed that freedom. I could do that all day long. But now, coffee.

"My guess is she's in Key West sipping a vanilla oat flat thing," Savannah said. "Or she's flying around on the modern equivalent of a broomstick."

"Then I'm going to find her," he said. "Right now."

"Can you do that?"

"We have two hours. I'll slip out without anyone noticing. Cover for me. Tell them I have to run to the B&B for something personal. I will be back in one hour, but I have to look for her. I have to talk to her. Should I start at that coffee shop?"

She made a face. "Nick, you can't go waltzing around Key West asking for your mother. People recognize you and it'll end up on social media, and you could be mobbed."

"I don't care."

"I do." She squeezed his hands. "Plus, you're not in any position to talk sense into her. I am."

"You?"

"I've been where she was at twenty. I know how it feels to cling to a baby because the alternative might mean losing everything. I'm not saying what she did— especially with the actor pretending to be your father— was right. But I think I can reach her. Do you want her here?"

He closed his eyes again as if in pain. "Yeah, I guess. But they'll never let you leave, so you're wasting your breath."

She frowned thinking about that, shifting her gaze to Sunny who stood on the other side of the French doors, watching with impatience etched on her face.

"They'd let me go if we promised Sunny the one thing she wants more than anything else."

"Drama?" he guessed.

"More than she'll know what to do with," Savannah said. "Come on. I'll take the lead on this one."

But as she tried to pull him away, he stopped her, sliding her body into his and adding a kiss. "Fine. I'll let you take the lead, but, Savannah Foster, are you going to marry me this afternoon?"

"I might have one set of eyelashes on, my hair half done, and walk down the aisle in these shorts, but I give you my word, Nick Frye, I will be at the altar to marry you."

"Well, we don't do anything conventionally, do we?"

"Why start now?" She kissed him again, just as Sunny walked out, and Savannah told her the plan.

She loved it.

WHILE ONE CREW filmed a heart-to-heart between Nick Frye and his long-lost father that would evoke tears and cheers, Savannah jumped in her car and took off to Key West with her lopsided makeup and hair, with only Hector and his handheld at her side.

He didn't talk much, but never took the darn lens off Savannah's face. After a while, she just forgot about him. On the way down, she called her mother and talked through the speaker phone in the dash.

"Full disclosure, this conversation isn't private," she warned after Mom picked up. "How's the mad screamer?"

"I just gave him a bottle and he quieted. Savannah, why in God's name are you on the way to Key West?"

"I'm going to find my future mother-in-law and get her to her son's wedding because he wants her there."

She answered with a dead-on, classic Beck Foster "Hmmm."

"And while I'm gone," Savannah said, "Oliver is going to give his son his first life lesson: to forgive and forget."

"Oh, Savannah. That's beautiful."

"If it works," she agreed. "If that's a disaster, then we... I don't know, Mom. This wedding might not happen live on TV."

"Is that so bad?"

"No, but I want Nick to be happy, and even as mad as he is at Diana, he wants her there. Family, warts and all, matters to him and I love that."

"So do I," her mother said. "How are you going to find her in Key West on a Saturday? The place will be a zoo."

"I know where she hangs out," she said on a laugh. "I have an hour to persuade her to come back, and get ready for the wedding, and...oh my God."

"What?"

"There's a *crap ton* of traffic."

Hector lowered his camera. "I think there's a Tennessee Williams festival. Maybe Hemingway. Some writer from Key West, so lots of people here."

"Great." She tapped her brakes as the car in front of her stopped. "If I can't find her, I'll go back, Mom. I won't miss my own wedding."

"Be safe, honey. Dylan is fine. He's sound asleep in his crib, and I have the baby monitor. Keep me posted."

"I will." Savannah used a few back streets that she'd learned since moving here, but even they were bumper to bumper. She glanced at Hector. "Would you kill me if I got on a scooter? It's the only way to quickly get to where I think she might be."

"I can shoot anything," he said, tapping the surprisingly small camera he could easily work with one hand. "Do it."

"Perfect." She slid into an illegal parking spot not far from the scooter shop. "And *Celebrity Wedding* can pay the ticket I will surely get for leaving my car here. Let's go."

With Hector on her heels, she hustled into the small shop and immediately recognized the young man behind the counter.

"Do you remember me? I was here with this woman a couple of weeks ago." She grabbed her phone and flipped through the last few pictures, finding one she'd taken of Diana holding Dylan. "You remember her?"

"The red-headed bitch?" he asked with zero humor or sarcasm, making her cringe because Hector never turned off his camera.

"That might be her," Savannah confirmed. "Has she rented a scooter today?"

"A few hours ago," he said, sparing a look at the camera, then leaning in to say, "She needs to take a chill pill."

"I brought them," she said. "Can we rent?"

A few minutes later, Savannah had a helmet on and was zipping through traffic on a scooter, leading Hector toward the only Starbucks in Key West. Moving on adrenaline, instinct, and hope, she threaded the traffic, flew through yellow lights, and studied every person on and off scooters for a glimpse of Diana.

But there was none. As they stopped at a light on Duval Street, she noticed that Hector had switched the camera for a cell phone.

"Sunny?" she asked.

He nodded. "Just letting her know the status."

"How'd Nick and Oliver do?"

"They're filming now."

Praying that worked the way she hoped, Savannah revved the engine and headed for the Starbucks inside the hotel at the furthest tip of the island. The afternoon sun pounded down, but the traffic opened up a bit when she got closer, giving her much-needed speed and a straight shot into the parking lot, where a scooter from the same rental company sat.

Bingo.

Hector followed with his trusty camera, five steps behind her as she whipped off her helmet and marched into the little Starbucks, spotting the back of a familiar auburn head at a window table.

She headed straight there and slid into the chair across from Diana, who gasped and, wow, looked like hell.

"What are you doing here?" Diana exclaimed, instantly turning to look around, spotting Hector. "You have to be kidding! Stop! Get...*go!*" She flung a hand in his direction, horrified. "Turn it off!"

Half a dozen people turned at her outburst, but Savannah leaned and whispered, "If you promise to talk to me."

"I'm not going back," she ground out. "I've already decided I'm going to the B&B to pack during the wedding because I know no one will be there. I'll drive back to L.A. if I have to."

"Just talk."

She narrowed her eyes at Savannah. "Not with him filming."

"Give us five minutes, Hector," she said. At his disappointed look, she tipped her head. "Please. Five private minutes. The rest is yours."

He turned off the camera and headed to the counter, leaving them alone.

"You're wasting your time," Diana said before Savannah could talk. "I am not going back to face...either of them. I've lost Nick, which I always knew was the direction this was heading."

"Diana, you were the one who showed up suggesting it."

She huffed out a breath. "I never thought he'd go along with it."

So he'd been absolutely right about that. "You called his bluff?"

"I thought he hated reality TV, and once he was 'forced' to marry you, he'd run."

"You were wrong."

Diana gave her a look. "Which happens so rarely."

"You were really willing to take that gamble?" Savannah still couldn't quite understand why she'd push for something she didn't want.

"I live for a gamble," she replied. "And I also..." She shifted in the chair, uncomfortable with whatever she was about to admit. "I wanted to see the baby."

"Oh. Well that gets you a lone point in heaven."

She snorted. "As if I'd ever get there after what I did."

"With Oliver?" Savannah guessed.

"Obviously. I did...the unthinkable."

Savannah couldn't argue that. "But not the unfor-giveable."

"Neither one of them will ever forgive me," she said on a sad sigh. "And I don't expect them to. I'm just hoping to...lay low. I'll change my name, move to...Canada. Start over."

"You're not moving to Canada, and you don't have to lay low. Nick is going to forgive you, and so is Oliver." She reached across the table and put her hand on Diana's. "I understand, you know. I almost didn't tell Nick about Dylan."

"But you did."

"Only after a brush with death, to be honest." She squeezed. "If you'd told that gorgeous Australian rugby player that you were pregnant, you know he would have insisted you move to Sydney."

"And I would have had to give up my dreams of show business," she admitted. "I really love everything about Hollywood. Everything. Movies were my escape as a child."

"Escape from what?" Savannah asked, suddenly intrigued by a story she'd never heard—Diana's childhood.

"A life not unlike the one I 'created' when I hired an actor in a trailer park. I ran away at sixteen and never—and I do mean never—spoke to anyone from my family again."

"That's so sad."

Her expression grew cold. "It is what it is."

"But my point is that you were alone, and this man—who you barely knew—would have wanted you to move across the world for him. Am I right?"

She looked away, as if she were remembering, quiet for a moment. "I was on the cusp," she whispered. "Peaking in my looks, finally getting some breaks, about to realize my dream of being a movie star, then, wham. Pregnant by a sexy athlete I met in a bar."

Savannah sighed. "Oh, Mama. Do I know that feeling."

"But I couldn't...not have the baby," she rasped. "I tried. I went. I almost did, but..." Her eyes welled up. "I went to a psychic instead."

"Well, it was Los Angeles. What did she say?"

She smiled. "She closed her eyes and touched my belly and said, 'This baby will be a star that shines brighter than all others. He is going to make your dreams come true.'"

"And he is a star," Savannah said as chills blossomed over her arms. "He made your acting dreams come true."

"Yes, but...I've been a terrible mother."

"Not true." Maybe a terrible person, but Savannah kept that to herself. "No one who raised a man with a heart as good as Nick's could be terrible." Then she frowned, thinking of the last conversation they'd had in this very same coffee shop. "What about the whole 'men leave' thing? Who left you?"

She rolled her eyes. "I made that crap up."

"You did? It was so...convincing."

"I'm an excellent actress," she said matter-of-factly. "But you aren't. And I can see that..." She took a breath like it pained her to say the rest. "You really love him, don't you?"

"Insanely. And not because he's Nick Frye, superstar, but because he's just the greatest guy who ever walked the face of the earth, held a baby in the middle of the night, or taught my niece how to deliver a line in a play."

Diana's eyes fluttered. "He is a good man."

"He's so good that he is ready to put his arms around you and tell you it's okay." She leaned in. "Diana, he wants you at our wedding."

She stared at Savannah for a moment, then blinked, sending a tear down her cheek. "I'm so ashamed," she rasped. "I'm just...burning with shame. Honestly, this is not acting. I am...mortified."

If she was acting, she deserved an Oscar. Also, proof that she must have had some moral compass after all.

"I've always known I was...flawed," she whispered. "But after meeting your family, your *mother*? She's a saint."

"Can't argue," Savannah said. "But, please. Look at me. Talk about flawed. And Nick loves me, so he can— and does—love you."

"It feels like a black hole, you know?" She pressed her hand on her chest, eyes filling. "Where my heart should be. My soul. My...tenderness. I have nothing."

"Act?" Savannah asked, terrified to fall for another one.

"Sadly, no."

Then she genuinely felt bad for the woman. "Look, you start over. Be kind. Be...less manipulative. Love your son and your grandson and...me."

She searched Savannah's face, her expression one of awe and fear. "You would allow me in your life?"

Savannah took both hands in hers. "Please be in our lives."

She let out a sob as more tears fell and she tried to wipe them. In her peripheral vision, Savannah could see Hector coming over.

"Excuse me," Diana muttered, jumping up and walking away, rushing toward the bathroom in the front of the store while hiding her face.

"Give her a minute," Savannah said, dropping back in her chair and looking right at the camera. "We had a good talk, but she needs to process what I said. She's going to come around. As soon as she's out of the bathroom, we'll zip back, return the scooters, and make the wedding with time to spare."

"Uh, you sure?" Hector pointed out the window, where Savannah caught a glimpse of red hair on a scooter pulling out to the street.

"Are you *kidding me*?" Forgetting Hector, she jumped up and ran out toward the parking lot, swearing under her breath as she swung her leg over the scooter and twisted the key so hard she almost broke it. She didn't even bother with the helmet swinging from her elbow.

How many times was she going to fall for this woman's act?

Without any hesitation, she revved the engine and headed toward Duval Street, which was packed with revelers and bikes and carts and tourists. Barely missing them all, she went flying after Diana, keeping that red hair in her sight until she zipped off down a side street and headed toward the wharf.

Now where was she going?

Savannah followed with no idea if Hector was behind her or not. She didn't care. She wasn't going to let go. She trailed Diana like the hounds of hell, refusing to let that woman out of her clutches. She was not going to get away with—

Holy hell. Diana was riding full speed toward the water. A group of people cut her off, slowing her down, and giving Savannah a chance to get within yelling distance.

"Diana!" she screamed over her engine. "Stop!"

Diana held up a hand and waved her off. But Savannah slammed the accelerator, threaded through a few pedestrians and called out again.

Diana swerved and had to work to stay upright, giving Savannah a chance to catch up.

"Will you please stop?" Savannah yelled when she was two feet away.

But Diana barreled forward toward the edge of the wharf. What was she going to do? Go flying into the water?

Yes, Savannah realized. That was *exactly* what she was going to do.

"Over my dead body!" Savannah screamed.

"No, mine!" Diana shot back, less than twenty feet from the edge of the wharf.

Savannah let the helmet hooked to her elbow fall into her hand, snagging the strap. It was her only hope. She lifted her arm and tossed the helmet full force at Diana, barely missing the bike, but making her gasp and lose control, swerving wildly and forced to drop to the ground to keep from eating it just a few life-threatening feet from the water's edge.

"What the hell are you doing?" Savannah screamed, screeching to a stop and easing the scooter to the ground.

"Ending it all."

Savannah almost laughed. "I sure do see where Nick gets his flair for entrances and exits." She abandoned the bike and closed the space between them, taking Diana's heaving shoulders in her hands. "You think it's that easy?"

"Nothing's easy," Diana sobbed.

Those were real tears, she realized with a start. Real, broken, agonizing tears.

"No, nothing is," Savannah agreed, working to catch her breath. "Starting with being a mother. Take it from one who has a few months under her belt." She forced Diana to look at her. "It's the hardest job in the world. We all make mistakes. Every mother does, even mine."

"I doubt it."

"She does." Although she couldn't think of one at the moment. "You need to forgive yourself, Diana, and the rest will come naturally. Your son, me, my family, even Nick's father. Everyone can be forgiven, but you have to do two things."

"What?"

"Change...and love."

Diana stilled in her arms. "Do you think I can?"

"Anyone can." She stroked Diana's hair, vaguely aware of Hector coming closer to them, camera at his eye, getting every juicy minute on tape.

"How can I?" Diana murmured. "This whole thing will be recorded for the world to know that I am the worst person who ever lived."

"Not the worst," Savannah said, turning to press her

lips to Diana's ear. "Work with me now and you'll see who's the worst."

"What?"

"Hector, she's hurt!" Savannah cried out. "Please, put that down and get over here."

He lowered the camera and hustled closer. "What's wrong?"

"Hold her, please! While I call 911!"

He instantly dropped the camera on the wharf and reached for Diana. As he did, Savannah turned and let her foot slide really hard to the side...and off went the camera with a noisy splash.

"What the hell!" he barked.

"Oh, I'll be okay," Diana said breathlessly, as if nothing happened. "I'm not hurt."

"God, I'm so sorry, Hector! My foot slipped!"

He took a slow inhale that made his nostrils flare, then let it out with resignation. "Are you okay, Diana?" he finally asked.

"I'm..." She turned to Savannah, her face ravaged but a smile working toward her eyes. "I'm better since this lady came into my life."

Savannah smiled. "The least I can do for the woman who gave the world Nick Frye."

As they picked up the bikes and helmets, Hector stood at the water's edge staring into the depths.

"You're quite an actress yourself," Diana whispered.

"And you are quite the mother-in-law."

"Not yet, but if we make that wedding, I will be."

CHAPTER TWENTY-FOUR
BECK

*J*ust as the sun landed like a fireball in the deep blue of the Gulf of Mexico, Beck watched her gorgeous daughter walk toward the wooden aisle that had been built for the sole purpose of giving Savannah her dreamiest bridal moment.

She chose to walk alone, which seemed perfect for a woman who was so strong and independent. No one was giving Savannah Joy Foster away. She'd always marched to her own drummer, living her life the way she wanted to, as unconventionally as she could. But that was what made her utterly amazing.

Under a canopy of flowers and tulle, far more elaborate than the little pink trellis they'd had for Jessie's vow renewal ceremony, four parents, three attendants, and one very happy groom waited. As the first notes of an instrumental version of "Wild Horses" started playing, the group in the chairs stood to honor the bride.

Beck stole a glance at Nick who, even when a little groom-nervous, looked shockingly handsome. Next to him, just as tall and handsome, stood his newly minted father, the resemblance strong, except for the eye color. Oliver's were impossibly dark but had a light that seemed to come from deep inside him. Nick stood between his parents, a loving hand on his mother's shoulder after all the tears had been shed and forgiveness had been offered.

Forgiveness.

How long had Beck struggled with that concept? Since the day Dan Foster sat at their dining room table, well over a year ago, and announced he was leaving her for another woman. Irony of ironies, that woman wasn't even here for the wedding of Dan's middle daughter.

But oh, so many people were. Family and friends she didn't even know existed that dark day up in Atlanta when she stared at her husband and literally felt her whole world collapse.

Now there was Jessie and Chuck, Heather, and her kids. There was a son she never dreamed she'd meet, and Josh, a man she'd always love...as a brother.

She spared a glance at Peyton and Callie, standing at the top of a small stage, their blue dresses the same color as the water behind them. And Ava, the world's best granddaughter, her gaze locked on Savannah, who'd become the role model the lost teenager had so desperately needed when she arrived.

And there was Lovely in the front row.

Talk about people Beck didn't know existed. From estranged, misunderstood aunt to precious mother, business partner and best friend, no two people had come further in the last year.

She caught her mother's eye as the older woman

looked to see if Beck was enjoying Savannah's slow walk. For a split second they held each other's gaze, the deepest love arcing between them, a message in her mother's eyes that she already recognized.

Forgiveness.

If Nick could hug his mother and tell her that her lifetime of deception was forgiven, and if Oliver could shake Diana's hand and murmur that he understood her decision, and if Savannah could risk missing her own wedding to personally let Diana know that she was worthy of love...well, then, couldn't Beck do the same?

As Savannah got closer, Beck let out a little sigh that came deep from her heart.

"Isn't she beautiful?" Dan whispered under his breath.

"They all are," she replied. "We made brilliant, beautiful girls, Dan." She looked up at him, seeing a face she'd loved with all her heart, until that heart was shattered by him.

He smiled. "You did all the heavy lifting, Beck. I just... had the blessings."

"I wouldn't change a thing," she confessed.

"Really?" His whole expression softened. "Because I'm so sorry, Beck. I am so, so sorry I hurt you."

The music grew a little louder as Savannah nearly reached the end of her long walk. But Beck held her ex-husband's gaze and smile. "I forgive you," she whispered.

And best of all, she meant it.

After that, it was all she could do to keep from weeping like a fool while her daughter gave her heart, soul, and life to a man who'd given up everything for her.

"I've got him!" Beck stepped away from the three hundredth family picture when Dylan let out a wail to say he'd had enough of this wedding. She took him from Savannah's arms with a wide smile. "I'll take him upstairs and get him fed and calm. You just keep smiling."

Savannah blew a bridal kiss. "Thank you, Momma! You're the best."

"Can I join you?" The low, accented voice sent an unexpected shiver through Beck as Oliver stepped away from the group to walk next to her. "I've had my picture taken enough today to last a lifetime."

"But at least the TV cameras are gone," she said, bouncing the baby as a little drool threatened to slide from Dylan's lips to her pale peach dress. "I heard you were masterful, though."

"I was honest, and so was Nick. I don't know who had the idea for that chat, but it was a great way to get to know my, uh, son."

She could hear the little bit of emotion in his voice when he said the word *son*. She so remembered that feeling from when she first met Kenny.

"It takes some getting used to, doesn't it?" she said as she gestured him into the house and toward the stairs that led up to Savannah and Nick's room.

He laughed. "I'm used to it, all right. Fact is, I'm not sure how quickly I want to leave now that I've found him."

"Then you should stay," Beck said. "Although I'm sure you have plenty to keep you busy in Sydney."

"Not that much, to be honest. I'm retired, and golfing,

surfing, and coaching rugby gets a bit boring after a while. My social life's taken a bit of a nosedive, I'm afraid. Haven't made the effort since...well. I do need to change that."

"If you decide to stay, I've got room at the B&B."

"That is a tempting offer."

They reached the master door as Dylan's cries reached a crescendo. "There are bottles up here in the fridge, if you'd like to feed him," Beck said. "Or you can head back down to the party and I'll handle things."

"I'd like to sit with him for a while, but..." He gave her a slow smile. "I've never fed a baby in my entire life. Can you believe it?"

"Well, it's time to change that."

"Okay, but..." His smile faded. "You will stay, though, Beck? I don't think I want to do it alone for fear of choking the lad."

"No one's going to choke. And yes, I'll stay." She walked across the oversized room to the crib, cooing softly to the baby, easily getting the bottle into the warmer with one hand. "No more crying, sweet Dylan. We're here." She held him close, getting a whiff of a scent she adored, kissing his damp, smooth cheek. "Grandma Beck is here. And so is..." She turned to find Oliver just a few feet away, gazing with some wonder in his eyes. "Grandpa Ollie."

"Please not Ollie, but...Grandpa?" His handsome smile grew wide. "Now that's a name I never dreamed I'd be called."

"Life has a way of surprising you, doesn't it?" She carefully offered the baby to him. "Take him over to the rocker and I'll bring you everything you need."

"All righty there, young one."

Beck watched as Dylan stopped fussing and looked up into Oliver's eyes. He stared as if he sensed there was a connection, but he wasn't quite sure what it might be. And then his little mouth lifted at the corners and he kicked against Oliver's arms and chest, making them both laugh.

"A feisty one, is that right?" Oliver muttered to him as he walked to the sitting area, getting comfortable in Dylan's favorite feeding chair, stroking his feather-soft hair as they got acquainted.

Smiling at the exchange, Beck gathered the warmed bottle, a soft towel, and Dylan's little blue bib, and brought them over.

"He's a handsome young man, isn't he?" He looked up at her with that "new grandparent" love that was so familiar to her, she could have told him exactly how his heart was currently filling and still making room for more.

"Diana says he looks exactly like Nick, but I see plenty of Savannah in him, too." She handed him the bottle and helped drape the towel over his surprisingly broad shoulder.

"All I know is he's spirited and healthy." Oliver slipped the bottle into Dylan's hungry lips. "And where I come from, those are the makings of a fine rugby player." He took Dylan's little fingers and squeezed them play-fully. "What do you say, mate? Are you a backline man or a scrum-half? Oh, maybe a tough little hooker or a prop?"

Sitting in the other chair to watch, Beck laughed, having no idea what he was talking about, but the words and accent were lyrical and his low voice was like a musical instrument.

"Stay in Coconut Key long enough and you just might teach him rugby," she said.

"Now that would be a good use of my life." He stroked Dylan's head again. "What do you say, little mate? Could you use a bit of coaching from an Ozzie like me?"

Without realizing it, Beck leaned forward, mesmerized by his voice and by...him. She felt her breath catch as he dropped a kiss on Dylan's bald head, her heart singing at the sweetness of the moment.

He looked up, laughing as if he were embarrassed at having been caught in the act of affection.

"It's fine," she assured him. "I get a little overwhelmed being a grandparent at times, too."

"You do?" His dark eyes danced as he let them slide over her face, then held her gaze. "You were right. I've never felt anything quite like...this."

"Very special feeling," she agreed.

"I hate to make you sit up here and miss the wedding," he said.

"I'm not missing anything. I love watching someone discover the joy of my grandchild."

"You are definitely witnessing me...discovering joy." He winked. "Words no self-respecting rugby player should ever say."

She laughed, and while Beck watched a man fall in love with his grandson, a new kind of warmth stretched over her chest. Something that felt fluttery and unexpected and indescribable.

Something that felt an awful lot like...*magic*.

You didn't think this series could end there, did you? Of course, there's more love and laughter, heartbreak and hope, and, always, family and friends in Coconut Key!

*Check out **A Promise in the Keys, Book Seven** in the Coconut Key series!*

And **sign up** for Hope's newsletter to get the latest on new releases, excerpts, and more! Sign up today and you'll also receive a special surprise — the recipe for Jessie's *Anniversary Crab Cakes!* Straight from her kitchen to yours!

Read the entire Coconut Key Series!

A Secret in the Keys – Book 1
A Reunion in the Keys – Book 2
A Season in the Keys – Book 3
A Haven in the Keys – Book 4
A Return to the Keys –Book 5
A Wedding in the Keys – Book 6
A Promise in the Keys - Book 7

ABOUT THE AUTHOR

Hope Holloway is the author of charming, heartwarming women's fiction featuring unforgettable families and friends and the emotional challenges they conquer. After a long career in marketing, she gave up writing ad copy to launch a writing career with her first series, Coconut Key, set on the sun-washed beaches of the Florida Keys. A mother of two adult children, Hope and her husband of thirty years live in Florida and North Carolina. When not writing, she can be found walking the beach or hiking in the mountains with her two rescue dogs, who beg her to include animals in every book. Visit her site at www.hopeholloway.com.